MORE THAN
MEETS THE EYE

Lena
Bena

Dear Reader:

Thanks for picking up *More Than Meets the Eye* by Michelle Janine Robinson. Once again, Robinson has proven that she has an invigorating and innovative style of writing. This time she tackles a topic that some might find unbelievable and others might totally be able to relate to.

What if you needed sex in order to survive? Literally? A lot of us love sex and swear that life is unsustainable without it but what if that were actually true? What if we would wither away and die without it? Well, in *More Than Meets the Eye*, there are many who have been walking the earth for hundreds of years with that exact problem. Yes, I said, "hundreds of years."

This novel will have readers so caught up, riveted until the very last page. Robinson makes the possibility of an incubus visiting you in your sleep so sexy that some will actually yearn to experience it. She almost had me there for a minute—I'm only serious.

Robinson has been a contributor to most of my anthologies, including the lead-in story "The Quiet Room" in *Succulent: Chocolate Flava 2*. Hot! Hot! Hot. Make sure you check out Robinson's first published novel, *Color Me Grey*, and her most recent release, *Serial Typical*.

As always, thanks for supporting myself and the Strebor Books family. We strive to bring you cutting-edge literature that cannot be found anyplace else. For more information on our titles, please visit Zanestore. com. My personal web site is Eroticanoir. com and my online social network is PlanetZane.org. Please join us for weekly chats on Planet Zane.org on Mondays, Tuesdays, and Wednesdays.

Blessings,

Zane

Zane
Publisher
Strebor Books
www.simonandschuster.com/streborbooks

ALSO BY MICHELLE JANINE ROBINSON
Serial Typical
Color Me Grey

ZANE PRESENTS

MORE THAN MEETS THE EYE

A NOVEL

MICHELLE JANINE ROBINSON

SBI

STREBOR BOOKS

NEW YORK LONDON TORONTO SYDNEY

Strebor Books
P.O. Box 6505
Largo, MD 20792
http://www.streborbooks.com

© 2011 by Michelle Janine Robinson

ISBN 978-1-59309-292-4
ISBN 978-1-4391-8267-3 (ebook)
LCCN 2011926869

First Strebor Books trade paperback edition June 2011

Cover design: www.mariondesigns.com
Cover photograph: © Keith Saunders/Marion Designs

10 9 8 7 6 5 4 3 2 1

Manufactured in the United States of America

For information regarding special discounts for bulk purchases,
please contact Simon & Schuster Special Sales at 1-866-506-1949
or business@simonandschuster.com

The Simon & Schuster Speakers Bureau can bring authors to your
live event. For more information or to book an event, contact the
Simon & Schuster Speakers Bureau at 1-866-248-3049 or visit our
website at www.simonspeakers.com.

Justin and Stefan
You are my air...

ACKNOWLEDGMENTS

While watching a film recently, one of the characters, in describing his messy apartment to a prospective roommate, said, "Excuse the mess, but I'm a writer and writers thrive on anarchy." His comment got me to thinking. Is that true? Do most writers "thrive on anarchy?" And, if so, does that also include me?

I must admit, if you pick up any entertainment magazine or newspaper, you would be hard-pressed to debunk the statement. Chaos, disorder and rebellion often appear to be the defining characteristics of many artists, including writers.

While New Year resolutions have never been my thing, I made a solemn resolve as 2010 came to a close to embrace the joy in life, to endure and learn from adversity and to hold dear those treasured loved ones who have stuck with me through it all.

Justin and Stefan, I thank you for allowing me the comfort of no pretense. I am more "me" with the two of you than any other human being on this planet. It is often such a challenge to wear so many hats and…and so many faces. Yet, when the day is done and "I let down my hair," I know all I have to be is me and that will always be enough for the two of you.

To Charles Trovato, I feel so very lucky to have met you. Yet, I'm not surprised, since I wholly believe in fate and destiny. It was predestined. You quiet my storm and remind me what's real. And, for that, I am ever-thankful.

To my family, there's something about getting older that allows you to appreciate your family even more. I am so lucky to have you all, with all your quirks, nuances and special attributes, I am in awe of what our family has evolved into. I can't wait to see what the next fifty years brings. And, yes, Justin and Stefan, I do plan to be here for the next fifty. Maybe, I'll take your advice and quit smoking, exercise more and modify my diet… Okay?

To all the folks at the Strebor/Simon & Schuster family who have made me feel so much at home, thank you for guiding and welcoming me. Zane, Charmaine and Yona, I appreciate your expertise and your willingness to help me be all that I can be.

To my girlfriends Christina Williams, Yvonne Landy, Lisa Millington, Joanne Schmidt, Tanya Davis, Denise Walcott and Debra Miami, although I don't spend nearly as much time with you all as I would like (our lives are all so very busy), I always know just how lucky I am to have friends that are among the smartest, sexiest and wittiest of the bunch. Love you!

To Mark Alexander, I want you to know I was literally

kicking myself when I realized I hadn't offered you a public thank you in my first book. Your support of me and my writing efforts has been constant and often well-needed. Thanks, Mark, for guarding my stories and keeping them safe for me, including providing a last-minute retrieve when I lost one of them…Oops!

To my fans, who have reached out to me via Facebook, Twitter, Myspace and e-mail, it thrills me each and every time I hear from someone who enjoyed reading something I have written. Without you, my publishing efforts would be in vain. Thank you for offering me wings to fly.

…And, to all of the angels, who left my life way too soon; my dad, Oliver Clements Robinson; my grandmother, Mabel Payne; my uncle Robert Payne, and my beloved friend Lamar Remouns, I miss you guys so much and think of you often. You teach me still, the importance of living each and every day, with love, peace and honor, for often there are no second chances.

Love,
Michelle

PROLOGUE

The crushing weight of him was strong enough to rob her of her breath. She struggled beneath him, sensing his next move, inhaling his scent. She could feel him, could just barely reach out her hands to touch him. Yet, as if she were suddenly blind, she could not see him; darkness enveloped every corner of her world. Her long, slender fingers, grasped at the sheets beneath her, reaching for anything, hoping to find the strength to scream. There was no warning, no time for her to run; not even enough time for her to panic and scream. He was so very heavy. As if 400-pound weights were laid flatly atop her body, she was immovable. But what was most confusing was her obscured sight. She could see nothing. Whoever or *whatever* was on top of her was so large, she couldn't imagine that she wouldn't be able to see him; even in the darkness of the night. Belinda's attempts to free herself were useless. He was everywhere. Muffled screams inside her throat, with nowhere to go, brought her nothing but pain.

Her T-shirt pushed aside, an ice cold object probed roughly between her legs, straining to gain entry. The prospect of being raped was horrific enough, but this was more than that. Her eyes were wide open and unconcealed, yet she saw no one, and though the feeling of a man's body on top of her was unmistakable, what was now forcing its way inside of her bore no resemblance to anything she had ever felt. She had at first feared that she was being invaded by some sort of object, but it was not. It was clearly a man inside of her. But, the temperature of his appendage could only be likened to what a dead man might feel like if his penis were capable of being inside of a woman. It was painfully large and stabbing at her relentlessly—and was as cold as a block of ice.

"No! No! Not this!" she screamed, beneath her invisible muzzle.

Indistinguishable hands groped roughly at her body, teeth bit at her flesh and a vise grip held her so tightly, she thought for sure her entire body was being ripped limb from limb. Lingering in the air was the feint scent of decay, transporting her to the edge of nausea.

She reasoned with herself, assuring her conscious mind that she was not crazy, only asleep.

"Yes," she spoke to herself, amidst her haze. "This is little more than an extremely vivid dream."

She prayed that was it. Because, if it were not, then it meant that she was dealing with something far beyond her own comprehension, or anyone else's for that matter. Or, even worse, maybe she was going completely insane.

When she was convinced she could do nothing but die, Belinda lost all consciousness.

ONE

The *nightmares* started soon after accepting a writing assignment with *Newsweek*. What started as some eagerly accepted freelance work seemed to be leading her down a path toward ultimate destruction. After years of battling the worst insomnia, sleep had become her enemy. She knew better than anyone what could happen when you slept. That's why she sat now in Starbucks at 8:45 p.m., downing her last of several cups of coffee before they closed. For the past several weeks she had devised artful ways of avoiding what she initially thought was some sort of stalker, angered by the story she was doing. It wasn't long before she discovered what plagued her was a great deal more than merely a stalker. She realized that her safety was short-lived and that, sooner or later, she would have to go home or, at the very least, she would have to tell someone what she had learned. But who on earth would ever believe what was happening to not only her, but countless others?

She watched him, just outside the windows, lurking in the shadows…waiting.

The words *be careful what you wish for* rang in her ears

once again. For months she had wanted little more than to get some work, any work. So when Cameron, over at *Newsweek*, had contacted her with a dream writing assignment, she had jumped at the chance.

It was hard to imagine it was little more than three weeks ago when she got the phone call. In three short weeks, she had gone from worrying about paying her mortgage to wondering if she would even live long enough to see the next day.

Despite months of agonizing insomnia, Belinda was overjoyed to hear the phone ringing that morning; even at such an early hour. Since the downturn in the economy, work had diminished significantly for her. After years of working at jobs that had left her feeling mostly dissatisfied, she had built up a strong client base of magazines and newspapers that called on her often to write for their publications on a freelance basis. However, for the past year or so, it had been an uphill climb to stay ahead. Most companies were cutting back and it was becoming apparent that her life-long dream of vocational independence would once again have to be put on hold and she would have to join the ranks of working stiffs on the edge of quiet desperation. That was what kept her from sleeping most nights. Now, her problems were far greater than anything she could ever have imagined. For now all of that would have to wait. The phone was ringing and she could see from the caller id that it was her editor at *Newsweek*.

"Hey, Belinda, how's it going?"

"It's going. How are you?"

"I'm good. I've got an assignment for you."

"I was hoping you'd call. Things have been a bit slow lately."

"I'm sorry about that. But, things have been slow all over; what with all the cutbacks. *Newsweek* is feeling the crunch as well. However, I do have an assignment for you; a good one."

"Great!"

"We want to do a story focusing on the number of people that go missing each year. You'd be perfect for this. According to FBI-NCIC statistics, there are over 100,000 missing persons listed in their system and over 6,000 unidentified persons. Washington, D.C. has more missing persons than any other city listed, but New York has the most unidentified. I'd like you to explore these statistics and dazzle us with a phenomenal story. Maybe you could use your New York contacts to find out more about the *unidentified*. It's got a good angle. This one could help put you on the map."

"Thanks, Cameron. You're right; it's a good story."

"I thought you'd like it."

"How much time do I have?"

"You've got some leeway; a couple of months, maybe. Keep me posted. Okay?"

"Absolutely!"

For the first time in months, Belinda was hopeful. All

it took was one really good story. She couldn't wait to call her girls and tell them the news.

"Summer, guess what?"

"Hey you, you're in better spirits than the last time I spoke with you. What's goin' on?"

"I've got a gig; a writing assignment. And, it's a good one!"

"Good, good. Even though I still say you need to relax. Nobody ever went to their grave saying I wish I had worked more. You need to enjoy the fruits of your labor and stop stressing so damn much. That shit will kill you. You have to remember, everything in life is temporary; even the slow economy."

"Yeah, yeah, I know. It's hard to stop stressing when you can't pay your damn rent, or in my case, my exorbitantly high mortgage."

"Sell the condo, rent a modest apartment somewhere and live to fight another day."

"I've considered that. But, I love my place; and not only that, this market sucks right now. I've put some feelers out and it's getting close to impossible to sell right now."

"You need to get out. You know what they say about all work and no play."

"That's one of the reasons I called. I thought maybe you, Diana and I could hit a club tonight and celebrate, maybe have some dinner."

"Sounds good to me."

"I'm gonna call Diana and then I want to get started

on this story. I might call Aidan and see if he can help in any way.

"Aidan, huh? I thought you were weaning yourself off that one."

"I am. This is business. He's a detective. I'm doing a story about missing and unidentified people in New York. What better person to talk to?"

"Okay."

"No, seriously. That's the only reason I'm calling him."

"I believe you. And even if you were calling him for other reasons, who am I to judge? That's not my thing. Besides that motha fucka is fine!"

"Summer, you ain't got no sense. I'll call you later. I've got work to do; finally!"

Before calling either Diana or Aidan, Belinda decided to work up the main idea for her article, so that when she did get in touch with Aidan, she could cut to the chase and ask the right questions right off the bat. She sat in Starbucks, trying to focus. But, instead of the initial excitement she felt at getting the assignment, she found her thoughts were just as lost as she had been lately. She was once again distracted, edgy; and worst of all, she found she still couldn't write. If she couldn't write, she couldn't pay her bills, and if she couldn't pay her bills, she was decidedly screwed. Worse than that, she didn't even have an excuse like the bad economy to fall back on. She had a primo story, yet she was still at odds. So, Belinda realized she had better get her act together and either figure out what the hell was going on with her state of upheaval or put it on a shelf somewhere until after she had written the article she promised.

For years, she had been successfully working as a freelance journalist, writing articles for both magazines and newspapers and had gotten to a place where she was able to make a substantial living at it. But lately, she had become disenchanted with her work. Even before the decline in the economy, her articles seemed somehow stale to her and she needed to write something she could feel proud of. That's what made this opportunity all the more of a godsend. Slowly, ideas began to come to her. She made a note to research the statistics for missing African-Americans and other minorities. She was sure she had read somewhere that people of color made up a larger portion of missing victims than the media represents. She could be the person to bring things to light. There were so many possible angles to the story, she couldn't help but get excited about it all over again. She also realized that this was something she *had* to write about.

Belinda decided she would call Aidan first and get started on her research before calling Diana. Her ideas were gaining momentum and she wanted to hold on to that while everything was fresh in her mind.

"May I speak to Detective Aidan Roberts, please?"

"Just a moment. May I say who's calling?"

"Belinda Wilson."

"Hey! You finally decided to return my calls, huh?"

"I've just been really busy," she lied.

Aidan realized Belinda was conflicted. The fact that he had a wife and kids didn't sit well with her. She never went into detail but, over time, their encounters had gotten less and less and eventually, she had stopped returning his calls.

"I was wondering if you were free for lunch?" she asked.

"For you, always."

His attempts at flirtation were not unrecognized, however, Belinda decided from the moment she picked up the phone to call him that she would keep this purely professional and would not fall into any old patterns of *play*.

"I'm writing an article about missing and unidentified persons in New York...not just New York, but mostly New York; and I was hoping you could help me a bit."

"No problem. Where are you now? I could come to you."

"I'm on 75th and First. There's a diner on 77th; Green Kitchen. You wanna meet me there?"

"I can be there in twenty minutes."

She and Aiden had had an affair for almost a year. He was married and had a family, but she had grown up with him and had had a crush on him for as long as she could remember. One night, she was out at a club when she suddenly had the feeling that someone was staring at her. She turned to find Aidan looking directly at her.

At first, she was put off by the blue contact lenses he was wearing, but eventually she got over it; especially since they seemed so natural. Belinda was in awe of his confidence. Even though the last time they had seen one another they had both been teens, she was impressed with how confident he appeared. Gone were all those years of awkwardness and insecurity. He was incredibly self-assured and she had to admit a certain curiosity about what had gotten him to this state of being. They talked and laughed all night and the inevitable happened. Breakfast after the club turned into a cup of coffee at her place and a night of the most incredible sex she had had in a really long time. That went on for about a year before her conscience and her emotions got the better of her. She never considered herself the sort of woman that would break up a family. Not only that, it was clear she was in a dead-end relationship.

Now, she sat in a diner waiting for him once again. This time she hoped she would keep her wits about her and stick to the matter at hand; writing a kick ass story, with Aidan's help.

"Hey, baby. You look beautiful, as usual."

He leaned in to kiss her and there was no mistaking how awkward the moment was.

"So, this sounds like some article you're writing, and *Newsweek* no less. They're big. I'm proud of you."

And with those few words, Belinda's cautious veneer melted away. The thought crossed her mind, that he really wasn't a bad guy. He just wasn't her guy and it would have to stay that way.

The rest of lunch progressed with ease and Belinda was happy she had called. She was surprised to find that he actually had more information to offer than had even occurred to her. Not only that, there was certain information that she was sure he was offering to provide that he probably was not supposed to make available to the public.

After leaving the restaurant, they stood lingering outside, well aware that another awkward moment had arrived.

"I'll email you what I find when I get back to the station and I'll keep it coming until you say when. Okay, baby?"

She hated her reaction to him whenever he called her baby. It was her last weakness with him. She could stop returning his calls, stop sleeping with him. But, those lips that had once given her such immeasurable pleasure mouthing the word "baby" were more than she could stand. Still, she understood that she would have to be strong. All it took was one good fuck and she'd be right back to where she started.

"Thanks, Aidan. I appreciate this very much."

This time, when he leaned in to kiss her goodbye, she didn't move away or turn her face. She was too distracted by an odd sense of deja vu. He suddenly reminded her of someone else. Even his scent seemed vaguely familiar; not his own scent but someone else's. She just wasn't sure whose. He kissed her lightly on the forehead and whispered, *I understand*. It was touching and seemed heartfelt and the two went their separate ways.

Belinda dialed Diana's office. Although it was regular office hours, the phone rang and rang. No receptionist answered; no service. It was odd. *What if she were a patient?* Next, she tried Diana's cell with the same result. Diana was a doctor and was very committed to her practice and *always* busy, but it seemed as though she was always impossible to get a hold of.

Belinda called Summer back before heading home.

"Yo, girl, what's up?"

"I *really* need to get out tonight. I saw Aidan and I swear, I wanted to fuck him right on the sidewalk outside of Green Kitchen. Not only that, I'm scared to death that if I don't ace this story, my career is going to be in the toilet. I haven't had a real date in God only knows how long and quite frankly, I *need* a drink; actually, I need several drinks."

"Damn, girl, you're only thirty-eight. Are you going through a midlife crisis already? Your career is fine. You got that bad ass condo on the Upper East and as far as a date, you date as much as you want to. I read something once that said each of us is in exactly the kind of relationship we want to be in. That includes you."

"Look who's sounding like the voice of reason."

"What? Like I don't offer up some pearls of wisdom every now and then. Don't let the spandex fool you. I know some shit."

"Summer, stop making me laugh; this is serious."

"That's the problem with you, Belinda. You take life *too* seriously. You're right. You need to get out and have some damn fun. Redemption it is."

"I've been trying to call Diana but I get no answer. I even tried calling her office. There's no answer there either."

"Now why you gonna go and ruin our good time? The whole point is for you to unwind. How you gonna unwind with Miss Uptight there?"

"Come on, Summer. Diana's not that bad."

"So you say. Not only is she that bad; I personally think she's running game. That girl got some brontosaurus skeletons in her damn closet."

"You're so crazy. Why is everything a conspiracy theory with you?"

"'Cause that's what life is baby; a series of conspiracies. The difference between you and me is I've embraced that fact. You investigate it, and still haven't embraced the reality. I don't get that."

"Maybe I want to remain my old naïve self. You ever think about that?"

"Even a little bitty baby isn't completely naïve. Reality has a way of seeping in, whether we like it or not."

"Point taken."

"I'm still calling Diana."

"Go ahead and call Her Highness."

"Summer, are you gonna behave or what?"

"I always behave."

"Yeah, right!"

"Alright, alright, I'll cut her some slack. But if she tries that condescending shit she does with me, it's on."

"Thanks, Summer."

Belinda tried Diana's cell and office number once more, but there was still no answer. This time she left a message.

"Hey, sweet pea! Tonight is party night, so don't even think about telling me that you can't make it. Call me. We're gonna hit Redemptions and wear something sexy!"

Rather than wait for Diana to call her back, she decided to make an impromptu visit to her office.

TWO

As he walked, it occurred to Dante that even some-one like him, someone ageless, could lament the passing of time.

Through the years, he had been known by countless names. For now, he was Dante Rivers. He stood outside the medical building that he visited each and every week and once again began to regret coming. He was envious of those with ordinary lives. How clueless some people could be about how much life had to offer even less than extraordinary lives. Most people were so intent upon living longer, being the most beautiful, making more and more money, they forgot about what the essence of true life could provide.

Those, among other thoughts, are what kept bringing him back here. It was a foolish lie he told himself. But lately, the semblance of normalcy was what he needed more than anything. For him, *life* was nothing more than an endless flow of half-lives strung together that seemed to continue with no end. There were those that would have coveted his existence. He could do nothing more than pity it. Therefore, it had become more and more important to establish some form of consistency. Diana was that consistency. She was his tie to both of the worlds he lived in. Somehow, she seemed to have embraced life's duality far better than he ever had. Her relationships were consistent. She worked as a *respectable* member of society. Diana walked a very fine line between two separate existences. Somehow, Dante never truly felt himself capable of doing the same. Diana had become his link with regularity. And despite his growing discontent with that link, he was fully aware that his choices were limited.

The incalculable number of women was so infinite he had lost track of names and faces long ago. Now, they were little more than sustenance; a means for him to continue. Lately, he had begun to consider the alternative. There was no joy, only survival. There was no beginning, no middle and no end. He found humor in those who took their lives because of their inability to handle some momentary pain or another. He had existed for years on nothing more than the will to survive.

Standing outside Diana's office, more than anything, he wanted to forego the tedium of fucking someone who neither sustained his energy nor provided him with any real devotion. Yet, what else did he have? He had grown bored with engaging in the tedious chore of luring women from clubs and restaurants simply to endure. He wanted—no, he *needed* more. Not only that, he was beginning to realize how much easier it was when he was younger. He was stronger then and could often snare a willing offering within minutes, with little more than an inviting glance. Though his power and strength were nothing short of herculean, he had become weaker and his will faltered with each passing day.

Dante sniffed the air, smell her in heat and waiting for him to offer her some temporary respite; her scent wafting past the doors and greeting him outside.

"Oh, what the fuck! Why should this week be different than any other?" he uttered to himself.

He decided it was best that he do exactly what he came there to do. Besides, Diana was a valuable comrade and he was sure she could be just as formidable an enemy if toyed with.

He was a striking presence; especially amongst the waiting room comprised primarily of women. But, it was more than his chiseled features and his stately air. He was simultaneously frightening and stimulating; tall and dark, with eyes that glimmered like stones floating atop water. Even the pregnant women in the office couldn't avoid being captivated.

"Mr. Rivers, the doctor will see you now."

As he passed by the receptionist's desk on his way to Diana's office, the scent of him was positively intoxicating; sweet and enticing but also mildly oppressive, like being confined in a seductive trap, of which there was no hope of escape.

Yet, she couldn't have resisted speaking to him again if she tried.

"You know where the office is; don't you, Mr. Rivers?"

She hoped the long, seductive glance she offered him was enough to convey her intentions.

"Yes, I do. Thank you."

Dante didn't miss her mild flirtation, but had decided long ago to steer clear of Diana's employees and patients.

He entered her office, then closed and locked the door.

"Hello, Dante."

"Hello. I see you have yet another new receptionist."

"You can thank René for that. I can't keep *any* staff, thanks to him. Thank goodness he knows enough to stay away from my patients; otherwise I'd have no practice to speak of."

"Can you see now why I've limited my contact with him? He's a threat in more ways than one."

They had engaged in this very same discussion more times than she'd cared to. For now, all she wanted was to wrap herself around his astounding member. For a moment, she lamented the fact that neither could sustain the other, and instead would eventually need to secure the services of another in order to maintain what they both needed.

"Is that what you came here to discuss; René again?"

"No, it's not."

His eyes burned through her, mentally devouring her, as he stepped closer to her desk, circled it and took her in his arms. His cock lay like granite against her thigh. His tongue entered her mouth with fierce determination as he released her hair from its tight bun. Her dark, unruly hair fell and cascaded past her shoulders as an audible gasp escaped from her lips. Ripping her panties from her, he unzipped his pants and entered her without ceremony. She had become accustomed to the cold steel of his cock reverberating inside of her. It felt so damn good. There were things they could do with one another that no other could withstand. As Dante drove himself further and deeper inside of her, increasing his speed and varying direction, she met each rapid thrust with equal momentum. His animalistic groans hypnotized the patients in the waiting room and, although his brief rendezvous within the confines of her private office would sustain neither of them, he took comfort in knowing that these weekly trysts were the one consistency he knew.

Their frightening series of physical transformations at a peak, her moans reached a melodic crescendo as she cried out, "Come with me, Dante! Come with me, now!"

Their union was one borne of dark and infinite secrets. Each sought comfort from the loneliness they sought to deny. When they were not seeking to sustain life, they were battling their true nature—an existence that didn't allow for companionship.

Under normal circumstances, patients anxiously waiting to see any other doctor would not only be agitated but would be complaining profusely. Instead, by the time

Dante exited the office, the patients all seemed lulled into some form of harmonious restraint, while Diana's receptionist sat daydreaming and twirling a lock of her hair.

There was something about sex with Diana that drained him. He quickly scanned the waiting area with his eyes, acutely aware of his unbelievable hunger for more.

The door to the waiting area swung open and ushered in with it the most breathtaking beauty. She was everything he never realized that he wanted, and he had yet to hear her utter even her name.

She was positively unearthly. Before the door could swing back into position, someone followed close on her heels. Dante recognized René's distinctive scent immediately and by the time he was close enough to see him, it was readily apparent that René could barely contain his glee.

Dante quickly cautioned him with his eyes, although he was unsure why he had, to which René simply smiled.

The subject of their interest headed straight for the receptionist's desk. Dante was hard-pressed to understand why this beautiful young woman was not affected by his presence. There was seldom a female that was not.

Dante joined René and establishing a tight grip on his arm, led him to the door.

"What the fuck was that about?"

"It's broad open daylight and Diana has lost enough receptionists for the time being. Don't you think?"

"I'm tired of receptionists. I'm thinking of moving on to patients. Did you see that one I came in with? I bet she's so good."

"So, where are we going tonight?"

"We're not going anywhere. I'm checking out Indigo tonight; alone."

"Oh come on, Dante; I hate to hunt alone."

"You see, that's exactly why I prefer to go it solo. Hunt? Why do you insist on such archaic interpretation? You're only drawing attention to yourself, and to me, by using such words. I've been around a whole lot longer than you have, René, and believe me, the stance you persist in taking can mean nothing but trouble for *all* of us. But, I can only give you advice; it's up to you whether to heed it or not. So, why don't we agree to disagree, and you go your way and I'll go mine?"

"Aw shit, man; you're too fucking uptight. We own this town. We're untouchable. We ain't got a damn thing to worry about, except where to get the most spirited pussy."

"No one is untouchable René; not even us."

"Whatever. I didn't want to go to that tired-ass Indigo anyway."

Dante chuckled to himself. René was going to show up at Indigo, whether he wanted him to or not; that's why he was going to Redemption instead.

René took too many chances and quite frankly, Dante could not care less what he did, but his actions could affect them all. And, that was exactly what he didn't want.

Belinda watched as Dante and René left Diana's office and she wondered why they were there. After all, it was a gynecologist's office and neither of them had left with a woman. She wondered if they were friends of Diana.

"Hi, uh, Rachel…right? Is Diana in? My name is Belinda; Belinda Wilson."

Belinda wondered if Diana's disposition was the reason she changed receptionists so frequently. She loved her, but she could see how Diana's haughty air could get on someone else's nerves. In fact, that was one of the things she was going to mention to Diana today. She was looking forward to hangin' with her girls and having a good time and hoped that Summer and Diana wouldn't get to bickering like they always did when the three of them got together.

"She's just getting out of a meeting. Let me see if she's free." The receptionist activated the intercom. "Doctor, Belinda Wilson is here to see you."

Diana replied, "Send her right in."

Belinda could smell the scent of sex in the air, but declined to mention it or even joke with Diana about it. Although they were very good friends, Belinda learned early on in their relationship that Diana was an extremely private person and she kept her sex life more private than anything else. It occurred to her that one of the men that she saw leaving might have been *visiting* Diana, or maybe both? It did appear that they were together. That would make Diana every bit the freak that Summer often accused her of being.

"Did you get my message? I've been calling you all day. I was starting to get worried about you."

"I'm fine, worry wart. I can't seem to keep a receptionist and quite frankly, I don't think this latest one is going to last much past the week. She's terrible."

"Oh no, don't tell me another one is gonna bite the dust."

"I think so. I got your message, but I don't know if I can tonight. I'm exhausted. I was just going to go home and get to bed early tonight."

"Come on. We never go out anymore. Please?"

"Okay, okay. I'll go. Stop begging."

"You'll wear something sexy?" Belinda reminded her.

"Yes, I'll wear something sexy. Although if I were a more sensitive person, my feelings might be hurt by how *many* times you remind me of that very same thing."

"It's just that…you tend to *hide your light under a bushel*, so to speak. You're so beautiful; you should flaunt that fact."

"Is Summer going?"

"Yes."

"Did you remind *her* to bring a bushel? Quite frankly, if you think I hide mine under a bushel, I should give her a bushel; she hides *nothing*.

Both Belinda and Diana laughed in unison.

"You've got that right," Belinda agreed.

THREE

B elinda was surprised when the doorman announced that both Summer and Diana were on their way up. She was sure they hadn't come together. As hard as she had tried to get Summer and Diana to get along better, it seemed as though it would never be. Instead, they had found some sort of *happy* medium in which they could be around each other for Belinda's sake, but that was about it.

"Oh, oh, oh, oh, oh! Party over here; party right there."

Belinda could hear Summer's loud ass all the way inside her apartment. Summer and Diana were getting off the elevator and walking toward her door. Along with Summer's loud voice, she could hear the clicking of her five-inch stilettos tapping against the Formica floors. Belinda made a mental note that one of these days she really had to sit Summer down and explain to her that she needed to tone down the girl from the hood act when she came to her apartment. Belinda wasn't one to judge *anyone*, but the ultra-conservative members of her condo board were sure to have a problem with loudness at all hours of the day and night. Belinda knew she had to have the conversation sooner or later. She just wasn't sure how to approach it diplomatically.

The doorbell rang. Belinda applied some red lipstick and took one last look in her full-length mirror. She was pleased–subtle, but sexy. She was wearing a black, form-fitting off-the-shoulder dress, black high-heeled sandals and her toenails were painted a vibrant red, the identical color of her lipstick. It was the beginning of Fall and although it was still warm during the day, the nights were often cool, so Belinda threw a red fringed shawl over her shoulders to complete the look, grabbed her black pearl-studded evening bag and keys and headed for the door.

As soon as she opened the door, Diana and Summer rushed in.

"Hey! I thought ya'll were gonna get here earlier than this."

"Sorry, B, I couldn't get out of work."

"And my sitter was late."

"Ooh, I love that shawl! I've got to get one of those."

"Thanks! I got it from Bloomies. It was the last one. I waited and waited until the price came down and by the time the price was where I wanted it, this was the only one they had left. I'm not into red. I really wanted a black one, but they said they probably won't be getting any more in."

"Oh well, my loss."

"I tried calling you after I left your office, but I got no answer at work or on your cell. Why doesn't your receptionist answer the phone? You don't have to be a rocket scientist to pick up the phone. Did she come from an agency? If so, I would say go with a new agency. I can even give you the names of a few."

"She's new and she's a bit overwhelmed. I get the impression this may be her very *first* job."

"See, I told you that you should've hired me for that job. At least I've worked as a receptionist before," Summer mentioned.

"I know, I know; as a receptionist, a hairstylist, a secretary, a writer, and the list goes on and on and on."

"No, you didn't. I know you're not judging me."

Belinda shot an eye at Summer, by way of her earlier conversation asking that she try to get along with Diana.

"So, how are you?" Diana asked.

"I can't complain; although, I'm a little bit stressed about—"

Before Belinda could finish her sentence, Summer loudly interrupted. "Girl, go on and have a seat. I gotta pee."

"Why don't you say it a little louder? My neighbors on the 10th floor didn't hear you."

"Oh be quiet, bourgeois. Don't these white folks pee?"

"Yes, Summer. They use the restroom. But they're not quite so vocal or specific about what they're doing in the bathroom," Belinda answered.

Diana stood there quietly, watching. As she listened to Summer and Belinda's banter, she marveled at the way the two of them interacted. Belinda and Summer couldn't be more different. In the four years since Diana had met Summer, she had held down no fewer than eight jobs. Belinda, on the other hand, was a very talented freelance journalist, with great aspirations. Summer's present job was a sort of "floating" bartender at various clubs. Basically, she worked with a club promoter and tended bar whenever and wherever he held his parties. Most of the parties were held in clubs in the midtown area. Much like most of the work Summer did, she had basically fallen into it; this time through her association with some friends of her ex-husband, Kaleel. Her ex's current residence was Riker's Island. He had killed a man and was presently serving 15 to 25 years in prison, thanks, in no small order, to his former profession as a drug dealer.

Diana couldn't relate to Summer very well. Summer was a smart girl. She knew all there was to know about politics, was highly skilled at math and was quite a talented writer. Diana and Belinda had gone to several clubs to see Summer perform her written works. But, Summer was rough as hell around the edges. She talked loud, dressed louder and associated with people most would never give the time of day. Diana was surprised to find that Belinda and Summer were such good friends. They were like night and day.

As Belinda explained it, she and Summer had grown up in El Barrio. They had both attended catholic school in their neighborhood and had attended the same vocational high school downtown. After high school was when their lives took different turns. Belinda attended New York University right after graduating from high school, while Summer got pregnant by Kaleel, got on public assistance, lived with her mom until she and Kaleel got married, then moved out of her mom's place and lived (rather well) off of her husband's earnings as a drug dealer.

The best thing that ever happened to Summer was when Kaleel got arrested. She finally realized she had to do something different with her life. She went out and got a job as a secretary at an insurance company, got a divorce from her husband, who was not only a murderer, but was also cheating on her while they were married. She found this out when a woman showed up at her door one day with a three-year-old in tow, aptly, if not offensively, named Kaleel, Jr. Summer's own daughter, Keyanna was only four years old at the time.

Belinda had even hired Summer for a brief period to work as her assistant when she was working at *Redbook* magazine, after Summer had lost one of her many jobs. Unfortunately, Summer thought working for Belinda meant she didn't have to actually work. She either came in late or didn't come in at all. When she did come in, she was loud, disrespectful and couldn't take an accurate telephone message to save her life. Not only that, Summer definitely did not fit the *Redbook* aesthetic. Eventually, Belinda realized to salvage their friendship she had to let Summer go. She was even able to get Summer a rather hefty severance package. Summer was pleased. It meant she could take off for a while. She hated any form of work.

While Summer was in the bathroom, Diana asked Belinda, "Weren't you about to mention something about stress?"

"Never mind, it was nothing important," Belinda answered.

"Yes, it was. It was important before Summer steam-rolled the conversation. What is it?"

"I'll tell you about it later. Okay?"

"Okay, but don't forget. Otherwise I'll have to bug you all night until you fess up about what's on your mind."

"Thanks, Diana."

"Thanks for what? I didn't do anything."

"Thanks for always being a friend."

"If anyone is going in the bathroom, make sure you bring along some Lysol," Summer said as she left the bathroom. "Them murder burgers I had tonight didn't sit well."

"God, Summer. You are so gross!" Diana replied.

"That's why you love me so much," Summer responded as she put her arm around Diana's shoulder. "I bring a little excitement to your otherwise humdrum life."

"I hope you washed those hands," Diana said as she wriggled from under Summer's hold.

"I'll never tell."

"Don't even listen to her, Diana," Belinda interjected. "She likes to fuck with you because she knows she can ruffle your feathers. She only does that shit to people she can get a rise out of. You should see her when she's in the hood. She's so quiet. You wouldn't know it was the same girl. But when she comes over here, she's all loud and obnoxious. She knows this building's tenants are very conservative."

"Let's call a spade a spade, with that conservative shit! Don't you mean that most of the tenants are white? Besides, Diana will never get to see how I behave in the hood; she's too scared to come up in there. Right, Diana?" Summer asked.

"I'm not scared," Diana answered. "I never have any reason to come uptown."

"I'm so glad you said that, sister-friend. My mama's havin' a barbecue next weekend at her place. You wanna come?"

Belinda couldn't wait to hear Diana's response. She was sure. She had never been anywhere near anything that resembled a ghetto. She had grown up with her parents in their home in Park Slope. Her Dad was a gynecologist and her mom was a pediatrician. And, when she bought her own place, she chose to live downtown in The East Village. According to Diana, her future had been written long before she was even born. It was always understood that she would be a doctor, just as her parents were. Diana had followed that plan to the letter, without argument. She had become a gynecologist, just like her dad.

It occurred to Belinda that Summer could be so mean sometimes. The projects that she and Summer had grown up in would not be a comfortable place for Diana. She had only invited her to fuck with her.

Belinda suddenly chimed in. "I didn't get my invite."

"Oh, now you want to go? Your ass just wants to go to protect your girl here. Don't worry, Diana will be alright. We won't make her carry a gun the first night."

"Diana, ignore her. She must've had a couple of drinks before she got here."

"Summer's trying to fuck with my head. From this moment forward, I'm ignoring her. And, by the way, Summer, I'll be carrying my own gun. Thank you very much!"

"Aw, aw. That's my girl. See, you need me as a friend. If it weren't for me, you wouldn't get a chance to see how much backbone you really have."

"And for that we all thank you, Summer. But, can we *please* go now?"

"I'm ready. I was waitin' on you guys."

"Yeah right," said Belinda.

"How we gettin' there?" Summer asked. "Are we takin' a yellow cab?"

"No, I called a limousine service," Diana answered.

"Now that's what I'm talkin' 'bout! We're travelin' in style. When we pull up in that limo, niggas gonna be all over us; especially as fine as we look."

"Jesus Christ, Summer, do you have to use that word?" asked Diana.

"What word?"

Belinda had to laugh. The two of them were like freakin' Laurel and Hardy.

Summer took one last look in Belinda's foyer mirror. She was wearing a canary yellow, see-through halter dress. Her nipples were visible through the dress. But that was Summer; the more she showed, the better. The girl had actually found a matching pair of yellow stilettos with a steel-tipped toe and heel. Summer had a big ass and she knew it, but that didn't keep her from wearing skintight clothing and tonight was as tight as Belinda had ever seen her wear. The dress was so tight and her ass was so big that the back of the dress pulled up, causing the dress to be longer in the front than in the back. Between the stilettos and the tight dress, Summer walking was a sight to behold.

Watching Summer, it amazed Belinda how flat her belly was with all the crap she ate; especially since she never exercised and had given birth. Summer was a very pretty, yet flashy girl. One of Summer's many jobs was as a hairstylist. She no longer did hair for a living, but she could still hook up a head. She was one of the few hairstylists who always made sure her own hair was as fabulous as her clients. Tonight she was sporting a burgundy weave. Belinda wouldn't have worn her hair that way, but it looked good on Summer.

The walk through the building lobby attracted much attention from tenants, visitors and the doorman alike. As soon as the girls left the building, they could see the black stretch limo sitting out front. Belinda wondered what the neighbors were saying about her and her friends. They probably thought they were hookers. Belinda tried not to care, but there was something about moving up the ladder of success that made you care what people thought of you. The doorman opened the door to the limo and Belinda handed him a tip.

Summer rolled her eyes. "Don't you pay enough money to live in this fucking money trap? Do you really have to give the doorman cash money every time he opens a fucking car door? I thought the limo driver was supposed to do that anyway."

As the limo left the Upper East Side to head to Redemption in Midtown, Belinda secretly hoped she would at least meet someone that was worth seeing again. She wanted more than merely someone to idle away the hours with; she needed sparks and fire. So often, she would start out trying her best to keep an open mind, until she realized she wasn't attracted to the person standing in front of her. Her friends and family would try to encourage her to build friendships that might later build into something more. But, she needed to feel that spark. If she couldn't feel even a glimmer of hope that she might start a flame, she lost interest. She wanted to get excited about the first date, about hearing his voice or reading a seductively written email or even better, that eager anticipation as she waited to see him once again. It had been such a long time since she had felt that for anyone. She was anxious to feel it once again.

As soon as they entered the club, men were trying to get Belinda and Summer out on the dance floor. Diana was pretty, but she was a little stiff, and it showed. It showed in the way she walked and talked. It especially showed in the way that she dressed. Tonight, she was wearing a gray wool coat dress. It was the sort of dress that could be worn sexy, if you tried, but was mostly conservative. It was made much like a jacket, with lapels, and was buttoned straight down the middle. Belinda had tried to encourage Diana to leave a button or two open (either top, bottom, or both), maybe show off a little leg, expose a little cleavage. But clearly that was not Diana's objective. Everything she wore seemed carefully chosen to conceal. She was model thin and Diana told her she had even done some runway work when she was in college. Although Diana's look clearly fit the magazine image, Belinda found it difficult to picture Diana in the role of a model. It seemed as though all she ever did was work at blending into the crowd. But maybe Diana was different in college. People do change. Diana's dark skin reminded Belinda of Australian Aborigines she had seen on *National Geographic*. She always wore her black-rimmed glasses, even though she only needed them for reading. Belinda had seldom seen Diana's eyes without her glasses, but when she had, she was struck by what beautiful eyes they were. Smoky was what Belinda would have called her eyes. They were very close to the color of her hair, a beautiful brown, similar to an amber stone. Not only that, there were times that Belinda could have sworn that the color of Diana's eyes changed at will, shifting into a kaleidoscope of colors, almost like the mood ring she had once owned in high school. Belinda was happy to see that, at least tonight, she had allowed her hair to hang free. She still had on those damn glasses though. Her beautiful long, brown, curly hair had grown to her waistline and people often assumed her hair was extensions. Belinda assumed it was Diana's Irish-American mother and Trinidadian father that were responsible for Diana's unique look. She was beautiful and self-assured when it involved professional matters. But when it came to men, Diana came across as painfully insecure.

They had met five years earlier at the gym and liked each other immediately. They would meet for coffee, work out together, and had gone to a couple of self-help seminars together, and soon became fast friends. Eventually, when Belinda thought it wouldn't be too overwhelming for Diana, she had introduced her to her other best friend, Summer. At first, their association had been a little rocky but eventually, they had become friends as well. The two of them had even gone to Paris together a couple of years ago. Belinda couldn't get away from work, so Diana had offered to take Summer free-of-charge. Of course, Summer had jumped at that opportunity. By the time they came back from Europe, they were much better friends. Belinda was ecstatic. She had wanted them to get along better, and their trip to Europe had served that purpose. Very often, Diana even confided in Summer when it came to men. Belinda believed it was because Summer was so overtly sexy and also because Diana wasn't as concerned about what Summer thought of her. On the other hand, Diana seemed to genuinely care what Belinda thought of her. Sometimes Belinda thought Diana cared a bit too much. She was amazed at how little confidence a woman like Diana appeared to have, especially when it came to matters concerning the opposite sex, from Belinda's point of view. It proved a point that she had always known; that all sorts of women, from all over the world and all walks of life, have self-esteem issues.

As Belinda, Summer, and Diana entered the club, they quickly surveyed the room.

"Damn!" Summer declared. "Is this scrubs night or what!"

"Give it a chance," Belinda responded. "We just got here."

"Easy for you to say. You got that fine as hell Aidan trailin' behind you."

"Lest we not forget, fine as hell Aidan's wife and three kids. Not only that, I told you I'm not seeing him anymore" Belinda whispered.

"Well, if you ever truly get tired of playin' with Mr. Fine, I'll take your sloppy seconds. I ain't proud."

Belinda looked over at Diana and thought she saw shock on her face. She wanted to tell Summer what a big fucking mouth she had, but presumed that would drag the issue out even longer. She had never mentioned to Diana that she was seeing a married man. There were certain things Belinda talked to Summer about that she didn't tell Diana. Summer and Diana were so very different and that was one of the very things Belinda liked about her two best friends. Belinda had lived two very contrasting lives and Diana and Summer fit nicely into *both* of those two lives. Besides which, Aidan had been little more than an on-again, off-again booty-call-on-reservation. When she realized her conscience couldn't handle sleeping with another woman's husband, she had quickly ended it.

Belinda and Diana shared a look that said they would talk later. One of the things Belinda liked about Diana was her gift for discretion. Belinda believed it was derived from Diana's upbringing, and her many years of doctor/patient confidentiality.

"Why on earth would you want anybody's seconds, thirds or fourths, for that matter?" Belinda finally asked.

"It's better than being alone," Summer said quietly.

"You're not alone," Diana chimed in, joining the loop. "You've got us. Now let's get this party started." She threw her arms around Summer and Belinda and the three friends made their way to the bar.

If there was one thing single New York women over the age of thirty had in common, it was the search for Mr. Right. Summer understood that better than anyone. She also knew that if you were a black woman looking for a black man, the search was twice as hard. She had recently read statistics that said 30 percent of black men were in jail, 25 percent were married, 20 percent were gay, 10 percent were with white women, 10 percent lived with their mommas and the other 5 percent were what a single woman had to work with; her and the thousands of other black women that were searching. Tonight, she was anxious to work on finding her 5 percent.

Summer, Belinda, and Diana took seats at the bar.

"What are you having? I'm buying the first round," Diana said.

"Well, if you're buying, I'll have a glass of champagne," Summer answered with a chuckle.

"You can't drink champagne by the glass. There's something anti-climactic about it. I'll order a bottle. Is that okay with you, Belinda?"

"That's fine with me, but what are we celebrating?"

"My new writing assignment."

"Hell no! Tonight we forget about work," Summer offered.

After the bartender poured the champagne, each of them raised a glass.

Belinda spoke first. "Here's to love."

"Fuck love; here's to being rich," said Summer.

"Trust me, being rich is highly overrated." Diana raised her glass and, with a rarely seen look of mischief, said, "Here's to that mind-blowing, soak-the-sheets, make-you-scream kind of *sex!*"

"I heard that," Belinda replied.

"See, Belinda, I told you Diana was a closet freak."

All three of the girls laughed and clinked their glasses together and said in unison, "To mind-blowing, soak-the-sheets, make-you-scream *sex!*"

FOUR

She suddenly noticed him out of the corner of her eye; the man with the awe-inspiring presence. He was magnificent. Summer's strongest desire was to be his. She was induced by a force more compelling than anything she had ever experienced. His power was unmistakable and frighteningly seductive. He was a cross between the most angelic of creatures and the devil himself. The word *beautiful* could never hope to come even close to defining him—from his striking olive-colored skin to his impressive muscular build. But most spectacular of all were his eyes. His eyes defied logic and were a color she had never seen before and would probably never see again. Yet, somehow they seemed vaguely familiar. From where she sat, they actually appeared to be shifting and changing from moment to moment to various shades of gray, green, and blue. His dark black, curly hair was impeccable and she guessed that it was probably softer than spun silk. Even the steel gray suit he wore was indefinable.

Summer's loins ached to feel the weight of his body

pressed against hers. She struggled to will herself to run with break-neck speed away from that place, yet she couldn't move. It was as though there was an electric current running through her that could not be broken. It appeared that everyone else around them felt his power as well. So much, in fact, that they had deemed him worthy enough to be granted a space of his own. Often the bar at Redemption was so jam-packed from end to end with people, a thirsty patron would be hard-pressed to get the attention of the bartender and eventually get a drink. Tonight, however, the bar created an opening, it seemed, especially for him. Within moments, the bar went from wall-to-wall people to a handful, primarily made up of Summer, Belinda, Diana, her mysterious stranger, and a couple of hypnotized onlookers. He seemed to be almost welcoming her. Who was she to ignore such an obvious invitation? Summer quickly and discreetly checked her face in her compact mirror, happy to find there were no remnants of the burgers she had eaten earlier left lingering between her teeth. Next, she surveyed her makeup. As Summer summoned the courage to rise from her seat and walk to the other end of the bar, she realized that the attraction she was feeling was not at all mutual, and the spell was broken. While Summer watched him, it seemed he was riveted by Belinda.

The moment he saw her, he was glad he had come alone. He could smell her from across the room. Her desire was unmistakable and greatly intoxicating. It was the scent of vitality and lust, fused with endless longing. It occurred to him that she was probably what had brought him there tonight.

René would have found Redemption to be a ripe hunting ground. Lately, Dante had taken to varying his routine and going to other clubs, not only to avoid René, but also to afford himself the opportunity to fall way below the radar. There were many of his kind living in New York. Most of them kept their presence a secret, understandably. Yet, lately, there were some of his kind, especially the younger ones, who had taken to living their lives out loud. They were running around without aim or purpose; simply taking whatever and whomever they wanted, wherever they wanted, with no view to the consequences of their actions.

Dante took great pride in his ability to still feel compassion and the fact that he never, ever, took more than he needed. He was very careful to leave behind as little evidence of his presence as possible. It was nothing more than a matter of survival for him. He had no evil intentions, no desire to harm.

Unfortunately, this life afforded him no room for long-lasting alliances and had, therefore, become unbearably lonely for him. Tonight, there was an impressive collection to choose from; all of them so full of spirit and energy. It made him feel so full of life, knowing that within a matter of moments, one of them could be his, but he wanted more. He wanted her, and he wanted her for more than just a fleeting moment. Yet, he realized that could never be an option.

The others paled in comparison to her. She was all things good and beautiful, magnified. Yet, within her, there was a desire for so *many* things. That made her a pleasing target. Hers was a soul longed for. His kindness willed him to choose another; or better yet, to leave the place altogether. Once he touched her, he would never be able to get enough. He was painfully aware of the end result of that kind of longing. His desire was strong and he was afraid it would not permit him the luxury of simply walking away. He needed her far too much.

He drank her in, gently massaging her existence with his captivating eyes, willing her to come to him. And, as Summer admired his succulent lips, silently agonizing over his intensity, his mouth curved upward in a slight smile and he rose from his seat.

"May I buy you a drink?"

Even his voice carried with it a certain strength; thick, yet soothing, like a welcoming blanket. Heavy and warm, but soft and inviting at the same time.

While Summer was ravenous and unafraid, Belinda was titillated, yet frightened.

"I, uh, uhm. No thank you. My friends and I were just enjoying a bottle of champagne...to..."

Before she could finish her sentence, he was gone. His exit was nothing short of haunting. One minute he was there and suddenly he was not.

"What the fuck just happened?" Summer asked. "That was some weird shit! I mean, what is he? A fuckin' magician or something? He just disappeared."

"Summer, what are you talking about?" Diana asked.

"You're gonna sit there and tell me that you didn't notice what just took place," Summer replied.

From Belinda's point of view, the conversation between Summer and Diana seemed to be happening from some far-off place. Their voices were low and distant and reminded her of what a voice might sound like if being heard through a vacuum. She struggled to hear, before getting the sense that somehow, some invisible button had been pushed, decreasing the volume all around her. Everything was coming in through Belinda's ears at a greatly reduced timbre. That is, until Summer snapped her out of it.

"Belinda? Belinda? Girl, are you alright?"

Finally, she could hear everything in normal mode.

"Yeah. Yeah. What? What were you saying?"

"Did you catch that? There was something weird about that man. He was either demon or angel and quite frankly, I don't think I want to know which."

"What man?" Belinda asked.

"What man? You gotta be kidding me! The man that just offered to buy you a drink; that man. The man that's been ogling you since we got here, before disappearing in front of our very eyes."

"I'll be right back," was Belinda's only response. Her actions were on autopilot as she headed toward the exit.

The person at the door stopped her before she could leave.

"You coming back?" he asked.

Still in a bit of a haze, she never answered. Instead, she nodded, extending her hand so that it could be stamped for her return.

She thought she recognized Cameron from *Newsweek* and was surprised to find her there since she lived in D.C.

"Cameron! Cameron!"

She was sure that was her, but still no response.

Suddenly, Belinda began to feel as though she was being followed. The street was surprisingly empty for a Friday night in New York City. Yet, she heard the telltale pounding of lone footsteps approaching her, quickening with each step she took.

She continued to walk in the direction she thought Cameron was going, and when she entered what looked like another club, Belinda followed. She silently admonished herself for leaving Redemption, without so much as a word to Summer and Diana as to where she was going. She wondered what had gotten into her. She was disoriented and more than a bit confused. She realized that this kind of behavior was very much out of character for her; out of character and possibly dangerous.

Along with the dense fog of smoke that hung in the air, she noticed the tangle of bodies writhing and squirming in unison on the cluttered floor the moment she entered. Though most of the bodies were drenched in sweat, a cool, icy wind blew through the open windows.

Not even two feet away, shards of glass littered the floor beneath the windows. Yet, the inhabitants seemed unfettered by it all. There were multiple couplings as well as an endless string of free-for-alls. However, the moans and cries seemed to peak in unison, almost as if it were a well-rehearsed song.

Before leaving, Belinda scanned the bodies; a bit embarrassed but curious if Cameron was among them. Just as she was turning on her heels to leave, he arose from the heap. His torso was reminiscent of what a half-man half-beast might look like. His imposing male appendage jutted forward, drawing her to him as if it were some twisted version of a divining rod leading her to water. One look in his eyes and she realized that there was no way she could leave, even if she wanted to. His eyes were something beyond human; a kaleidoscope of colors that shifted and changed to suit his desire. As she made her greatest effort to run, those very same eyes appeared to boil red beneath the sockets, just before changing to an oddly familiar shade of blue.

"Come to me. You have no free will here."

"I, we, every…everyone has free will," she stammered.

She realized how out-of-place and odd her words were for this situation. It almost seemed silly under the circumstances.

"That is nothing more than a foolish mortal perception…Belinda. Now, come to me. I need you."

"How do you know my name? I didn't tell you my name!"

Belinda summoned enough strength to lift her feet from the floor and run as fast as she could.

Despite the fact that the streets were more than just a little familiar to her, she couldn't figure out which direction she needed to go in order to return to Redemption and the safety of her friends.

She was being followed. That urgent pounding of footsteps against the pavement returned, almost mocking her, reminding her that she was helpless. A quick look at the large street clock she passed indicated it was 8:45 p.m. It was pitch-black outside and there didn't appear to be another soul on the street, besides her and the lone footsteps that echoed behind her.

She only dared make a quarter turn to glance behind her. That's when she saw him. He was dressed all in black and a hood covered his head, making it impossible for her to see his face. She dared not look directly at him again for fear that any action on her part would seal her fate; possibility would become probability, and she would never again see the light of day. So, she hastened her pace. The mad thumping of her heart was relentless, yet it at least reminded her that she was indeed still alive. In an instant, she once again turned and found he was gone.

"Get a grip, girl; you're really beginning to lose it," she spoke nervously to herself.

As she was about to breathe a huge sigh of relief, she faced forward, only to find him standing before her, blocking her path, daring her to take another step. As he removed the hood of his cloak from his head and reached for her with his massive hands, she suddenly recognized how much danger she was in. If she didn't get away from him now, her life would probably be over. She might very well join the ranks of the missing persons she was investigating. But, where could she go. What could she do? As his towering figure loomed large above her, she attempted to scream, but remarkably, there was no sound. All she could hear was the ominous sound of his voice, painfully quiet, yet foreboding.

"I promise, I won't take too much," he whispered with a sardonic smile.

As his hot breath hovered closer to her face, she was suddenly devoid of fear. She no longer possessed the desire to flee from him. Her entire body was rooted to the spot, incapable of moving. He was in control.

FIVE

At the very moment Dante thought his benevolence might rule out over his passion; he had approached her and invited her to join him in a drink. She appeared to be turning him down and he was surprisingly relieved and prepared to concede defeat; that is, until he saw René enter the club. That's when everything changed. Dante had no other choice but to stay close, if only to protect her. At least, that is what he convinced himself of.

As soon as René entered, it was readily apparent to Dante from her actions that René was controlling her. To the untrained eye, her sudden lack of focus might have gone unnoticed. Dante had so often used the same manipulation, and therefore noticed her shift immediately. As quickly as he averted his attention from her to deal with René, she was gone. She left her friends and exited the club, with René close at her heels.

Dante followed them both, watching as René led her exactly where he wanted her to go. Dante had known René long enough to know what he would do. He would get her away from the comfort of her friends and the other club-goers, to where she would be defenseless.

She walked a block or so before he led her directly to a club his kind frequented, called Potion, as both he and René watched from a distance, each with conflicting objectives. Despite his intended purpose to only protect her, he couldn't help but be drawn to her, mesmerized by her every action. Every movement was a dance. This creature before him, more than any other he had ever encountered, was captivating. However, the realization that René lurked only a few feet away, brought him back down to earth. He could smell her fear. She knew there was danger and his heart ached for her. The last thing he wanted was for her to feel even a moment of alarm. Yet, timing was everything and he had to wait and see exactly what René had planned.

Watching them both from a distance, Dante felt no kinship to René, only repulsion at his caricature of his kind; the long black cloak, the makeup he had purposely applied to lend a paleness to his skin. He was a child playing a dangerous game; one that he couldn't hope to predict the consequences of. René likened himself to a vampire, but they were so much more than mere vampires could ever hope to become. They were the future; a future human kindness would never welcome with open arms. Therefore, their presence had to remain a secret; at least for now.

As Dante watched and waited, it didn't take long before

his suspicions were confirmed. René indeed had plans for the beautiful young woman. As she walked, René, played a game of cat and mouse that only Dante could recognize. He knew better than anyone that René could have taken her at any time. But, he enjoyed the physiological change that her ever-increasing levels of adrenaline were creating within her. He fed on it. So, he followed just closely enough that she knew he was there; that is, until he would eventually and inevitably, capture her.

Dante, however, refused to allow it.

At the precise moment that René prepared to take her, Dante stopped him.

"I thought you were going to Indigo."

"I changed my mind."

"Yeah, right," René snorted.

"Leave this one," was all Dante said.

"Why should I?"

Dante was not enjoying the game that René was playing. "Because I said so."

"I don't think I can do that. I think I'm in love." He laughed while roughly fondling her breasts.

Dante's anger bubbled dangerously to the surface at the sight of René touching her. "I said, let her go."

"You still haven't told me why."

"For the same reason I've been telling you for months now. You're going to fuck things up for all of us, with your constant showboating. You have the same powers we all possess, René, and there is no question of the strength we *both* possess, but nothing or no one is all powerful; not even us. What? You don't think anyone will notice her missing? You lured her from a club full of people, including two of her friends."

"And, how exactly would you know all that, unless you were watching her as well? Maybe it's you who's in love, huh? Or, is it that you think she's the one; the one to bring longevity to your power? That's it, isn't it?"

That thought hadn't even occurred to Dante until then. Maybe that was the reason he was there, not merely to restore, but to build even greater power—through her.

"Besides, speak for yourself, Dante," René continued. "You've developed a soft spot for these humans in your old age. As much as you think my attempts at amusement will cost us, your compassion for them will come with an even greater price."

"LET...HER...GO!"

Dante's words were measured; limited, but specific. However, those words were spoken with such intensity, René responded immediately.

She had collapsed from the very moment he touched her and now lay unconscious in his arms. He passed her along to Dante.

"Do with her what you will, Oh Great One," he said, sarcastically. "This game was beginning to bore me anyway."

Before Dante could utter another word, René was gone.

Despite his hasty departure, Dante realized that he had

not seen the last of René. He would have to prepare himself for the backlash that was sure to follow.

But for now, he decided, he would focus his attention on her. She was as light as a feather in his arms and so very helpless. He gazed at her angelic features, her brown, doe-like eyes, her flawless caramel complexion, and the sexy black mole that dotted the right side of her full lips, reminding him of a period at the end of a sentence. He couldn't help but smile; his first genuine smile in quite some time.

The only thing left now was what to do with her? More than anything, he would have liked to have done what he came there to do; to replenish and then spirit her away with him. But, somehow, he couldn't. Instead, he decided to quietly and safely return her to her friends and awaken her with no memory of what had taken place.

SIX

Belinda entered the club just as he had intended; with no memory of what had taken place. In fact, the last thing she remembered was walking away from the bar.

"Belinda, where the hell have you been!" Summer exclaimed. "We were worried sick. You just left, without so much as a glance in our direction. I considered going after you, but Diana talked me out of it."

"I went to the bathroom."

"Oh really? Is that why you smell like the inside of a smoking lounge?"

That's when Belinda noticed that her hair and clothing reeked of smoke.

Belinda shrugged her shoulders. "I don't know. Maybe someone was smoking in the bathroom."

Summer turned Belinda's body so that she was facing in the direction of the bar.

"See that," she said, pointing. "That is where we were sitting. The bathroom is in that direction. When you left the bar you walked in this direction...the direction of the exit door. Belinda, I don't know what's going on and if there's something you don't want to tell me, that's cool, but you're acting a little strange. You definitely didn't go to the bathroom. I saw you head straight for the front door."

"Maybe I had too much champagne. I'm not saying you're a liar or anything, Summer. I truly don't remember leaving the club. If I did, I'm sorry that I didn't say anything. Maybe I did have too much to drink and needed a little air. It's no big deal. Let's find Diana. Didn't we come here to party?"

Summer watched as Belinda made her way through the club. She wasn't quite sure why, but she was worried. She had the uncanny feeling that something was terribly wrong.

"Hey, Bee. Where you been?" Diana asked, as she approached Belinda from the other side of the club.

"Well, according to Summer here, and her overactive imagination, I've been up to some espionage shit or something."

Summer tried not to show it, but she was pissed that Belinda seemed to be poking fun at her. Instead of her customary, lambasting response, she decided to let it drop and started dancing with an old friend she saw on the dance floor.

While Summer danced, Diana and Belinda talked.

"I didn't want to say anything tonight, with Summer sitting here because she always thinks everything has some kind of supernatural influence, with her talk of premonitions and ghosts and goblins and shit, but I've been feeling so strange lately, sort of out of it, a little paranoid. I don't know what it is. It might be anticipation about this new writing assignment or maybe just a case of the lonelies, but I can't sleep. I jump at the slightest noise, and a few times I could've sworn that someone was watching me, right inside of my own apartment. I realize that it sounds crazy as hell. I need to get it out of my head and talk about it with a rational human being. So, do you think I'm insane or what?"

"Belinda, you know me; I don't necessarily subscribe to Summer's concept of things. I'm a doctor. I operate from a scientific perspective, but I'll admit one thing; I don't believe everything is as simple as what it appears to be. It's very easy for all of us to believe only what we've seen with our own eyes. It's hypocritical not to recognize that there must be so much more in the world that some of us have never seen and may never see. But, simply because we haven't seen it, doesn't mean it doesn't exist. As far as your inability to sleep and your jumpiness is concerned, that can all be explained very logically. You're jumpy because you haven't been sleeping and you haven't been sleeping because you've obviously got a lot on your mind. If you'd like, I can prescribe something for you; something mild, so you can get some sleep. If you want to bounce whatever is rattling around in that head of yours off of someone, I'm here as a sounding board, or I can refer you to a therapist."

"I might take you up on two of your offers. Maybe not

tonight, but I'll take you up on the offer to talk and the offer of some chemically assisted sleep. I'll think about the therapist. Thanks, hon."

"No problem. What are friends for? I need to stretch my legs a bit. You feel like taking a walk? I was thinking about checking out the downstairs."

"No. I'm going to sit here a while; try to clear my head."

"Okay, sweetie," Diana said.

Diana motioned to Summer that she was going to take a walk downstairs when she stood up, then turned to Belinda before she left and whispered, "Would you just look at those two."

Some big ole boy was bumping and grinding against Summer's ass as she gyrated to the music. The two of them were creating quite a scene. He got all the way down to the ground, despite his rather massive 250-plus pound frame. Summer's crotch was so close to his mouth, Belinda was sure things were going to go from an 'R' to an 'X' rating.

After sitting alone for a few minutes, Belinda decided to find Diana downstairs since Summer seemed to be otherwise occupied.

Belinda found the tone of the smooth jazz music playing downstairs to be just what the doctor ordered. That is, until she noticed what appeared to be an argument between Diana and a tall handsome gentleman she didn't recognize. Belinda was sure she knew all of Diana's friends, of which there were very few. In fact, most of Diana's acquaintances consisted of other doctors at her practice. It occurred to Belinda that the person she was arguing with might be a stranger, but she thought she detected a certain familiarity in their exchange, so rather than attempt to rescue Diana, Belinda decided to hang back and watch from a distance. She had only been watching for a moment when the disagreement arrived at a hasty conclusion. Belinda wondered if Diana had noticed her watching, despite her efforts to hang back and be discreet.

Rather than put Diana on the spot, Belinda decided she would go back upstairs and see what Summer was up to. She found her at the bar having a drink alone.

"What happened to your nasty friend?" Belinda joked.

"Oh him. That ain't nobody but Pookie. He's one of Kaleel's homeboys from back in the day. He obviously was smarter than Kaleel; he got out of the life and now has a straight job working at a law firm somewhere. That boy used to try to get with me all the time when Kaleel and I were together. As crazy as Kaleel was, he probably would have killed him if he knew that. But Pookie seems like he's calmed down quite a bit."

"He didn't look like he was calm, rubbing against your ass on that dance floor."

"Girl, we were just havin' some fun. You startin' to sound like Diana. Loosen up. Speaking of which, where is Diana? I haven't seen her since she went downstairs. Is she still down there? The only reason anybody stays down there is if they hooked up. Did she meet some-body?"

"Yeah, she's still down there, but I don't think she met anybody," Belinda lied. "You know how Diana is; clubs aren't really her thing."

"Yeah. Yeah. Clubs aren't her thing."

Belinda didn't notice the sarcasm in Summer's voice. Summer was recalling a particular incident that she had never mentioned to Belinda.

One night she had gone out with some girls she used to work with at the hair salon and was completely shocked when she noticed Diana on the dance floor, wearing a tight leather corset and black jeans, her make-up and hair all done up and sexy. For a moment she was sure that her own eyes were playing tricks on her. But, it was definitely Diana. She was glued to some guy that appeared to be at least a decade younger than her. She was touching him and whispering in his ear. Then, as quickly as Summer saw the two of them standing not two feet away, they were gone. She had never told Belinda about it. But, often, when she and Diana were going at it, she considered mentioning Diana's out-of-character walk on the wild side. Yet, she always stopped herself.

Belinda and Summer enjoyed the rest of the night dancing and talking and it wasn't until the club lights started to go up that they realized they hadn't seen Diana all night.

"You think maybe they're kicking us out?" Belinda said.

"Yeah. Where the hell is Diana? I haven't seen her all night. The last time I saw her, some pale-ass guy was following her downstairs. I hope she's not hooking up with him; that was a weird-lookin' motha fucka."

"Listen to you. I know you're not talking about anybody's choice of men, because we've all had some doozies." Belinda laughed.

"No, for real; you didn't see him. He looked like he was straight out of some doggone horror movie. I mean, he wasn't ugly, but he looked weird. You had to be there. You'd know what I was talkin' about if you'd seen him. Not only that, he had bad news written all over him."

"Well, Diana's a grown woman and she's a big enough girl to pick her own men. I'm happy to see she's still in the game. Sometimes I worry about that girl. For a minute there, I was starting to think she was asexual. I never hear her talk about men, or women for that matter."

"I keep tryin' to tell you the girl is a closet freak."

"Summer, you think everybody's a closet freak."

"That's true." Summer laughed. "I know one thing; she better not have left without telling us, or the next time I see her, I'm gonna cuss her ass out."

"What makes you think Diana would do a thing like that?"

"You have a lot more faith in people than I do."

"You wanna go look for her downstairs?" Belinda asked.

"I'm not walkin' anywhere but out of this club. My feet hurt like hell."

"I'll go look for her then. She's probably downstairs."

Just as Belinda was about to descend the stairs, Diana arrived.

"Ho, where you been?" Summer asked.

"It was too loud up here. I was downstairs listening to some jazz."

"All night?"

"Well, no. Not all night. I was up here for a while and then I went down there."

"We haven't seen you all night."

"Oh come on, Summer; there you go exaggerating again. I motioned to you that I was going downstairs."

"Yeah, that was like three hours ago."

"Belinda, can you believe this one? She has no concept of time. I was not down there for three hours. It was one hour tops."

"Yeah. Okay," was all Summer said. "Anyway. Are we ready to go? Not that it matters, because the lights are going up. They're kicking us out, regardless. You know what they say: *you ain't gotta go home, but you gotta go.* We gonna do our usual?"

After a night on the town, they would always have breakfast at Green Kitchen. It was Belinda's favorite neighborhood diner. She had been eating at that diner since she was a little girl. Her father had been a clerk at a nearby library and every Friday, after he left work, he would take her there to get a cheeseburger and a cherry coke. It was a tradition she loved. It made her feel special. Whenever she missed her dad the most, she would remember those Green Kitchen cheeseburgers and those extra sweet cherry cokes and smile.

"What you grinnin' about?" Summer asked.

"Nothing. Just thinking about my humble beginnings; that's all."

"Well, I'm ready to get my grub on. All that dancin' and sweatin' with Pookie has got my appetite in full effect."

They stepped outside to find the limousine was still there waiting.

"I can't believe you had the limo wait all night. This must be costing a fortune," Belinda remarked.

"It's actually isn't as expensive as you'd think and it's worth it for the convenience. Besides, how often do I splurge on anything?"

"Very true."

"You don't hear me complaining," Summer commented. "Now, let's go eat. I'm fuckin' starvin'."

Diana visibly flinched as Summer spoke. She had stopped admonishing Summer for her vulgarity long ago. It didn't change anything and if anything, it only made Summer worse.

They got in the limo and Diana told the driver where they were going. "77th and York Avenue please."

"Would you like me to wait, ma'am?"

"Yes, thank you. After that, if you could just drop each of us home, you'll be done for the night."

"No rush, ma'am. I'm yours for the night, for as long as you need me," the driver mentioned.

"Hmmm," Summer said. "Yours for the night, huh? For as long as you need him? Sounds like an invitation to me. I think he wants you, Diana dear, and he is kinda cute, in a low-rent sort of way. If I were you, after you and the driver drop us off, I would *wear that dick out!*"

"Geez, Summer, he can probably hear every word you're saying," Belinda said.

"So, it's not like he wasn't thinking it himself. Three fine ass women in the back seat of his limo in the middle of the night, smelling good. What, you don't think his dick is hard? I bet you if I touched it right now, it would be solid; solid as a rock."

Summer started to sing the chorus to that old Ashford and Simpson song.

"Solid, yes, it is, solid as a rock. Ah, and nothing's changed it, ooh, the thrill is still hot, hot, hot, hot, hot, hot , hot , hot."

All Belinda could do was laugh, while Diana pretended not to fume.

All the girls had seen of their driver from behind the wheel was his face and his upper body. He had short black hair that was receding slightly in the back. He had what seemed to be a Greek accent. His upper body was appealing enough. He wasn't a bodybuilder or anything, but he was easy enough on the eyes. Belinda had noticed from the very start of the evening that he was a little heavy-handed with the Paco Rabanne, but it was livable. A cologne update that included scents from this millennium, maybe a baldy, instead of the receding hairline, and he might actually be a '7.'

After pulling up in front of Green Kitchen, the driver got out and opened the door. He reached for Diana's hand to help her out of her seat and Belinda thought she could see Diana visibly flinch. There were definitely some sparks flying between Diana and the driver. He could forget about it, though. Diana and her family were slaves to the caste system. It often amazed Belinda that Diana would even hang out with Summer, or herself, for that matter. After all, both she and Summer were pretty much hoodrats. Whatever her reasons were, Diana definitely did not come by her decision to spend time with the two of them easily.

They entered the restaurant and took their favorite booth by the window. Everyone that worked at the restaurant knew them well. They had been in Green Kitchen so many times.

"Good morning, ladies," said the owner. "Would you like something to drink? Some coffee maybe?"

"Yes, thank you. I'll definitely have some coffee," Diana said.

"And I'll have a mimosa please," replied Summer.

"Make mine an orange juice," was Belinda's answer.

"Okay, ladies. Do you need some time to look at the menu?"

"Yeah, thanks. Give us a couple of minutes," Belinda responded.

"I'll bring your drinks."

While the owner was getting their drinks, Belinda was doing a mental countdown…10-9-8-7-6-5…

"So, what's the dealeo, girl?" Summer asked. "Where the fuck were you all night? Tell the truth; were you blowin' some guy in the men's room? You can tell us."

Belinda was impressed with how well she knew her friends. She didn't even make it to number one before Summer asked about Diana's whereabouts all evening.

"I told you what I was doing. I was sitting downstairs listening to some jazz."

"Yeah, but what about Bèla Lugosi?"

"What the fuck are you talking about?"

Suddenly, the table was silent. Belinda didn't think she had ever heard Diana use a four-letter word. For the first time in God only knows how long, Summer was silent.

Recognizing the impact of her words, Diana made an attempt at levity.

"What? I suppose you guys didn't think I ever swore. What do you think? I'm Mother Teresa or something?"

Belinda was not convinced. Summer had touched a chord. There had obviously been something going on at the club with the man she saw Diana arguing with, but she decided the best thing to do was to change the subject.

"So, how about those Knicks?" she joked.

It worked. Both Summer and Diana laughed and by that time their drinks had arrived, the waiter had taken their breakfast order.

"What about that big ole boy you were dancin' with tonight?" Belinda asked Summer. "He was all up in there when I saw him. I thought for sure you were takin' him home tonight."

"Despite what ya'll may think, I'm not the ho that I appear to be. In fact, lately, I've been going through a drought that would rival the Sahara. What nobody seems to get is despite my colorful demeanor, I do have principles."

"Colorful, huh? That's an…interesting way to put it," Diana said.

"That's right, colorful. But, let me finish. You see, just any brotha won't do. I've scraped the bottom before, but those days are over. After Kaleel, I'm ready for something good; something healthy for a change. That whole situation really opened my eyes. I mean, for a while there, I was actually riding that fuckin' bus; taking my daughter to see her father behind bars. Shit like that can't help but open your eyes. I talk a lot of shit about fine and all that but on some level, we *all* need to be careful. Some of these brothas. Let me correct that; not just brothas. Some of these men be walkin' around lookin' as fine as they want to be, but a large percentage of them are full of shit and so much more. All I'm tryin' to do, at this point, is not get caught out there with the Triple G's."

All three girls chimed in with their special mantra, "GIMME, GOTCHA, GONNA GIT!"

"Like I always say," Summer continued. "When in doubt, ask yourself three questions."

"Question one?" Diana volunteered. "Is the man in question gainfully employed?"

"Question two? Did Mr. Wonderful give you his home phone number?"

"Drum roll please. Question three? And, I might add, my most important question? Is money a frequent topic of conversation?"

"As long as we all keep in mind all the signs of a Triple G, we'll be fine. Then we can commence to doing our respective thangs."

"Thanks for the love lesson; we don't know what we would do without you," Belinda said."

"Glad to help."

"I got this," Belinda offered when the check came.

Both Diana and Summer thanked her. Belinda laid her American Express card on the table. She didn't add a tip to the sales slip. Belinda always liked to give the waiters a tip in cash. She even tipped the busboys. Belinda had worked as a waitress on more than one occasion, while she was a student, and could relate to having cash on hand.

Belinda, Summer, and Diana left the diner and got back in the limo. The driver first dropped Belinda off. She only lived a few blocks away on 68th Street and 1st Avenue.

"Goodnight, Diana," Belinda said. "Thanks for the limo ride."

"Don't mention it, sweetie. Thank you, for breakfast."

"Goodnight, Summer. I'll see you tomorrow afternoon. Remember, we're supposed to go to Bloomies tomorrow."

"Hell yeah; I remember. You said you were gonna buy me those Pradas I saw on sale; an early birthday present, right? Just make sure it's not too early. A sister's gotta get her beauty sleep."

"Don't worry; I won't call before noon."

"Okay, that's good; not before two. Talk to you then."

"Now you know two means four to you. We're gonna get there just about closing time. Later!"

Belinda closed the door to the limo, said goodnight to the driver, and went inside her apartment building.

The driver watched Belinda go inside and say good morning to the doorman, then pulled off, heading for El Barrio, where Summer lived. Summer got out of the limo and said goodbye to Diana. But before she left, she winked at Diana and motioned toward the driver. Diana couldn't help but smirk.

"Where to now?" the driver asked.

"How about you take me home? By the way, my name is Diana and your name is…?"

"Oh, I'm Vladimir." Vladimir turned and shook Diana's hand. "My friends call me Vlad."

"Vlad, do you like scotch?"

"Yes, as a matter of fact I do. It's my favorite."

"I happen to have a very special bottle of scotch in my apartment and no one to share it with. Would you like to have a drink with me?"

"I'd love to. So back to where I picked you up earlier this evening?"

"Yes," Diana answered. "The address is 75 Christopher Street."

Two years earlier, Diana had bought a $2.5 million home on Christopher Street, in the Village. The neighborhood was so out of character for her. But, that was what she liked about it. It was such a departure from her surface lifestyle. Her practice, and its Upper East Side medical office, was day and her apartment, it…it was night.

Entering Diana's apartment, Vlad couldn't believe what he had lucked into; especially given the fact that he had considered not working that night. It wasn't as though he never slept with his passengers, but this woman was clearly the crème de la crème of his very short list. Although she was a bit plain, her beauty was impossible to camouflage, even behind her woolen dress and horn-rimmed glasses. Given the fact that she had invited him back to her apartment, she obviously wasn't the shrinking violet she appeared to be. In fact, if he were going to bet on it, he was sure she was probably a hell-cat.

"Have a seat, Vlad. I'm going to take a quick shower, if you don't mind. Feel free to help yourself to anything you'd like. The scotch is on top of the sofa table."

"No problem; no problem at all. I'll wait here for you."

As Diana exited the room, she couldn't help but chuckle slightly. It was always so very easy; a smile, pleasant words. Were all men that easy?

The combination of scotch and anticipation wouldn't allow Vlad's hard-on to subside. He gently stroked himself through his pants, glancing occasionally to ensure that Diana wasn't exiting the shower. He would have liked nothing better than to join her—no preliminaries, no conversation—and fuck her until she spoke Russian as well as he did. But, he wasn't sure what the protocol was in a situation such as this one. He decided that she'd have to be the one to take the lead. Just as he was removing his hand from his raging erection, a sound that bore a striking resemblance to velvet glided gently to his ears.

"Don't stop on my account."

She stood in the doorway, her body naked and glistening against the backdrop of the full moon shining brilliantly through the apartment's picture windows. Her breasts were perfection, pert, erect nipples, inviting him to taste. Her body was curvaceous, yet slender, and bore little resemblance to what could be seen beneath the gray frock she'd worn earlier. Endless waves of thick, unruly, curly hair cascaded past her shoulders and ended near her waistline.

Diana sensed his discomfort at being discovered touching himself. Truth be told, she derived great pleasure from his unease.

"Cat got your tongue, baby?"

"No, no. It's just, you are so very beautiful," he stuttered.

"Thank you, Vlad. I'm sure your cock is equally as beautiful, but I can't see it beneath those pants. Remove them, please. I want to see what you've brought to me tonight."

Vlad stood, quickly removing his pants, hoping that she would be satisfied. His cock jutted forward, with a mind of its own, as soon as it was released from its confines.

"Hmmmm. I'm pleased. Come to me."

Her fingers motioned for Vlad to join her, but it was her eyes that beckoned him; green, mesmerizing eyes, liquid pools of desire that were simultaneously enticing, yet somehow frightening, as they seemed to shift and change hues at will. For a moment, Vlad considered his wife, his five children, his job. He considered putting on his pants and taking himself and his hard-on home where he belonged…for a moment. Instead, he crossed the room and she led him, her hand massaging his now pulsating cock from behind her back. She led him to her bedroom and she shut the door.

SEVEN

"Good evening, Ms. Wilson."

"Good evening, Javier."

Belinda couldn't help but smirk. She could see her doorman discreetly looking for Summer. Summer often spent the night at her house and although Javier always maintained his professionalism, there was no mistaking that tell-tale look of lust in his eyes every time Summer passed him by.

Belinda couldn't remember when she felt more exhausted. She and her friends had been partying together for years and this was the first time she ever remembered feeling so drained. She even considered calling Summer and canceling their shopping spree for later that day. Instead, she decided to get some sleep and, if need be, she would give Summer her credit card and let her pick out what she wanted. That would make up for her canceling. She would wait and see how she felt when she woke up.

Once inside her apartment, Belinda got an eerie feeling; almost as if she weren't alone. She had been having that same feeling for weeks now, but with each passing day, it had gotten stronger and stronger. Tonight was the most intense it had ever felt. As if the paranoia were not bad enough, she had been plagued with the most frightening nightmares she had ever experienced. She was starting to think that maybe she had ghosts.

"Come on, Belinda," she spoke aloud. "Chill out. You're freaking yourself. There is *no one* and *nothing* here."

She turned on the TV and found that she was a bit hungry, so she popped a little bit of leftover naan from her favorite Indian restaurant, Apna Taj, in the micro-wave, sat down with the naan and some tamarind sauce, flipping channels on the TV until she realized nothing was holding her attention. Belinda found that candles always relaxed her, so she lit a few candles on the dresser in her bedroom and took a quick shower. By the time she was done with her shower, she was tired and decided she should probably go to bed and get some rest. Within minutes, she had drifted off to sleep.

"Belinda. Belinda."

A voice called to her in the middle of the night. At first, Belinda thought she was dreaming, but finally, she opened her eyes. As soon as her eyes were opened, a brisk wind washed over her bedroom, quickly extinguishing the candles she lit earlier. It was as though a window or door were suddenly opened; or maybe it was exactly what it felt like; like someone had exhaled their breath. And there it was again.

"Belinda. Belinda."

"Who's there? What do you want?"

"You. I want you, Belinda."

EIGHT

"I thought you would come," René sneered, without even bothering to turn around.

"I thought I told you to leave this one alone."

Dante stood in the doorway of Belinda's bedroom in his true form; wings fully extended, jagged teeth bared. Colossal horns sprouted from both the sides of his head and at his shoulders. Angered by René's actions, his eyes actually appeared to be boiling from beneath their sockets; rippling and blood red. Red lines pulsed and contorted beneath his skin, tangling themselves together, like vines on a tree.

"I thought you understood that this is our one true purpose. I most certainly shall not be diverted from that purpose by these mortals."

What could only be described as a growl emanated from Dante's grotesquely formed lips, as spittle dropped and fell to the floor. His wings prepared to take the stance of battle.

"If you care anything at all for this mortal, I'd be very careful about your next move. You see, I'm still inside of her and if for the sake of my own protection, I was forced to say, take my natural form, she'd never survive it. Besides, there's no need to scold me now, big brother; I was finished anyway. I have one question for you, Dante. Did you really think you could keep her to yourself? You, of all people, should know by now, that this is not how we do things. I'm willing to share; why can't you? In fact, she's still alive. Why don't you replenish *now?* You look like it's been quite some time since you've restored."

In fact, Dante had not taken another woman since he'd laid his eyes upon Belinda. It was a precarious position. He couldn't survive without satisfying his basest desires, yet to do so was to forsake everything he stood for. He wanted her, but he wasn't sure he would be able to control himself if he were with her. Too many times he had seen what could happen to a mortal if his kind did not exercise control. Through time, he had learned how to get what he needed without killing. It meant that he would often have to take women without their consent in order to supply the large numbers he needed. To depend on one woman, or even a few, meant that someone surely would die. And survival, not another's death, was his only purpose.

"I, unlike you, understand my fate, René. Our survival does not require a human bloodbath."

"Who said I wanted a bloodbath? I just want to have some fun."

"Why do you insist on pushing my buttons at every turn? One of these days..."

"Brother, it's best you not finish that sentence. No need to set unnecessary wheels in motion; at least not yet. Not while I'm still enjoying myself. Let's agree to disagree while we play with this one. I assure you, there's enough of her to satisfy both of us."

Eager to rile Dante, just a bit, René began a partial transformation and traced his talons along Belinda's face, continuing the length of her body, and drawing blood at her chest.

Never in his entire existence had Dante ever possessed such a strong desire to destroy one of his own. Until now, René had never been more than a slight annoyance to Dante. He had now progressed to a full-blown liability.

Within seconds of withdrawing from Belinda, René transformed into a smaller, lighter-hued replica of Dante, spread his wings and took flight. His evil laughter could be heard floating out upon the night air as he departed. In the distance, Dante could hear his last words mocking him.

"She...will...*never*...be yours...Dante. I'll...see...her...die...first."

With René gone, Belinda began to stir, moaning in her sleep and eventually progressing to tortured wails. Dante watched her, tossing and turning; eager to bring her some comfort. Eventually, she settled down. Dante sat there in the corner of her room, cloaked in darkness, in case René decided to return.

He had every intention of quietly departing long before

sunrise. Yet, he found it difficult to will himself to leave her side.

After tossing and turning in her bed, Belinda's alarm clock sounded at its usual 6:00 a.m. Rising from her bed to stumble sleeplessly into the bathroom, she was at first relieved to find that she was not blind, but couldn't help but notice the shooting pain that ricocheted off of her temples. The only time she had ever experienced a headache quite this bad was the one and only time she had ever gotten really and truly…drunk; and this pain was ten times worse than anything akin to a hangover. Even the sockets of her eyes hurt.

Once her feet were firmly planted on the ground, it was readily apparent that her head was not the only thing in pain. There was a dull ache throughout her entire body. Her legs moved as though they were treading through quicksand and her arms felt like lead. However, the most fear-provoking of all was the focal point of where her pain seemed to settle. At her core, her body echoed the signs of a woman who had engaged in a vigorous night of sex. She could barely walk. Yet, she remembered nothing more than having been alone all night.

In the interest of stilling her already rising panic, Belinda reasoned that she had to have been masturbating in her sleep. After all, what other explanation could there be?

"Hell, why not?" she spoke aloud.

Hadn't she read a story a few years back where this

woman was on trial for murdering her husband and it was discovered that she had killed him while she was sleepwalking? If a woman could kill someone while she was sleepwalking, why couldn't she have gotten a little rambunctious with herself beneath the sheets, while under the influence of sleep? Sure, it was a stretch. But, when she considered the alternative, it was the very best she could come up with to keep from completely losing her mind.

By the time she had awakened, Dante decided it best to leave quietly and discreetly; that is, until he saw the remnants of René's visit etched upon her body. Dante's power to be unseen in the face of mortals was a valuable tool; especially at moments such as this. He watched her painfully rise from her reclined position in her bed. When she attempted to stand, with difficulty, it took every bit of restraint within him to keep from assisting her.

As hard as she tried, Belinda could not ebb the fear that brewed inside of her and it became even more difficult to do so when she entered her bathroom. She walked in, looked in the vanity mirror, and the first sight that met her eyes were the telltale bruises that covered her chest. Upon closer inspection in the full-length mirror behind her bathroom door, she realized that the bruises didn't stop there. They were all over her body; her arms, her legs; her torso were all covered with black and blue marks. Between her legs were patches of dried blood.

"Oh my God!" she shrieked.

Although he had not been the one that had done this to her, he imagined himself no different than René. After all, hadn't he depleted literally thousands of *Belindas* throughout his existence? How, then, was he so different from René?

Dante knew full well what the end result would be once Belinda took a look at herself in the mirror, so he prepared himself for what he would do after she returned from the bathroom. As soon as she completed her frantic call for help to her friend, Summer, Dante convinced himself that the only way to properly care for her and protect the knowledge of his kind's existence would be to take her to his home; to someplace safe.

Wings outstretched, he enveloped her until she was barely visible. Within moments, he was flying high above the city with her in his arms. His secluded Chelsea apartment was his destination and her comfort was his intent. He would need time to think about what his next move would be and she would most probably sleep for hours, maybe even days, depending upon how much damage René had inflicted upon her. She was asleep, yet every now and then she would whimper. She was so very defenseless, like a wounded puppy. Suddenly, while he still soared through the skies, she opened her eyes and gazed at him. Where he expected to see fear, there was none. Before he had fallen from grace, he heard tell of a curious emotion—love. He wondered if the look in her eyes was what love looked like. Although he was sure he would probably never know.

NINE

J arred out of a restful sleep by the ringing of her
telephone at slightly past six in the morning, Summer
couldn't imagine who might have the nerve to wake
her that early; that is, until she glanced at her caller
ID and realized it was Belinda.

"You know you my girl and all, but you better have a
damn good..."

Summer didn't get a chance to finish her sentence.
Just as she was about to tell Belinda she'd better have a
good reason for calling her so early, she heard Belinda's
last words before the phone went dead.

"Summer! Summer, help me! Help me, please!"

And she was gone.

From the moment the phone went dead, Summer
sprang into action. She dressed, called a neighbor to
come over and watch her daughter, and then raced downtown in a taxi from her El Barrio apartment to where
Belinda lived on the Upper East Side. She sat in the cab,
impatient and on edge, drumming her fingers against
her lap, the door, the window, fearful of what might be
waiting for her when she arrived at her best friend's home.

"Can't you drive any faster than this?"

"Miss, this is as fast as I can go."

"Fuck!" she uttered to no one in particular.

Finally, she arrived at Belinda's place, only to be met with resistance from the doorman.

"Ma'am, it is not building policy to open the door to a tenant's residence without expressed permission from the resident."

"I don't give two shits what your fucking policy is! My best friend called me and said she needed help. For all we know, she could be dead. Now, open the goddamned door!"

Summer was agitated, sweaty and sleep-deprived, and in no mood for the annoying doorman who, in the past, had ogled her each and every opportunity he got, yet now pretended not to see her or to even know who she was.

The doorman indeed knew Summer well and he had had enough run-ins with her before to know she wasn't going to give up easily. Yet, he couldn't open the door to a resident's apartment without permission.

"Ma'am, the best I can do is call the police and then, with their permission, I can open the door."

"For Christ's sake, would you stop fuckin' callin' me ma'am? Do I look like a fuckin' ma'am to you?"

A pair of skintight blue jeans clung to Summer's ample ass and she wore a form-fitting red Lycra shirt, and no bra on her size 40DD breasts, which left very little to the imagination. Her hair was bright red…today. On any given day, the doorman had seen her head go from black to brown, to platinum blonde to this reddish hue she had come up with. He hated to admit it because she was so very crass and vulgar most of the time, but his pants legs rose a little bit more each time he saw her.

"Okay, okay, calm down. I'm calling the police now."

Within minutes, the NYPD was entering the building and while they engaged in questioning banter with the doorman, Summer interrupted the animated exchange.

"I know you got here fast as hell and all; or, at least a lot faster than you would've gotten to my neighborhood. But, do we plan on spending all day discussing what might be wrong with Belinda, or are we going to get our asses upstairs and find out for sure?"

For a moment, the female officer considered lashing back at Summer, but thought better of it. She surveyed Summer from head to foot and Summer, very aware of what she was doing, gave it right back. As far as Officer Hernandez was concerned, she knew her kind well. Her overall perception was that she was probably some convict's baby mama that did hair somewhere on The Avenue and her girlfriend, Belinda, was probably her best friend since they were kids; one of a few who had made it out of the hood successfully, judging from the Upper East Side condo. Each and every day Belinda's friends from her new life probably questioned why the hell she still hung out with tacky-ass whatever her name was. Yes, she thought she had her pretty well pegged. According to Hernandez, she was one of those women who lived her life in Technicolor twenty four hours a day, seven days a week.

As if completing her thoughts, her partner, Officer, Wilson spoke. "And, your name is, Ms...."

"My name is Summer...Summer Johnson. I don't think that's going to help my friend if she's upstairs dying," she answered sarcastically.

"Okay, why don't you stay here? We're going upstairs now."

"Hell to the no! You think I'm going to stay down here twiddling my thumbs while my girl is upstairs going through God only knows what? I'm coming with you!"

"No, Ms. Johnson. I must insist that you stay here. It's a safety issue. As you said yourself, we have no idea what's going on upstairs. The longer I stand here explaining that to you, the greater danger your friend could be in. So, please, let Officer Hernandez and me do our jobs, and you wait here. We'll be sure to call you if we need you. Okay?"

For the first time in a long time, Summer was quiet. She couldn't help but think that this had something to do with last night. She had gotten an eerie feeling while she was out with Belinda and Diana. It was the same feeling she always got when something wasn't right. Even though no one ever believed her, Summer believed she had been endowed with some form of clairvoyance; a certain sixth sense. Despite the naysayers, her premonitions were seldom wrong.

"Belinda, Belinda honey; are you okay! Where is she? Is she here?" Summer called out.

"No, she's not here," Officer Wilson responded.

"Ms. Johnson, I thought we asked you to wait downstairs?" the female police officer barked at Summer.

Summer was trying her damnedest to keep her cool, but J. Lo, the hood cop, was starting to get on her fucking nerves. She had gotten away with the obvious attitude she was giving her downstairs, but her patience was wearing thin.

"I waited long enough and what do you mean? She's not here?"

"And what gives you..."

"Officer Hernandez, why don't you go downstairs and get a statement from the doorman?" Officer Wilson interjected.

"I..."

"We've seen all we can see here. I'll take Ms. Johnson's statement and you can get started on the doorman's statement."

Officer Hernandez walked away in a huff, but not before she stopped for a moment to stare directly at Summer.

"Feeling froggy?" Summer asked.

Officer Hernandez glared at Summer. "Excuse me?"

"The statement, Hernandez," Officer Wilson said.

The last thing Wilson wanted to do was break up some unnecessary conflict.

Officer Hernandez stomped off, slamming the door as she left.

"What the fuck is her problem, slamming my girl's door like she ain't got no damn sense? She on the rag or something?"

Wilson smiled. He couldn't figure out if it was what she had said or the fact that she was clearly a tough woman. Wilson had grown up in a family full of women and they were all just as strong.

Wilson said, "Maybe men are not the only ones that have dick slinging contests."

Under different circumstances, Summer would have had a good laugh about what the officer had said. Not only that, she would've probably flirted with him shamelessly. But right now, all she could think about was Belinda.

"Yeah, I guess that's true," was the most she could muster.

"Before I take your statement, I'm going to first tell you what the problem is."

"What problem?"

"The problem is that although it appears that something did go on here, judging from the broken glass and the blood on the sheets, there's really nothing I can do. There isn't enough blood to justify being called a crime scene. The broken items could be easily explained away, as well as the blood."

"What about her phone call?"

"What did you say she said when she called? What exactly?"

"Her exact words were something like 'Summer, help, or Help me, Summer, please!' Something like that."

"Exactly; even that could be explained away as something far less threatening than your friend being a victim of a crime."

"But, she and I were supposed to get together today. Belinda would never disappear like this. It's not like her."

"I completely understand where you're coming from and if it were one of my sisters or my mother, I would feel the same way. But, unfortunately, my hands are tied. The protocol dictates that I can't even file a missing persons report, since Ms..."

"Ms. *Wilson*, the same name as yours."

"Yeah, I should have remembered that. I'm sorry, Ms. Wilson is not suffering from any sort of mental illness and doesn't require life-saving medication of any sort."

"So, basically what you're telling me is there's nothing you can do?"

"In a nutshell, that's exactly what I'm trying to tell you. If it were up to me and if we had the manpower, I'd work on this myself, but I simply can't. I will, however, need to take a statement."

Summer was glad it was Officer Wilson taking her statement and not the Latino psycho-bitch downstairs.

Summer wanted to make things easy for the officer. Since he probably couldn't leave her in Belinda's apartment, she left of her own accord.

"Oh, Ms. Johnson, I will tell you something that I noticed and found a bit odd."

"What was that?"

"Your friend's windows were open and although she's

on the sixth floor and there's no fire escape, there was a piece of cloth caught on to the window. The cloth appeared to be ripped from the clothing of someone that was in the window."

"Why is that odd?"

"It appears that from the direction of the cloth, the clothing was exiting the window, not entering it. It almost seems as if someone jumped or was pushed out the window. I wouldn't worry, though; the only thing that drives a hole through that idea is if someone had jumped or was pushed, there would be a body."

"Unless of course, if the person that did the pushing took the body and disposed of it."

"Trust me, Summer, that would be a bit difficult in this neighborhood; especially with a doorman."

"True, true. So do you have any suggestions?"

"The only thing I can suggest is that you stay near a phone and if you know anywhere that your friend might be, try reaching her. I guess those are both pretty obvious. In the meantime, if you think of anything or if you have any thoughts, don't hesitate to give me a call directly."

Officer Wilson handed Summer a business card and they both made their way out of the apartment.

By the time they got downstairs to the lobby, Officer Hernandez was outside in the police car.

Summer made it a point to flash her most wicked smile at Officer Wilson, just to fuck with the female officer.

"Thank you," she said in parting. "I'll give you a call if I think of anything."

"Why do you always attract the nut jobs?"

"I don't know, Hernandez; I thought she was pretty cool."

"Yeah, and those tight ass jeans and forty triple Ds didn't hurt any either."

"I didn't notice anything of the kind. As far as I'm concerned, she was just another witness. But, you sure seemed to notice."

"Fuck you!"

"Promises, promises."

As the police car drove off, Summer considered her next move. She wondered if maybe Diana knew where Belinda was.

She pulled out her cell phone and called her home. Diana's voicemail picked up. "Diana, call me as soon as you get this message. It's an emergency."

Summer considered calling Diana at her practice. But, it was seven-thirty on a Saturday morning. Where on earth could she be? Unless she was jogging. They had all gotten home so late the night before, or actually, early that morning. Summer decided to call Diana on her cell...nothing.

"Diana, I left a message on your voicemail at home, but I figured I'd try you on your cell. Give me a call whenever you get either of these messages. It's about Belinda. I think something is wrong."

Even though her neighbor had offered to watch Keyanna for her, Summer told her she could go. There was nothing she could really do until Belinda called or showed up.

The police had been no help at all. They had looked over Belinda's apartment and pretty much concluded that there was nothing that indicated she might be in danger and nothing they could do. Summer knew what had to be next. If the police couldn't help her, maybe the criminals could.

Pookie had given her his business card the night before when they were at Redemption.

"Hey, Pookie."

"Hey, beautiful. What's goin' on?"

"I know you've gone legit and all, but do you still have any connections?"

"What exactly do you need?"

"You know my friend, Belinda; the sista I was with at Redemption last night? Well, she called me early this morning, distraught as hell and asking for help. She dropped the phone before I could find out what happened and by the time I got to her place, there was nobody there."

"Where does she live?"

"She's got a condo on the Upper East."

"That's not really my area, Summer. I'm a hoodrat."

"Yeah. This is true. Do you know anybody that might be able to help me?"

"I can ask around, but most of the people I know spend their time well past 96th Street."

"Yeah. I hear ya."

"I'm startin' to think there's some weird shit goin' on with Redemption. There's always some buzz going on about something that took place at that club."

"What kind of buzz? I've been kind of out of the loop lately, with the kid and all."

"Another bartender from there disappeared recently."

"What do you mean, another bartender?"

"You gonna tell me you didn't hear about that bartender that disappeared last year? It was even in the newspapers."

"No, I didn't hear anything about it. What happened?"

"I would think that you, of all people, would know something about it."

"Why me?"

"Your girl was one of the first people they questioned when the first guy disappeared."

"Are you sure? Belinda? I didn't realize that she knew the bartender."

"Oh. No. No. Not Belinda. I'm talkin' about that other one you was with at Redemption last night; the redbone one."

"Diana?"

"Yeah. That's her name; Diana. A club full of people saw her leave with Sam; that was the bartender's name. Anyway, a club full of people saw her leave with him and he was never seen or heard from again. To this day, almost a year later, he's never been found."

"You're kidding!"

"I probably wouldn't have even remembered any of that,

except that a few weeks after she was questioned, I was at this dive called Potion. It's a real cesspool kinda place and who should I see but your friend. I didn't really know her, except for seeing her with you and Belinda and that she was a doctor. But, who should I see one night at Potion but your conservative doctor friend. She wasn't wearing her usual granny-wear. She was half-naked and dry humping any dick she could connect with. It was a real Sodom and Gomorrah situation. She even came on to me and I ain't gonna lie, I considered it. I am a man and all. But she scared the shit out of me and my Momma didn't raise no fool. After that, every time I went to Potion, she was there. In fact, one night in particular, I was hangin' wit my boys and she laid this stare on me that I gotta tell you. Them fuckin' eyes of hers scared the shit outta me. I never went back to that fuckin' place again after that."

"Come on, Pookie. Are you shittin' me or what? Are we talkin' about the same Diana?"

"One and the same. I wouldn't lie about no shit like that. There's something off about that girl."

"Pookie, I need a little favor and if you do it for me, I'll owe you big time."

"Oh hell no!"

"Come on, Pookie. You don't even know what the favor is. Just hear me out."

"How long have I known you, beautiful?"

"Hell, since we was kids in Catholic school."

"Exactly. So what makes you think I don't know exactly what you're about to ask me? Your crazy ass wants me to take you to Potion. Am I right?"

"Oh, come on, Pookie. You're the only person I can ask. If this place is anything like you said, you're not gonna let me go there by myself, are you? I gotta figure out what's goin' on. I'm worried about Belinda."

"You ain't gonna find Belinda at Potion; that's for sure."

"I'm just tryin' to follow a trail; that's all. All of these events are somehow connected. I'm simply following my instincts. Come on, Pookie. Please?"

"Okay, okay. But, when did you suddenly turn all Nancy fucking Drew and shit? I'll pick you up at your spot at eleven sharp. I'm tellin' you, Summer, if you're not ready, I'm takin' my happy ass straight home. You hear me?"

"Loud and clear. Eleven; I promise. Pookie, can I ask one more favor, though?"

"Girl, don't you know how to quit when you're ahead?"

"Oh come on; you know you love me."

"Yeah, I love your ass. Otherwise, I wouldn't be marchin' my ass right back into the outer reaches of hell for you. So, what do you want now?"

"Can you give me a lift to Park Slope?"

"That I can do. No problem. What's in Park Slope?"

"Maybe I need to go to the source, if I'm gonna find out anything significant about Ms. Diana."

"Is that where she lives? If so, I'll drop you off a few blocks away, if you don't mind."

"No, she lives in the Village."

"Figures; all the freaks live in the Village."

"Now how you gonna go and generalize like that? Suppose somebody said all the criminals lived in Harlem and the Bronx."

"That shit wouldn't offend me. There are a whole bunch of criminals in Harlem and the Bronx."

"You know that shit ain't right, Pookie."

"Yeah, but is it true? That's the real question."

"I'm not even gonna dignify that with a response. Hell, you're talking to a Harlem baby."

"See how you went and made my point for me?"

"Fuck you, Pookie."

"That's what I been tryin' to do, but you so stingy; won't even break a brotha off some."

"This is me ignoring you, Pookie."

"You ready to go to Park Slope or what?" he asked.

"Yeah. Just let me make a phone call first."

Although Summer didn't know Diana's parents all that well, she had met them before and decided to give Diana's mom a call.

"Hello, Mrs. Crandall, I'm going to be in Brooklyn today and I've been trying to reach Diana regarding something urgent, but she hasn't returned any of my calls. You see, Belinda is missing. I'm a little frazzled and I was wondering if it would be okay if I stopped by to see you."

"What do you mean, Belinda is missing?" Mrs. Crandall asked on the other end of the call.

"She's missing. She called me early this morning, frantic. She sounded like she was in some sort of trouble. She begged me for my help and then hung up. By the time I got to her place, she was gone; there was blood in her bed and a lot of broken glass and furniture. I called the police, but they were useless. The first person I thought of calling was Diana and I've been calling her all day with no response. I'm just not sure what to think. We all went out last night and that's the last time I saw either of them."

"I'm sure they're fine, but come on by. I'll be here. Do you have the address?"

"Yes, I saved it in my cell phone the last time we visited."

It only took Pookie and Summer about twenty minutes to get to Mr. and Mrs. Crandall's brownstone.

"If you don't mind, I'm gonna leave," Pookie said. "Quite frankly, the mere fact that Drucilla used to live here is freakin' me the fuck out."

"Pookie, you're so damn crazy. Thanks a lot; I'll see you tonight. Eleven; I'll make sure I'm on time and ready."

"How are you gonna get home from here? I can pick you up when you're ready. Give me a call. You have my cell."

"I'll be okay. I'm gonna take the train. This isn't so far from Manhattan."

"Okay. I'll see you later then."

"Pookie?"

"What now? Before you finish that sentence, let me

warn you that you used up your favors for the day; hell, for the month. I ain't got no extra kidneys or livers or none of that shit lyin' around."

"I was just gonna say thank you, fool. Thank you."

Summer remembered the place as soon as she walked in. She loved The Crandall's home. Mrs. Crandall clearly had beautiful taste.

"Hello, Summer. Have a seat. Would you like something to drink?" Mrs. Crandall asked. "Are you hungry at all?"

"No, I'm fine. Thank you."

"So what brings you here? You mentioned that Belinda and maybe Diana were missing."

"Yes. I've been sort of snooping around; asking people questions, hoping that maybe someone noticed something. Anything that might point me in the right direction. I'm really worried about Belinda, since the police found blood in her apartment…on her bed."

"They found blood and they couldn't do anything?"

"Yeah. I also thought that was crazy. I don't understand it. I guess you have to actually have a body before the police will intervene."

"Our tax dollars at work. So, what would you like to know? Before you continue, let me first say that chances are Diana is fine. She's been executing these disappearing acts for years."

"Really? That sounds so out of character for Diana."

"I see you don't know our Diana as well as I thought you did."

"Why do you say that?"

"Well, because Diana is what you might call a conundrum wrapped in an enigma. If I were to be totally honest with myself, I would admit that she's been that way as far back as when Warren first brought her home."

"I'm a little confused, Mrs. Crandall. You said, when Warren brought her home. Was Mr. Crandall married before? I mean, is Diana your stepdaughter?"

"Not exactly. It's a complicated story, if you have the time?"

"Absolutely."

"Mr. Crandall and I were married for about three years when I found out I couldn't have children. I was devastated. I had this plan for my life; you know, the career, the white picket fence; the two point five children. So, I go to the doctor and I sit there while he tells me that I'm infertile. The fact that Warren was a gynecologist made it all the more painful. Here he was delivering babies for other people and we couldn't even have our own children.

"Our marriage began to suffer; I started drinking. Warren started staying away from home more and more; that is, until he was jogging through the park early one morning and heard these cries coming from the woods. It was a woman and she was pregnant and in labor. This was long before the days of cell phones and Warren knew he was fully qualified to deliver the baby, so he did. What he wasn't prepared for was the condition of the baby after he delivered it. Whenever a doctor delivers a baby under unusual circumstances, he is prepared for the possibility of some level of trauma. But, nothing in all of Warren's years of training prepared him for what he saw that day. At first, he thought the baby was dead. There was no pulse, no heartbeat. Then, suddenly, it moved, writhing around in his hands. Yet, there was still no pulse…no heartbeat. He realized that he was probably a bit rattled and checked her again; still nothing. The mother didn't appear to be faring very well after the delivery and Warren decided he needed to get help as soon as possible. He walked to the road and tried to flag down a passing car, but no one would stop. When he realized it was going to be next to impossible for him to get someone to stop, he went back to where he had delivered the baby, only to find the mother gone and the baby lying in the grass, still moving, but still with no heartbeat or pulse.

"By the time I got home from my practice, he was sitting in the living room, baby in hand, with a sheepish grin on his face. He believed it would solve our marital problems and give me the family that I had always wanted. He told me the story and at first, I thought he was stark-raving mad. A baby with no pulse and no heartbeat but alive—until I held the baby myself and checked even more accurately with a stethoscope. He was right. Initially, I tried to convince Warren to turn the baby in, but when he explained to me what would probably happen if he did—the experimentations that would probably take place. After all, it was a medical miracle.

"Warren made sure that I spent more and more time with the baby. It was my idea to name her Diana; after my great-grandmother. Eventually, I grew to love her as if she were my own. By the time Diana was six or seven years old, she was suddenly normal. She had a pulse and a heartbeat like any other child her age and we both figured that without the original limitations, she could begin to live a normal life; spend time with kids her own age—those sorts of things.

"It wasn't easy, but we were able to forge a few papers and get Diana enrolled in school. That's when we started to notice that she wasn't your typical seven-year-old. Diana had an unusual effect upon people, men especially. They were putty in her hands; Warren included. She could manipulate most situations and pretty soon, I was starting to question where she had come from. Diana didn't like that. She made sure I knew that she didn't like that. She could have done a lot more, but in some respects, she felt she owed me something. I wouldn't use the word love. The word loyalty would be more accurate."

"I don't understand, Mrs. Crandall. What do you mean when you say she had an *unusual* effect upon people?"

"Exactly what I said, although I misspoke, slightly. She didn't *have* an unusual effect upon people, she *has* an unusual effect upon people; and she's only become more powerful through the years."

"But, you make her sound almost…dangerous."

"I've never seen anything concrete or tangible that I could give anyone examples of, but trust me, this isn't the ravings of a jealous, paranoid wife. There's something bubbling below Diana's surface that's extremely volatile."

"Tell me the truth. Do you think Diana could've done something to harm Belinda?"

"If I were going to guess, I would say no. Diana seems to genuinely like Belinda. But, if any of what I'm saying has any basis in fact, I could very well be wrong about where her alliances lie. Although she is for all intents and purposes my daughter, I've just described a sociopath. We all know what sociopaths are capable of."

"Mrs. Crandall, you're clearly an intelligent woman and I have the utmost respect for you, but I've got to tell you, I'm hoping that you're either paranoid or crazy. If you're not, then Belinda's life very well could be in danger."

Summer was already outside waiting for Pookie when he got to her apartment. Her babysitter had arrived an hour earlier, and Keyanna had already been in bed two hours before the sitter got there. She was ready to go.

"Dag, you weren't bullshittin.' Already outside and waitin.'"

"Ye of little faith," Summer said. "I told you this was important. I don't fuck around when it comes to family; and Belinda, she's family."

"Don't worry; you're in good hands now. Just make sure you stay close once we get to Potion. There are some mad freaks up in that place."

"Which would explain why you go there. Oh, oh, I'm sorry. I forgot. You don't go there anymore."

"You got that right. I already told ya. That place is straight up Sodom and Gomorrah. And your girl, Diana, she's its leader. My man, Duggan, he hooked up wit' her a few months ago. I saw him like a few weeks after they hooked up and Duggan looked like he had gotten instant AIDS and shit. He was all drawn and his skin was dry and crackin' and shit."

"Okay, Pookie; now you're sounding crazy."

"If you'd seen him, you would've said the same thing. The weird thing is, he's another motherfucka that fell off the map. Nobody's seen him in months."

By the time Summer left The Crandalls, she was feeling a little guilty about contacting Diana's mother and a little stupid for starting to believe what she was believing. At one point, she even considered calling Pookie to cancel their plans to venture out to Potion. But, then she called Diana yet again and got her voicemail, yet again. There was no mistaking the fact that the balance of things had shifted and even though she wondered for a moment if she had succumbed to the evils of paranoia, she trusted her instincts and reminded herself that one plus one still equaled two and no matter how many times she did the math, something didn't add up.

Potion was everything Pookie said it was. Riding crops and chains hung from the ceilings. At the front door there was a display case full of dildos, nipple clamps, leather collars and chokers, harnesses and masks, along with the requisite assortment of condoms.

Pookie was amused with Summer's reaction; especially since she was the last person he ever expected to be shocked. Yet, she was. It was written all over her face. He didn't know if it was the combination of sexual devices, the techno music, or the fact that this was the first time he had come here with a woman, but his dick was suddenly harder than he had ever felt it. He always joked around with Summer about hooking up with her, but truth be told, he saw her as much more of a sister than he did a fuck buddy. Although this latest development was clearly contradicting that. He really wanted things to remain exactly the way that they were and the last thing he wanted was for Summer to become aware of his raging erection, so he turned around and focused on something else, trying to block out the music, the toys—and Summer, until his erection could subside. By the time he turned back around, Summer was nowhere to be found. Instead, Diana was standing directly behind him, pressing herself firmly to his back, her hand gripping his cock, dashing any hopes of his hard-on going away.

"Hello, Diana," he said, trying to play it cool.

"Hey, Pookie. Have you come to play?"

"What exactly did you have in mind?"

"Come with me and I'll show you."

The head on his shoulders was telling him no, but the head in his pants followed her like a puppy enticed by a shiny new bone.

Diana led Pookie straight to the nearest bathroom. There was such a combination of sucking and fucking going on in that bathroom and the tell-tale scent of sex wafted through the air. As Pookie's feet stuck to the floor, he wondered what he would eventually find clinging to his shoes.

Diana found an empty stall and latched the door. In her other hand she held two sets of handcuffs. With lightening swift accuracy, she smacked a set of handcuffs on each of Pookie's wrists and before he had an opportunity to truly recognize the precarious position he found himself in and put up a greater struggle, she had attached each of the handcuffs to a hook in the ceiling. Pookie looked up, surprised, since he had never noticed the hooks that were strategically placed in the middle of each stall ceiling area.

"Okay, Diana, you've had your fun; now unlock these handcuffs. This ain't my thing."

"That's where you're wrong Pookie, I haven't even begun to have fun and before we're done, you will most certainly be *into it*."

"Goddamn it, Diana! I'm not fuckin' around! Unlock these damn handcuffs."

From the waistband of her skimpy satin skirt Diana withdrew a small blade. At first, Pookie was sure he was going to die right then and there. Instead of cutting him with the blade, he was happy to find that she was only going to use it to remove his pants. Ordinarily, he would have been pissed, but under the circumstances, and given his initial fears, he was willing to see where this was going; especially since his dick was now eager for some pussy.

Diana traced the blade from the waist of his slacks to right about where his dick stopped, cutting along the way. Pookie got a little nervous about a blade being that close to his family jewels, but as soon as his dick was free and she put the blade away, he was back to thinking about how tight her pussy would be wrapped around his dick; and whether or not he would be able to get some head.

Pookie had always been proud of his nine by four—as he so often called it.

"Well, there it is. What are you gonna do with it?"

"Just you wait and see."

Diana held firmly to the handcuffs extended above Pookie's head and in a move that Pookie himself was quite impressed with, she raised her entire body off the floor, while only holding the cuffs, mounted his dick and fucked him virtually in mid-air. Pookie was surprised to find that she didn't miss a stroke. And, just when he thought that nothing in life could feel any better than this, he caught a glimpse of her face. For a moment he thought maybe she had donned some sort of a Halloween mask. But he knew better. Out of nowhere he thought of what he had told Summer earlier: *His Momma didn't raise no fool.* Apparently she did. With each stroke, her pussy got tighter and smaller; and at first it was pleasure beyond belief, but the greater the transformation of her face; the decaying skin, the bloody horns emanating from her neck, the rancid spittle dripping from her lips, the more pain he endured. It was as if hidden within her were a set of strategically placed, jagged teeth, gnawing at his manhood. Worse than that, when he tried to speak or cry out for help, he felt strangled, like every attempt at vocalization tightened an invisible noose around his neck, cutting off his air supply. Her head and body twisted and revolved with such speed, he was unable to see a thing. It was like watching a set of rotors spinning wildly out of control.

Eventually, she had extracted all that she could from him. Dried up and lifeless, his hands slipped through the cuffs that bound him and his entire body fell in a heap to the floor below.

Before exiting the bathroom, Diana glanced in the mirror. With each restoration, with each soul, she looked younger and younger.

Diana could see Summer looking for Pookie. Her eyes darted from left to right.

"Shit!"

Diana chuckled to herself. Summer probably thought Pookie had left her there alone. She would have liked nothing better than to have a little fun with Summer, but thought better of it. No. It was time for her to make a hasty exit.

If it had been anyone else, Summer might not have noticed. But even with a quick glance of her from the rear, as she exited, the look of Diana Crandall's signature windswept hair was unmistakable.

TEN

Belinda slept peacefully for the first time in weeks. Her frightening, fitful dreams were replaced with loving touches and the gentlest of hands. Cloaked in the safety of unconscious sleep, she silently wished all her nights could be like this. She dreamed of a beautiful, kind man protecting her; a powerful man, who sheltered her from harm. He swooped down, took her in his arms and spirited her away.

Consumed with guilt, he sat quietly next to her, tending her cuts with a warm cloth. His touch was so soothing and reminiscent of affection. But, she realized that she should probably fear him. He was a stranger and she had very little recollection of how her body had come to be in so much pain or why they were here, together, in this place that was foreign to her. He could very well have kidnapped her; especially considering she didn't remember anything.

Belinda attempted to speak, but her throat was dry and constricted. She licked her lips and tasted blood. As quickly as she became aware of her bruised, cracked lips, he attempted to ease that pain as well. He raised her head and brought a straw to her lips. The ice-cold water relieved what felt like several days worth of dehydration. She drank too quickly and coughed. Water trickled past her lips out the corners of her mouth and he dabbed away the droplets of water. Lost in the moment of touching her, he forgot his earlier resolve to keep his distance and lightly traced her lips with his finger…and she shuddered. Aroused by the feel of her lips beneath his touch, but even more aroused by her response, Dante quickly rose from the bed and hurried to the kitchen.

"Are you hungry, Belinda?"

Large chunks of her memory were missing. She couldn't remember who this man might be. The last thing she remembered was Diana and Summer meeting her at her apartment for a night on the town. What happened after that was completely blank. Yet, she felt compelled to stay. There was something welcoming about this place. For the moment, whatever happened to her was a distant memory. And, maybe that was for the best.

"I, I… Yes, I guess I am a little hungry. How long have I been here?"

"I brought you here yesterday morning. You've been asleep ever since."

"I don't understand. Why did you bring me here?"

"I was visiting a client in your apartment building," he lied. "I heard screams coming from the apartment next door…your apartment. Your door was open and I walked in and found you lying on the floor. You had a few cuts and bruises, but you seemed okay otherwise. I couldn't wake you and I considered taking you to the hospital, but you seemed more asleep than unconscious. I wasn't sure whether or not that was what you would want when you woke up. It occurred to me that it might have been someone you know; maybe a boyfriend or husband or something, who caused those cuts and bruises."

Under normal circumstances Belinda would have voiced an objection to his implication, but she was so drained, she didn't even have the energy to protest.

Dante was surprised to find he still had a conscience. It had been so long since he had felt anything close to regret for the things he did. Somehow, though, with her he did. He hated lying to her. But, the truth was not something she was prepared for; at least not yet.

"I considered calling the police. I realized I didn't actually know what happened. I thought about waiting with you until you woke up. Then I considered all the variables in such a situation and thought better of it. You know, you wake up, scratches and bruises on your body and bleeding, with a stranger in your home. Not a good spot for me to be standing in. So, I decided to bring you here. I watched you for a few hours and decided that you were not badly injured, just shaken. Do you remember anything?"

"No. All I remember is going out with my friends and then I woke up here. I did have the most horrible dreams though. I also had a really good dream…one of those crazy dreams you don't want to wake up from. I was flying."

"Really?" he asked a little too quickly.

"I was flying beneath the most majestic wings and then I saw a face. The face looked a lot like yours."

"Let's get some food in you."

While she wasn't afraid of him, Belinda wasn't quite so confused that she didn't recognize his frequent attempts at evasion. But why?

"Can I use your phone? My friend, Summer, must be worried sick about me. We were supposed to go shopping…um, yesterday, I think. Yeah, yesterday. What day did you say it was again?"

"It's Sunday. And, no, I don't have a phone. But I will make sure you get in contact with your friend. But first, you have to eat."

For the first time, Belinda looked over her body. There were bruises everywhere; on her legs, her arms, along with a few scratches. Her body felt as though she had fallen down a flight of stairs. Her lips were sore and her breasts were in an equal degree of pain. Between her legs was a cloth of some sort and she wore a pair of men's underwear. She was suddenly extremely embarrassed. Had she suddenly gotten her period in the midst of all of this and her handsome stranger decided to improvise? If so, that was way above and beyond being hospitable.

Belinda was exhausted and decided to rest her eyes

until he returned with some food. Then, after she ate, she would go home and call Summer and tell her all about her two-day melodrama. But, not before she asked Summer what the hell she was drinking at the club on Friday to get her so fucked up.

She awoke to find him sitting in a chair next to the bed, watching her. Although it seemed as though she had only slept for a few minutes, it was now dark outside.

"I'm sorry. You were sleeping so peacefully, I didn't have the heart to wake you."

"I don't know what's wrong with me. I'm so tired. I've never slept this much in my life."

"Your body probably needs the rest. I went out and got you a phone while you were sleeping; one of those prepaid ones."

Before Belinda could ask the most obvious question, Dante answered as if reading her thoughts.

"I think I left my cell phone at your apartment when I was there and I don't have a land line here. I'm not home enough to make it worth it…the land line.

"You said you were visiting a client when you found me. What is it that you do?"

"I'm an accountant."

"Funny, you don't look like an accountant."

"And what are accountants supposed to look like, Belinda?"

"You know, I just realized something. You know my name but I don't know yours."

He stretched his hand very formally and shook Belinda's. "Hi, Belinda. My name is Dante. Dante Rivers.

"What an unusual name. It's very nice to meet you, Dante…and thank you for being so kind. There aren't a lot of New Yorkers who would do what you've done. This would make an interesting human interest piece. I'm a freelance writer. Stranger Rescues Woman from… That is, if I could actually remember what it is you rescued me from or even if it was a rescue. For all I know, I could've fallen and hurt myself…bumped my head or something. Did you happen to notice if there was any broken glass in my apartment? Maybe I hit my head on my coffee table or a window or something. Summer always jokes about how clumsy I am. Oh my God, Summer. She's probably got the search party out after me by now. None of this makes any sense. I'm not a heavy drinker. I don't do drugs. Yet, I've lost two entire days."

"Your memory will probably return once you have eaten and…regrouped. In the meantime, why don't you call your friend?"

"Yeah. You're probably right. Speaking of which, something smells so good. I hope you didn't go to too much trouble on my account."

"No trouble at all. I only wish that I could do more."

"Are you kidding? You've already gone above and beyond."

"Would it be possible for me to wash up before I eat?"

"Of course. The bathroom is right down the hall on the right," he said and motioned toward the hall.

Belinda modestly gathered up the sheet and grabbed the phone before heading to the bathroom.

Once in the bathroom, she dialed Summer.

"Yes," Summer answered with annoyance, not recognizing the phone Belinda was calling from.

"Summer, it's me, Belinda."

"Oh my God! Belinda, are you okay? Where are you? Where have you been? I didn't know what happened and the police were no fucking help! Do you know you have to show evidence of foul play or the person has to be a mental case or on medication in order to file a missing person's report? Television is full of shit! Every time you watch a program they're like…oh, you have to wait twenty-four to forty-eight hours to file a missing person's report. That's bullshit!"

"Summer, Summer, your mouth is running a mile a minute."

"You have no idea how fucking scared I was. Belinda, I thought… I thought you might be dead or kidnapped or something. I don't know."

"I'm so sorry. I'm sorry you were worried. And, I really don't even have an explanation that makes any sense. It's almost like I've lost two whole days and I have no idea why."

"What are you trying to say? You mean you have amnesia or something."

"Not really amnesia, but there are definitely some holes in my memory. Everything seems to get fuzzy after you guys came by my house on Friday. Did anything strange happen, that you remember?"

"Hell to the yes. I tried to tell you and Diana. There was some weird shit goin' on at that club. Strange people coming and going...or at least stranger than usual. Two in particular."

"You think maybe someone slipped me a Mickey or something?"

"I don't know, Bee. You guys think I'm crazy and shit most of the time, but I believe there was something goin' on Friday that defies logic. I believe there might've been something supernatural goin' on."

"Summer, come on. What are you trying to say?"

"I got a really weird vibe on Friday. Really weird. And, it centered around two people at that club...two people who I bet know one another. The funny thing is I was feeling a bit fuzzy after I left the club on Friday, too. Maybe not as bad as you, but I tried to recall what those two guys looked like and somehow the memory of their physical characteristics completely escaped me. All that's left is the feeling...a heady feeling...sort of like I'm drunk, but not quite. That's not like me. You know me, Belinda. I never, ever forget what a man looks like; even if I've only seen him for ten seconds."

"Summer, that's exactly the way that I've been feeling. Like I've been on a two-day bender or something. I told

Dante I was going to ask you and Diana what I had been drinking on Friday."

"Who is Dante?"

"Oh. I didn't finish telling you where I am."

"You're not at home? And, whose phone are you using?"

"No. I don't know what happened, but I may have been attacked or maybe I fell or something. I really don't know. I have a few cuts and bruises. It's nothing serious, but someone heard me screaming or something in my apartment and he brought me here, to his place."

"He? Who is he and why would some stranger bring you back to his place? Who does that? Why didn't he call the police or something? I don't know, Bee; I don't like the sound of this."

"It sounded weird to me, too…at first. But, it made sense when he explained his logic."

Belinda could hear his footsteps approaching the door, seconds before he knocked, calling her name.

"Belinda, are you okay?"

"Summer, I've got to go. I'll explain it all to you when I see you."

"Wait, wait, Belinda, where are you?"

Belinda hung up the phone before she could answer her.

"I want you."

"What did you say?" Belinda asked from inside the bathroom.

Dante hadn't realized he had communicated his thoughts to her. He seldom made such a mistake. The only time he ever did that was when he was trying to control someone. Yet, somehow, she had heard his thoughts, his innermost desires. And, yes, he did want her…more than anything he had ever wanted during his entire existence.

"Nothing…nothing important. I…I was wondering. You mentioned your dreams; you know that some were bad and some were good. And, you mentioned that in one of the dreams you saw a face that looked like mine. Was that one of your good dreams or one of the bad?"

Belinda opened the bathroom door.

"It was a good dream; a very good dream. The man in my dream was saving me. So, maybe it was you. I mean, you did save me, didn't you?"

"I don't know if I saved you from anything," he lied.

"In fact, it's more like I was being nosey and suddenly realized once I was in your apartment, how bad it would look with me being there. So, I actually saved myself from who knows what. So that headline you were talking about didn't say something like 'Intruder Caught in the Act: Professes Innocence.'"

"You've got a point there."

Dante could do nothing to avert his attention from her lips. Curved, ever so slightly in a smile, she was the most beautiful creature he had ever laid his eyes upon.

Belinda was sure she heard him say something else from the other side of that bathroom door. In fact, it sounded as though he said that he wanted her. The trouble was, if he had said that she wasn't sure what her response would have been. It was a bizarre feeling, standing there with this stranger, scantily clothed in his home, while he looked at her that way. Yet, somehow, she felt as though she had known him her entire life.

Dante lent Belinda a jogging suit to go home in. When it was time for her to leave, she lingered at the door, unsure of what to say. Finally, she extended her hand to shake his.

"Thank you so much, Mr. Rivers. As I said before, I don't think anyone else would've been as gallant as you've been. You're a lifesaver. If there's anything I can ever do for you, please don't hesitate to ask."

"That would be very difficult, unless I decide to break and enter your home again. I don't have your phone number."

"Do you have a piece of paper and a pen?" she asked.

Belinda scribbled her phone number on the paper and handed it to Dante.

"Would it be okay for me to call, even if I don't need anything? Would it be okay to call you simply to say hello, or get a bite to eat?"

"I would love that."

"Are you sure you're okay? I could see you home, if you'd like."

"No, I'm fine. You've done enough."

Belinda was slightly disappointed that Dante hadn't made some sort of concrete plans with her, other than coming to her aid once again. After leaving his apartment, she realized she had no wallet, no metro card, and no way to get home. She considered going back to Dante's apartment, but thought better of it. Instead, she found a pay phone and called Summer collect.

ELEVEN

Within twenty minutes, Summer was downtown, anxious to pick up her friend. She couldn't help but notice how tired and slightly disheveled Belinda looked.

"Some people will do anything to get out of taking a friend shopping," she commented, lightheartedly. "I'm not even going to get into these weird ass hours you keep calling me; early in the morning, late at night. You need to start having your crises at a more reasonable hour, young lady."

Belinda was thankful for Summer's levity, under the circumstances. "Summer! Thank you so much! I don't know what I would've done without you. And, I promise, I'm gonna make good on that shopping spree."

"Yeah, yeah, yeah. Get over here. Do you know you scared the shit out of me? I was thinking all sorts of things. And you know what a vivid imagination I have." Summer grabbed Belinda and hugged her. "Let's get the hell out of here. Have you eaten anything at all? And what may I ask are you wearing?"

"Dante let me borrow this. I wasn't wearing anything but a nasty old T-shirt."

"This is definitely not a restaurant conversation. You're coming to my house. I'm going to fix you something to eat, or some tea or coffee if you'd like, and you're going to tell me exactly what's been going on for the last couple of days."

"You might not believe this, but I don't know what's been going on the last couple of days."

"Hold that thought while I get a cab."

By the time they were in the taxi headed uptown, Belinda was asleep again.

"Belinda, Belinda. Honey, we're here."

Belinda practically jumped out of her skin. All she heard was her name being called. She made no connection at all to Summer, but instead was reminded of the last time someone called her name. It was like flashes of memories. In this particular one, her name being called was the prelude to impending doom.

"Sweetie. Calm down. It's just me."

In her attempt to wake Belinda, Summer shook her shoulders. The slight touch was enough to startle Belinda and elicit a scream.

The cab driver, who until now had his eyes fixated on the road, turned to look in the backseat to see what was going on.

"Everything's okay. My friend was in a deep sleep; that's all."

Belinda was finally awake and was beginning to become aware of where she was.

"Oh my God, Summer; I'm so sorry. I didn't hit you, did I?"

"No, you didn't. But you came pretty damned close. I've got just what you need in my apartment. And, don't fight with me either. Also, you're going to stay here, at least for tonight, and we can go to your apartment tomorrow, if you'd like. If not, you can stay here as long as you want."

"Damn, you're bossy."

"Hell yeah. I'm a mother; I'm supposed to be bossy. Speaking of which, you want me to get rid of motor mouth for tonight, so you can get some rest? She's gonna lose her mind as soon as you walk through the door. That girl loves her some Aunty B."

"No I wouldn't dream of it. It'll be nice to have Ms. 'Busy Lizzy' around. I have to admit, I'm still a little freaked by the events of the last couple of days, or at least what I can remember of it. It'll be nice to have a noisy distraction."

Keyanna was on alert as soon as she heard the key turn in the lock. "Hi, Aunty B!"

"Hey, Keyanna. I haven't seen you for like a hundred years."

"Did she behave herself?" Summer asked the babysitter.

"Yes. She was a perfect little angel."

"Whose kid were you watchin' because I know you weren't watchin' mine? Perfect little angel, my foot."

"Really; she's no trouble."

"Thanks again for stopping by on such short notice. You want me to call you a cab? It's kinda' late."

"No problem. I'm good; I can probably get a yellow on the street."

Summer handed the sitter some cash and walked her to the door.

"You wanna see my room, Aunty B? Mommy fixed it up for me and it looks like a grownup room."

"Really. Well, in that case, I'd love to see your room."

Summer smiled. Belinda was better with her daughter than she was. She had a lot more patience. She couldn't wait for the day when Belinda was married with her own children. She was going to be a great mother.

"Keyanna, leave Aunty B alone. She's not feeling well and the last thing she needs is you burning out the last little bit of energy she has left."

"You can lay down in my room too, if you want. I have two beds now."

"It's okay, Summer. It'll be fun to hang out with Little Miss Keyanna."

With that, she tickled Keyanna mercilessly until she was giggling and trying to break free so she could run to her bedroom.

"I'm coming to get you! The Tickle Monster wasn't finished yet!"

Belinda went running behind Keyanna and Summer could hear the two of them jumping up and down on the beds.

"Ya'll break those beds down and you and Aunty B will be sleeping on the floor tonight."

"Yay! You're spending the night! Hip, hip hooray! Hip, hip hooray!"

"I don't know if I'm going to stay!" Belinda shouted to Summer. "I don't think Keyanna is happy enough about me spending the night."

"Yes I am! Hip, hip hooray! Hip, hip hooray!" HIP, HIP HOOOOOORAAAAAAYYYYY!"

"Okay that's better."

"Keyanna, you better quiet down in there. It's kinda late and you know how much our neighbors complain about noise."

"Okay, Mommy," Keyanna whispered. "We have to be quiet, Aunty B, because our neighbors are trifling mother..."

"Keyanna!"

Summer entered Keyanna's room just in time to hear her own words coming out of her daughter's mouth.

"Ms. Keyanna Singer, didn't I tell you not to repeat what you hear me say!"

"I'm sorry, Mommy."

"Okay, don't do it again."

"Uhm, uhm, uhm, do as I say and not as I do. Miss Summer Chantal Johnson, you know that don't work."

"Yeah, yeah, yeah. Whatever."

"What do you feel like eating?" Summer asked Belinda. "I know you don't want those tater tots and hot dogs I fixed for Keyanna tonight."

"I'm not really hungry. I'm sleepier than anything else."

"Girl, you sure you ain't pregnant? You're using condoms with Aidan, aren't you?"

"Hell yes! Do I look stupid? And, for the record, I cut Aidan loose. He was getting boring, always talking about his miserable home life and the sex wasn't even all that good. If I'm going to be smack-dab-in-the middle of a bad marriage, complete with mediocre sex, it's at least going to be my own bad marriage and my own mediocre sex. The fucked up part is right before we split, he became an animal in the sack. It was like he was a different person. I still had to let him go, though. I've got too much of a conscience to go on fucking a married man. Speaking of which, I can't believe you mentioned that shit in front of Diana on Friday. I don't tell her the same things I tell you. I thought she was gonna have a coronary."

"Oh sure, she can't remember a thing about Friday night, but that she remembers. That's what I call some selective damn memory."

They both laughed.

"But seriously, Belinda, I don't think I've ever seen you so tired before."

"Ain't it crazy? I slept at that guy's house…Dante's,

for like two days straight. That's so unlike me. Usually it's impossible for me to sleep in a stranger's home. I can barely sleep in a hotel room. Lately I haven't been sleeping at all in my place."

"You sure he didn't drug you or something? Are you sure he's not the one who attacked you in your apartment in the first place?"

"I never say never to anything, but I really don't think he had anything to do with what happened to me. If anything, he was a good Samaritan. In fact, I'm not even sure I was attacked."

"A good Samaritan, huh?"

"In fact, he was kinda fine. All beat up and lookin' tore up from the floor up and your girl here was hopin' he asked her on a date."

"That's shocking 'cause your picky ass don't like nobody. He must've been fine."

"He was. He had the most beautiful eyes. They were practically blue. I've never in my entire life seen a black man with blue eyes."

"Are you sure he was black?"

"Yeah. His skin color was a bit different too, sort of olive-colored, but he was definitely black; or maybe he was multiracial. And, a body to die for. Silky, curly hair. He was absolutely yummy."

"Wow! He sounds familiar."

"Stop tellin' that lie." Belinda laughed.

"No, for real. The way you just described him. It was

strange; almost like déjà vu. I couldn't tell you where I could have possibly seen him, but the description truly sounded like someone I've seen somewhere before."

"I don't know, Summer. This is the sort of man that would be hard to forget."

"Just because you've had such a hard couple of days, I'll be nice, make the supreme sacrifice and give up my bed to you, and sleep with motor mouth."

"No, Summer. I'm not gonna kick you out of your bed. I'll be fine with Keyanna. I'm just happy I don't have to go back to my place alone."

"You know my offer still stands. You can stay here as long as you like and if you want, I'll go with you to pick up some things from your house."

"I'll see how I feel when I wake up tomorrow morning. I know one thing, though. I'm gonna need my laptop. I'm supposed to be working on this story. The last thing I need is to lose a client because I don't follow through. That's the tough thing about freelance work. When you're on staff you can get fired, but when you're freelance, your reputation is absolutely everything. Unreliable doesn't go over big."

"You can use my computer."

"I may do that to check my emails and stuff, but I need my computer in order to work. I have everything on there." Belinda paused. "You mind if I take a shower?"

"Oh now you're acting like some damn guest. You know where everything is. Make yourself at home. Now, I know you done gone and bumped your head."

Belinda couldn't help but laugh.

Summer was a TV addict and had it on mute until she saw a picture of someone she recognized on the local news. She turned up the sound.

"Oh my God, Belinda, hurry up! Come look at who's on the news! Quick!"

"What are you trying to do? Kill me? I almost broke my neck, trying to get out the shower. What the heck is going on?"

"Forty-seven-year-old Vladimir Shoelenko, a driver with Delta Car Service has been missing since Friday evening. His car was found abandoned and stripped in an alleyway in Harlem. Shoelenko's dispatcher at Delta became concerned when radio calls made to Shoelenko went unanswered and Mr. Shoelenko failed to return home to his family. Foul play is suspected. According to Shoelenko's wife, he was wearing a black suit and tie, white shirt and black shoes when he left for work on Friday morning. Anyone who may have seen Shoelenko or knows anything about his whereabouts is asked to contact NYPD's CRIMESTOPPERS Tips Line at 800-577-TIPS.

"We were staring at the back of his head all night, but I could swear that's a picture of the driver we had on Friday."

"What driver?"

"I swear, Belinda; you've been a space case ever since that night, even before you went home and supposedly bumped your head; now this. Some freaky shit went on that night we went to Redemption. I'm not sure what. I find it difficult to believe that all of this is coincidence."

"All of what, Summer? For the sake of argument, let's say that guy was our driver. This is New York. People go missing in New York every day, at alarming numbers. Not only that, he drives a car for a living. That's a dangerous job in and of itself. Trust me, I know. It's my job to know. I see stories like this all the time. In fact, that's what I'm supposed to be writing about for *Newsweek*; how many people go missing each and every day in New York City and remain unaccounted for."

"So, as a *professional* you're going to tell me that you wouldn't question a connection between our missing driver and your two days of fatigue and amnesia? Belinda, you may not want to believe you were attacked, but one look at you and even I can tell your injuries were not the result of some fall. I mean, really, have you taken a good look at yourself…the cuts, the bruises, from head to toe. Not to mention Diana. I've been calling that girl ever since you disappeared and nothing. You'd think that your absence would've been obvious, but nothing. Not one response to my numerous calls. Does that make sense?"

"Summer, I really am trying to look at this objectively, but I'm a journalist. I deal in cold, hard facts and the things you've mentioned could all have far less ominous explanations. I'm not saying there isn't a possibility that something strange is going on that ties all these events together. I'm just saying that there's possibility and probability; and that the probability of all of these events you mention being somehow tied in together falls into an even lower percentage than the possibility."

TWELVE

Her eyes were glassy and transfixed; engulfed by the great pleasure he was giving her. And, just when she thought she couldn't possibly cum again, his tool rose to new lengths and expanded to such depths, she rained down upon him with the veracity of a raging river.

"Give yourself to me. More, more," he whispered to her. "I want *all* of you."

Maybe if she had even a small inkling of what his words truly meant, she might have at least tried to escape. Although, admittedly, it would have been to no avail. Instead, with each word he spoke, she met his bombardment of thrusts with an equal degree of lustful abandon; clawing at his back with her bright red fingernails, digging the heels of her feet into his thighs, tightening her pussy around him; anxious to feel every inch, every bulging vein, every corpuscle of his majestic cock.

"Fuuuuccccckkkkkk me!" she screamed when yet another earth-shattering orgasm rocked her to the core.

Satiated, yet drained, more than anything she needed to rest. Instead, like any junkie, she craved more. His cock was intoxicating, his cum addicting, and she needed to fuck him like most people need air.

"In my ass now. Okay?"

He liked this one. But, not the way that most men like a woman. He liked her the way that a man loves a dog. Not only did she provide what he needed, but she was obedient and sturdy. She had lasted far longer than any of the others. Not only that; she didn't ask a lot of questions. His kind were seldom able to engage willing partners. There were always so many questions. Even when they took a typical human form, there were certain things that could not be changed. Somehow, though, Desiree liked that his penis was not the same temperature as the rest of his body. Plain and simple: Desiree was what mortals called a freak; a freak that was addicted to what he was giving her.

"I will fuck your ass extra deep with my cock, if you will do something for me."

"I'd do anything for you. What is it?"

"The night I met you, there was another with you; the blonde one. Do you think she'd like to join us next time?"

She was at first jealous, but that jealousy was quickly replaced with loyalty when she felt the tip of his cock lingering at the entrance to her anus. She wanted him there. She was always so tight there and it seemed to please him so. And, more than anything, she wanted to please him. At that very moment she realized if she had to provide him with a consistent flow of women to keep him happy and fucking her, then that is what she would do. These were all new emotions for Desiree; jealousy, selflessness, such a strong desire for sex with one person, with no money changing hands. She couldn't understand or explain it. But, more importantly, she didn't care to.

"Please baby, please don't...don't...don't tease me. I want it...so...so...baaaaddddd! Awwwww!"

He entered her quickly and deeply and with his mouth hovering inches from her ear reminded her of what he wanted.

"Bring her to me."

René's level of control far surpassed any mere mortal. He could last for hours. There was a time when he would have taken a woman to the very edge; to a place where his restoration lasted far longer and she was nothing but a mere shell. But René knew some of what Dante had told him made sense. This city was a large place; one in which he thought no one would ever notice the disappearance of a girl here and there; especially with all its many nooks and crannies. Not only that, New Yorkers were habitually transient; milling about, migrating here and there. One of the reasons he had settled in New York was because the hunting ground seemed limitless. He had been wrong. With all its nooks and crannies and all its nameless faceless people, New York was also a city hell-bent on sensationalism. Most New Yorkers craved gossip and the next engaging story or incredible mystery. That was severely limiting René's ability to simply feed.

When the first story of a missing girl hit the papers, it was just another young woman fallen prey to peril.

That is, until the number of disappearances increased. His hunger was all-consuming. He should have controlled himself, but he couldn't. Even after Dante figured out that René had been responsible for most of the disappearances and confronted him, he still couldn't control himself. But, with time, he began to understand more of what it took to go undetected.

René had little respect for humans; he considered them a lower life form, but even amongst the humans there were those possessing a greater degree of strength. On one of his very forays into the night, René had met a woman unlike any other he had ever come into contact with. She was a sexual dynamo; capable of sustaining her lifeforce without being completely drained...like most of the women he encountered.

"Do you always read a book in a titty bar?" she asked.

"Only when I'm not sufficiently entertained," René answered.

"Well, I guess I'll have to do something about that."

Initially, Desiree was just working it. This was what she did for a living; a lap dance here and there, a flirtatious word or two to garner bigger tips. But, she had to admit, there was something decidedly more intriguing about this one.

"What exactly did you have in mind?"

And, with that, she lowered her top to reveal two full, inviting breasts. Both nipples were pierced and two small hoop earrings dangled from each.

René was intrigued by the things mortal women did with their bodies. Yet, on occasion when he was forced to visit one of them in the night without their prior invitation, they would scream, yell, try in earnest to get free. While others, like Desiree here, would actually intentionally pay someone to drive a hole through something as obviously sensitive as her nipples. He couldn't understand it.

After lowering her top, she knelt between his legs, jiggling and bouncing her boobs in front of him, licking her fingers and trailing a line around her nipples. She danced to the music, bending over to reveal her impressively round ass. Intermittently, she would lightly caress his checks, his neck, trail a line down his torso and slightly graze his cock, long enough to ignite enough of a fire for him to give her a really big tip and maybe even request a second round (she hoped). The finale involved her grinding hard and deep against René's impressive hard-on. René was well-acquainted with the rules, but was not so accustomed to following rules. Each time she bent down in front of him, he was tempted to mount her from behind and take exactly what he needed. But, he allowed himself to be patient; knowing that he would soon have his chance.

He could feel her wetness through her skimpy purple thong as she ground her pussy harder and deeper against his cock. He could smell her longing.

Through the years Desiree had become desensitized

to the physical effects of her job. She had done so many lap dances in her eight years working the clubs that she could count on one hand the number of times she was actually turned on. And, even those few times in the past couldn't begin to come close to what she was feeling now. Without even feeling him inside of her, she had cum. The last thing she wanted either him or anyone else in the club to know was that he had gotten to her. After all, she was a professional.

When she was done, Desiree was surprised to find that she had left remnants of her sticky offering clinging to the front of her patron's jeans. And, she was sure she detected a slight smirk on his face.

"Thank you; you are entertaining indeed."

He handed her two crisp $100 bills.

Desiree didn't want to let on that that was more money than she had ever gotten for a simple lap dance. Instead, she tried to come off calm, cool and collected. She failed.

"Usually, I would ask if you'd like another dance, but since you are thoroughly entertained, I'll forego asking if you'd like another."

"I think maybe you didn't hear exactly what I said. I said you were entertaining. But, 'thoroughly' entertained; no I am not, at least not yet. I believe thoroughly entertained is something that sadly cannot be offered within the confines of this club."

"What did you have in mind?"

"There is so much more I would like to do with you. Is that a possibility?"

Every now and then Desiree would extend a bit more than just a lap dance, under the right circumstances. But, it was not a service she offered everyone. This man, however, would have to be an exception. She wanted him the moment her pussy touched his cock.

"I think something can be arranged."

"Wonderful! Your place or mine?" he asked.

Desiree's place was a mess and she had two roommates. Somehow she thought it would be far more enjoyable if she went to his place instead.

"I have two very annoying roommates, so I'm thinking your place would probably be best."

"Absolutely. Shall we go?"

"I'm off in a half-hour. Can you wait?"

"Of course. I can finish reading my book. That is, unless you want to entertain me some more."

As much as she would've liked to fulfill his request, there were other customers that required her attention. She would have more than enough time to indulge both of their desires.

For months, Desiree sufficed. She was indeed entertaining and served to supply René with enough sexual sustenance to keep him going. However, she would soon prove to be more trouble than she was worth.

"Why can't I move in with you?"

"That is not the nature of our relationship, Desiree."

"I can't keep going the way that I've been. The longer we're together, the less energy I seem to have. It's becoming more and more difficult for me to be with you and work at the club. I don't understand it. It's almost like you're draining me."

"You say this like it's a bad thing. You enjoy fucking me just as much as I enjoy you."

"I do René, I do, but I...I can't explain it. I've never felt this way with anyone. Each encounter I have with you makes it harder for me to do...anything; let alone work."

"I keep telling you to take the B vitamins, but you won't."

"But why? Why do you want me to take B vitamins? I feel like there's something you're not telling me. Are you sick? Have I contracted some sort of illness from you?"

"No, I'm not sick and there's nothing to tell. B vitamins help to restore energy. That is what you've been talking about right; your lack of energy?"

"It's more than that. I feel like I'm fading away."

"I want some of what you've been smoking," he joked.

"What's that supposed to mean?"

"I'm screwing around with you. You're being a bit paranoid. You probably need a little break from everything; me included. As much as I enjoy your company, if you need to take a breather, I'm okay with that."

René realized she had served her purpose well and that she might be worth more to him if he used someone else for a while. The last thing he needed was someone, even her, asking a whole lot of questions. Despite Dante's belief that he was a loose cannon, René was not a fool. He began spending less and less time with Desiree and more time making nightly visits to strangers. His ability to move about unseen proved invaluable and he quickly realized that most women were not so quick to announce their sexual encounters with an unseen force.

Desiree realized that the less time she spent with René, the more her energy and vitality were restored. It was as though he were literally sucking the life right out of her. Obsessed with not only him, but the mystery she found herself a part of, she began following him.

At first, she was convinced he was just seeing other women. Although jealous, she was reassured that there was nothing more menacing going on than a sexually powerful man wanting a wider variety of pussy. That is until the first story surfaced in the *Daily News*.

MANHATTAN—Police are looking for Kimberly Swanson, 34, who they say has been missing since Friday. Neighbors of Swanson at 1125 St. Nicholas Avenue say they heard screams coming from her fourth floor apartment. Swanson's eight-year-old daughter was asleep all night in her bedroom and heard and saw nothing. According to Swanson's daughter, she may have been wearing a pink t-shirt and black stretch pants when last seen. Swanson is black, 5-foot-2, about 100 pounds and has light brown, shoulder-length, wavy hair. Anyone who sees her is asked to contact NYPD's CRIME-STOPPERS Tips Line at 800-577-TIPS.

Desiree recognized the address and the description.

Not only that, she too had heard the screams coming from the woman's apartment that night. It was the same night she had followed René. On that particular night, she assumed the sounds she heard were sounds of passion, but now she wondered if there was more going on than that.

What Desiree didn't know was that René was fully aware that she had been following him; and now with the story in the paper, he was convinced of what he had to do.

"Hey, René. You didn't tell me you were coming by the club tonight."

"I wanted to surprise you. It's been a while since we've seen each other and things seemed to end on such a sour note the last time we were together, I thought I'd make it up to you."

"Oh."

Desiree was clearly uncomfortable, but René had a quick fix for that. He had never needed to use his power with Desiree, but now it was a necessity. He did not think she would come to him as willingly as before.

"I would love one of those spectacular lap dances."

"Of course."

Desiree moved and swayed to the seductive music. Until now, he had always held back. He was satisfied enough with what she had to offer, to encourage him to keep her around; that is, until she had proven to outlive her usefulness.

"Is there someplace we can be alone?"

"Yes," she answered, still mesmerized.

There were private rooms at the club that some of the girls (Desiree included) sometimes used to make a little extra cash on the side. Desiree shut and locked the door, eager to give René what he wanted.

His spell temporarily broken, Desiree was suddenly frightened.

"I don't know if this is a good idea. They're going to be looking for me on the floor. Maybe we should continue this after I get off work."

"But I need you now. I don't think I can wait."

He approached her slowly and deliberately. The closer he got to her, the greater her fear was. The chemical reaction brought on by her fear was tantamount to sexually released pheromones for him and his evolution was complete. He was sure to suppress her ability to scream or even move. And, by the time he reached her, his wings had opened and he engulfed her, drawing her up mid-air along with him, spinning wildly as he made her life his own, withdrawing her spirit with each plunge, until she was little more than a lifeless shell.

THIRTEEN

"I cannot believe how long you slept. I got Keyanna ready for school, dropped her off, came back, and you were still sleeping. I'm starting to get a little worried. Maybe you should go to the doctor; make sure you're okay."

Belinda woke up around 11:00 a.m. Summer had been back from dropping Keyanna off for hours and she was sure her puttering around the house would have awakened Belinda much earlier.

"I did a load of laundry, put some dishes in the dishwasher, watched a little Maury, and you were still sleeping."

"Damn, I missed Maury," Belinda joked.

"Hell yeah, you missed it. And, he was…not the father!"

"So how many of them ran to the back and dropped to the ground crying?"

"Only two this time."

Both girls laughed.

"You ready for some breakfast, coffee?"

"I could definitely use a cup of coffee."

"You know where the kitchen is. I just made the coffee, so it's fresh."

"I'm ready to go home. I needed a night to regroup."

"See, I told your ass you should've slept in my room. Keyanna probably drove your ass crazy. That's why you wanna go home."

"No. You need to stop. That's not it. I miss my place, my things. You know how I am about my apartment. Besides, I can't stay away forever."

"You need to take your behind to the doctor. Have you looked in the mirror lately?"

"Oh gee. Thanks, Summer. Don't hold back or anything; tell me exactly what you think."

"No. Don't get me wrong. You always look beautiful. But, really, Belinda. You look so tired. You look beat up; not just because of the bruises and scars. You look like you've been through it."

Just as Belinda was about to respond, the phone rang.

"Where the fuck have you been? I've been calling and calling your ass and nothing…no response."

"Who's that?" Belinda mouthed.

"It's Diana," Summer whispered back.

"Yeah. She's here. Yeah, she's alright; a few bumps and scrapes, but she's okay. I'll let her tell you. Hold on."

Summer rolled her eyes and handed Belinda the phone.

"Hey, girl. Yeah, I'm alright. I'm not really sure what happened. I'm a little bruised, a couple of scratches; otherwise, I'm good. My memory's a little fuzzy though. I'm starting to think maybe somebody drugged me at

Redemption on Friday. It's the only explanation I can think of. I don't know. I went over and over it in my mind last night and every time I think I have it figured out, it doesn't make sense. At first I thought maybe I might've fallen in my apartment, but now I'm not sure. Yeah. I don't think Summer has anything planned. She's got a club job tonight, but that's about it. And, I've gotta work on my article. Otherwise, we could probably meet for an hour or two. Where?"

Belinda hung up the phone.

"What did that heifer want?"

"Okay, Summer, why are you so mad at her? It's not her fault."

"That girl got some shit with her. She walks around like butter wouldn't melt in her mouth, but mark my words, she ain't just got a few skeletons in her closet. When those doors open whole fucking graveyards be fallin' out."

"Summer, you ain't got no damn sense." Belinda laughed. "So what did she want anyway?"

"She wants us to meet her for brunch."

"Oh yeah? Now she wants us to meet her for brunch. When you were missing and I thought you were laying dead somewhere, her ass was nowhere to be found. Where are we going?"

"She's gonna meet us at Green Kitchen, which is perfect. When we leave there, I'll be close to home and you guys can stop off with me; since, truth be told, I'm still a little scared to go home."

"See. I knew you were still scared. I don't know why you don't stay here a few more days. It's not like you have to stay forever."

"You know what they say: there's no time like the present. The longer I stay, the harder it's going to get to leave. Besides, it's nothing but fear of the unknown, since I don't have a fucking clue what happened anyway."

"True. True."

"You know I'm only meeting her for brunch to find out where the fuck she's been for two days, right?"

"Summer, I've known you since we were little girls, kicking each other's asses playing kickball. I know you like I know the back of my own hand. And, you wouldn't be you if you let Diana off the hook."

"And, she better be paying."

"You know what, girl? You're priceless. You gonna fuck with the girl and make her pay for your meal."

"Well, we know your ass ain't paying; or have you forgotten you've got no pocketbook, no wallet, no credit cards—no nothing. In fact, I just thought of something. Do you even have keys to your own apartment?"

"No, but that's one of the advantages to having a doorman. He can let me in with no problem."

"Or, Diana could always let you in with her set of keys. I still can't believe you gave her a set of keys to your apartment. You've only known her for four years. We've known each other all our lives and I don't have a set, but she does. You have a set of my keys."

"I keep forgetting to give you a set. And, you know why you never got a set. When I made the set of keys you were still dealing with Kaleel. You my girl and all, but I wasn't trying to come home one day and find out one of those junkies Kaleel was selling to stole my keys from you and was up in my crib robbing me blind."

"Damn! It's like that! You didn't trust me to protect your keys?"

"It wasn't about you. Even you can't guard shit around the clock. I'll make sure I make you a set of keys; especially given recent developments."

"Hell yeah. I called the police when you did your disappearing act and after they investigated things inside, they wouldn't even let me stay. One of the cops was nice, but he still wasn't trying to let me stay in your place. If I had a key I could have come back and did my own investigation."

"I'm gonna take a quick shower," Belinda said. "I'll be ready in fifteen. Okay?"

"No problem. She'll just have to wait. I had to wait on her."

"Oh boy. I can tell how this is gonna go. Just don't act up in Green Kitchen. You know that's my home away from home."

By the time Belinda and Summer got to Green Kitchen, Diana was already there, sipping on a cup of coffee.

"Well, if it ain't the Prodigal Daughter," Summer announced.

"Hello, Summer. Hey, Belinda! You okay?"

"So, Diana, did the police contact you?"

Oh brother, Belinda thought. Here we go.

She was curious to see where Summer was going with this one.

"Contact me about what?" Diana answered.

"Have you been under a rock or something? The driver you hired on Friday…he's missing. Not only that, one of the bartenders at Redemption has done a disappearing act as well, coincidentally, the last time anyone saw him was on Friday as well."

"So, why would the police contact me? Why is that my problem? Did they contact you?"

"No, but I wasn't the one who hired the driver and I wasn't the person they questioned about the last Redemption bartender that disappeared. I would think that they will probably contact the driver's most recent customers. Not only that, he was last seen on Friday; the same day that you hired him. He waited for us all night and by the time we were done, it was Saturday morning. We were his last passengers. And, you did order drinks from the bartender."

"Yeah…and so did you and Belinda. Not only that, you may not have hired the driver, but you were passengers right along with me in his vehicle. But, to answer your question, no. No one contacted me."

"Maybe you should contact them?"

"Why? I have nothing to tell them. He dropped you off, then me and then Belinda."

"Actually, Diana, he dropped me off then Summer and then you."

"Oh, sorry, I must have forgotten. I thought you said you had amnesia or something. Is your memory coming back?

"Kind of. It's sort of scrambled up. Things are coming back but in no particular order and it's in bits and pieces.

"Besides which, where have you been the last few days?" Summer continued. "I've been trying to contact you for days. I called your cell, left a message on your voicemail at home. I even called your practice. Where were you?"

"What is this, an inquisition? I have a life just like everybody else. I don't question you when you're running the streets. And, I don't go see your parents."

"Summer, you didn't!" Belinda exclaimed.

Summer sighed. "Yes, I did. Hell, I thought something might have happened to her, too. How was I supposed to know she was fine and just ignoring me…if that was all she was doing. What would you have done? As far as I was concerned it was an emergency."

"I know your memory is fuzzy and you mentioned on the phone that you had a couple of ideas, but Belinda, what do you really think happened?" Diana asked.

"I don't know. I'm back to thinking maybe I took a fall

in my apartment and bumped my head. Somehow, I ended up in this guy's apartment. He heard me screaming or something from my apartment while he was visiting a client and he took me back to his place. But, I think before he got there, I somehow managed to call Summer and ask for her help. By the time she got there, I was gone."

"What day was this?"

Summer jumped in to respond. "She called me early Saturday morning, around six, and I've been trying to reach you ever since. Quite frankly, I was surprised when you called today. I thought Belinda would be the first person to hear from you; especially after you dropped off the map the way that you did and didn't bother to return any of my calls."

"Summer, I'm a gynecologist. I'm basically on call twenty-four seven. I'm not a nine-to-fiver. I work when my patients need me and sleep when I can. If I didn't get back to you when you expected me to it was probably because I was delivering a baby or catching up on all the sleep I missed. There's no great conspiracy. No deep dark secret. I was simply living my life, such that it is."

"I understand all that, but I gotta tell you, in all the years I've known you, this is the very first time it's been so difficult to reach you. You hear where I'm comin' from? And what's with the *'you were probably delivering a baby or catching up on all the sleep you missed?'* Either you were or you weren't, or do you have amnesia, too?"

"Hey," Belinda said to Summer. "I take offense to that amnesia remark."

"No offense intended, at least not to you."

"I must say, Summer, I don't really see where you're coming from," Diana said. "Spell it out to me. What are you saying? What do you think? I have my driver bound and gagged somewhere in my basement or something?"

Summer replied, "You said it; not me."

Belinda had had enough. "Okay, ladies, neutral corners. Isn't the most important thing that I'm fine, alive, and kicking?"

Diana grinned. "I don't know about Summer, but that was all I was worried about when I called today."

"Yeah, you were so worried that it took you two, almost three days to contact anybody," Summer stated sarcastically.

Belinda glared at Summer. "Come on, Summer; lighten up."

"And there you go again, taking her side," Summer replied. "She's been walking around for years, judging me about my lifestyle, etc., etc., etc., but when she fucks up, all is supposed to be forgiven. Hell to the no!"

Diana was sick of trying to be cordial to Summer. "Summer, if you came here to argue, I might as well leave; that's not what I came here for."

"You know what, Diana? You don't have to leave; I'm leaving. Belinda, give me a call later, when you're alone."

Belinda shook her head. "Aw, Summer, come on. Don't leave."

Summer decided to get one last jab in. "I'm sorry, Belinda, but I've always had my doubts about this one. She's hiding something and I've now graduated from doubts about her to an all out lack of trust."

Summer stormed out of Green Kitchen, and planned to hail a cab to go pick her daughter up from school. Instead, she turned around and came back to the restaurant. As she marched over to the table, Belinda suddenly was afraid of what she was going to do. She went over what had just been said between Summer and Diana and figured nothing was said that might initiate any physical violence on Summer's part.

"Oh, by the way Diana, I forgot to ask, will you be wearing that tight black silk number to Potion? I think I may have a gig there bartending."

Although her comment elicited no recognizable response from Diana, she knew that she would at least have some explaining to do to Belinda.

FOURTEEN

Belinda wasn't sure what she would find once she got to her apartment. Despite the tense encounter between Diana and Summer, Diana offered to go with Belinda back to her apartment and Belinda was glad she had.

She was hoping that Javier was not on duty, so that she would not have to go into a lengthy explanation; at least not yet. She had no such luck.

"Ms. Wilson! Thank goodness! Are you okay? The police were here and your other friend, Ms. Johnson, was here. She was very, very angry with me. I tried to tell her that I couldn't let her in your apartment. I'm so sorry, Ms. Wilson, but it's the rules."

"No, Javier, don't worry about it. You did the right thing. You're not supposed to let anyone in. Really, I understand. You did the right thing."

"Thank you, Ms. Wilson, but are you okay? We were all very concerned."

Belinda didn't like the sound of that *we*. She wondered if he meant *we*, like him, Summer, and the police;

or *we*, like the entire building. Somehow, though, she realized the answer to that question. As if it weren't bad enough that she felt like she was constantly being watched by her fellow tenants, now she would be the 'black tenant' who had been the subject of a police investigation.

"Everything is okay. I bumped my head on an end table in my apartment. I was unconscious for a bit and then a friend came and took me to the hospital," she lied. "Ms. Johnson and the police must have gotten here right after I left."

"Oh well, if you need anything, please let me know.

"No problem, Javier. I should be fine."

"Why did you lie?" Diana asked, once they were in the elevator.

"It seemed easier that way."

"Oh damn! I should've gotten Javier to open the door."

"That's okay; I have the set of keys you gave me."

"You carry them with you?"

"No, not all the time. I figured you might need them."

Once they got to the door, they realized they didn't need the keys after all. Although closed, the door was not locked.

"I'm so stupid. I don't know why I didn't ask Dante to bring back my pocketbook and keys and stuff."

"Who is Dante?" Diana asked.

"My gallant rescuer."

"Do tell."

Belinda told Diana the story of how she had come to

meet Dante and was relieved to find that Diana didn't seem concerned about who Dante was or what he was doing in Belinda's apartment, as Summer had been. That's when she realized exactly how much she was hoping to hear from him.

"That story you told Javier might actually have some ring of truth to it. Look at your coffee table. It's all cracked and there are shards of glass on the floor."

Belinda was beginning to feel hopeful that a simple fall was all that had happened to her when she went into her bedroom and saw her bed. There was blood on the sheets and every single window in her apartment was wide open. She never left the windows open; especially not all of them.

"I don't know, Diana. There's blood on the sheets and each and every one of my windows are open. You know me; I'm cold all the time. I would never have all of these windows open."

"Maybe Summer or the police opened them when they were here. And the blood, that might have happened as a result of the fall."

"I don't think it was Summer. She said they wouldn't let her stay in the apartment and why would the police open my windows? And as far as the blood is concerned, I have a couple of cuts and scrapes, but not enough to produce that much blood. Don't get me wrong; it's not like it's a gallon of blood, but it's enough.

"Maybe they were investigating or maybe Summer

opened the windows while the police were still here. I don't know. And you know how much blood even a finger stick can produce sometimes. You've got several cuts all over your body and a lot bigger than a couple of finger sticks."

Diana got a message on her BlackBerry.

"Is everything okay?" Belinda asked her.

"Yes. Everything is fine; just a patient in labor. I've got a little time. Do you need anything before I go?"

"No, I'll be okay. Besides, I really need to focus on getting this story done. The last thing I need in this economy is to lose another magazine." Belinda paused. "There is one thing."

"What?"

"Could you please do me a favor? Take the things Summer says with a grain of a salt. You haven't known her as long as I have. Half of the things she says she doesn't really mean. She's probably regretting what she said at brunch today as we speak. So, please don't judge her too harshly. You both are my best friends in the world and I couldn't bear it if you weren't getting along."

"I bear no grudges against Summer, but I don't know if she feels the same. You're right; you do know her better than me, but it sure sounded to me like she meant each and every word she said to me today."

"Well, trust me, she didn't. But, there was one thing I was confused about. What was that she mentioned about a Potion? Something about her job tonight."

"Oh that," Diana replied. "Potion is a club. I made the mistake of letting one of my colleagues talk me into going there. I didn't realize that it was a sex club until I got there. I think she thought if I went there with her, I might be enticed into getting involved in some kinky sex with her. She's sort of had this crush on me since we started working together. No big deal. I left right after I got there. I guess maybe Summer saw me there and jumped to conclusions."

Belinda nodded and laughed. "Yeah. That sounds like Summer."

Diana asked, "Anything else?"

"No, I'm good. Call me later to make sure I'm okay. I'd call you, but it sounds like you're going to be busy."

Diana hugged Belinda and left.

Belinda tried to return her apartment to its original state. She gathered up the glass from the coffee table, put most of it in a garbage bag, and pushed the base of the table into a corner of her living room. Then, she went into the bedroom and stripped her bed of the sheets. After removing the sheets, she sat down on the edge of the bed for a moment. Somehow, she thought the solitude and being back in her home would help to return her memory. However, nothing concrete surfaced. That's when she decided she should knuckle down to some writing.

Belinda's blank computer screen stared back at her and words escaped her. She had committed to writing the article, and she usually completed her assignments way ahead of schedule. But, her mind was a million miles away. She couldn't stop thinking about Dante or the events of the past few days. She wondered if she would ever see him again. She decided she was getting nowhere within the four walls of her apartment and needed a quick caffeine boost. With her Mac in tow, she headed off to the Starbucks around the corner.

Initially, she was beyond excited. However, she had gone from excited to once again worrying about her article. Now, she was bordering on something akin to paranoia. She convinced herself it was all the research she had done into the many ways people go missing; especially in a city as large as New York. But it was getting more and more difficult to justify certain occurrences; like the never-ending feeling that she was being followed. Sitting and staring out the window, she was sure the reflection of the man sitting behind her was someone she had not only seen before, but someone she had seen often and, for just a moment, she considered confronting him. Instead, she shook it off and decided to call Diana.

"Diana, it's me, Belinda."

"Hey. What's up?"

"Diana, I know that you planned to call me later but I couldn't wait. Any chance you've got the name of a good therapist?"

"Like I told you before, sure; I know plenty of them."

"I'm starting to feel like I'm going out of my mind."

"Where are you now?"

"I'm in the Starbucks, near my house."

"And how many cups of coffee have you had? More to the point, how much sleep have you had?"

"Point well taken; sleep hasn't exactly been my best friend lately."

"My suggestion is that you go home, get some sleep and give me a call in the morning when your mind is clearer. Okay? Then, if you still want a therapist, I'll help you find one."

"Okay."

Belinda hung up the phone and finished her drink.

"Who are you? Why won't you answer me?"

Every night it was the same question, met with no response. More than anything she wanted to believe that her mind was playing tricks on her, but it was all too real; physical manifestations that stepped outside of her dreams. She was a victim with no recognizable assailant. Even when she didn't come home, somehow he found her.

What was even more confusing was the shift in his nature. There were nights when he was unapologetically violent. Yet, other nights he was almost kind. And, still other nights, there was a startling sense of familiarity.

She tried to block it all from her mind; tried not to

make sense of what was happening to her. It was almost easier to believe that she was slowly going insane.

This night, she thought she recognized him.

"Aidan, is that you?"

For a moment it appeared as though she might be right. He skipped a beat, if only for a moment.

"Aidan, please answer me. Is it you?"

It occurred to Belinda that her paranoia might be nothing more than disenchantment with her life, compounded by pangs of guilt. She had become more aware than ever of her ticking biological clock. The fact that she had no apparent possibility of a husband in the near future and no children caused her to cling to her career. Now it seemed her confidence in that area was slipping as well. It seemed as though she were constantly searching for more. Maybe that was how insanity started.

"Aidan, please answer me," she implored.

She saw nothing; could hear…nothing. Yet, he continued to ravage her body and soul.

Strong gusts of wind blew inside her bedroom, despite the windows she was sure she had locked earlier. Curtains flapped, items toppled from the top of her dresser. Inside her mind, she prayed for it all to stop. But she knew this would all continue to go on until he was satiated and it would not end before that time. When the invasions first started, she convinced herself she would use every bit of strength she possessed to fight him off. She soon learned, however, that it was impossible; especially for an assailant she couldn't see. Not only that, each morning following the "visits" she was painfully exhausted and often unable to function normally. There were days when she slept fifteen hours or more. However, this night she resolved to fight off whatever fatigue she might be feeling the following morning and do what any good reporter would do. She would have to research and investigate. She wasn't comfortable sharing her experiences with anyone, for fear the boys in the little white coats might come and cart her off. But, she could always do some research under the guise of a prospective story. She lay there, powerless, hoping he would be done, and soon.

FIFTEEN

Now committed to keeping Belinda safe, Dante had taken to watching her from a distance. As she exited her apartment, Dante considered whether or not he should close the gap between them. As he considered, Belinda spotted him.

"Dante? Mr. Rivers, is that you?" she asked, tapping him on the shoulder.

"Hi."

At first, to Belinda's surprise, he seemed to not even know her. He was always so careful at going unseen that Dante was surprised at how easily he had let his guard down; just long enough for her to spot him. After all, wasn't he supposed to be watching her from a distance? So, when she called out to him, he couldn't think of what to say.

"It's me, Belinda. The damsel in distress. How soon we forget!"

"Of course. Of course, I remember you. I was a bit distracted; head in the clouds, you know?"

"Yeah, I know the feeling. I was about to grab a latte

at Starbucks; got a wicked case of writer's block. You wanna join me?"

"Sounds good."

"So were you visiting your client again?"

"Huh?"

"Your client; the one you were visiting the weekend you found me?"

"Oh yes. Yes, I was visiting my client; some papers to sign."

"What did you say his name was?"

"Excuse me?"

"You really are distracted. I was just asking the name of your client. I thought maybe I might know him."

"Some of my clients like to keep their business matters very confidential...even the fact that I'm their accountant. I try, whenever possible, to maintain that confidentiality. I hope I'm not being too cryptic."

"Uh. No, no. I um, I understand. I'm a writer, so I can definitely relate to the whole confidentiality thing; sources and all."

"So, what do you write about?"

"Right now I'm supposed to be writing about all these stories of missing women that have been popping up in the news lately."

"Really. What paper do you work for?"

"I don't work for a paper per se. I've made some really good connections with several magazines and a couple of newspapers, so I do freelance work. When I first started, the work was pretty sporadic, but over the last year or so, it has picked up enough so that I don't have to worry about being pinned down to a desk. That whole nine-to-five thing has never been quite my cup of tea."

"I could see that."

"Really?"

"Yes. You're clearly an unchained spirit," Dante replied.

"Wow! And, here I thought I was simply undisciplined. Thanks! I needed that."

"I don't believe there is anything undisciplined about you. The theory of discipline is all relative. You, my dear, are a visionary."

"And how can you tell all this after just two encounters?" Belinda asked.

"It's part of my job to know people," he lied.

"Is that really part of an accountant's job? I thought all accountants did was crunch numbers."

"Do you know the two main things most people lie about?"

"No. What?"

"Money and sex." Dante paused and grinned at Belinda. "As an accountant, I'm typically at the helm of what is happening with someone's money. I can't realistically do my job well, if I have no awareness of the psyche or intentions of the people I am dealing with. That's where my instincts come into play."

"So, Dante, do you also lie about money and sex?"

He laughed. "I guess I did say most people, didn't I? I don't know, do you?"

"Way to answer a question with a question."

"I think that's a question better answered over dinner."

Belinda blushed. "Are you asking me out on a date?"

"That I am."

"I accept."

"Do you need to go home first?" Dante asked.

"Truth be told, the last thing I want to do is go home. I've always loved my apartment, the location, everything about it, but recent events have left me feeling quite powerless. Now I understand how Alzheimer's patients must feel when the disease first starts to take hold. It's like the information is there, right there, but I can't grab hold of it."

"I can imagine, it must be awful; especially for a woman like you."

"A woman like me? What's that supposed to mean?"

"You strike me as a woman who is accustomed to being in control."

"Yeah, I guess I am. I've always had to be. My parents died when I was pretty young and I was never one of those kids who had a lot of friends. Most kids thought I was a bit strange. I enjoyed spending time alone and I always did so well in school. It was almost as if everything I touched turned to gold; science projects, spelling bees, everything. Kids don't like kids like that. I must've gotten beaten up at least once a week and threatened pretty much every day. Then, in the seventh grade, this loud, scary girl joined our classroom and the teacher sort of paired me up with her. In hindsight, I realize that teacher was quite a visionary. She was trying to offer both Summer and myself an opportunity for exposure to something we both badly needed. Summer was popular and scared of nothing and she had a great family, but her study skills needed some work. I had no friends and was afraid of my own shadow and no real family to call my own, but I was an A+ student. We were, and actually still are, two halves of a whole.

"Summer, is that the friend you called while you were at my place; the one you were supposed to go shopping with?"

"Yes. A lot of people think Summer is abrasive, but to me Summer is just Summer. She's a loyal friend. She would go through fire to save me and I would do the same for her. We're more like sisters than best friends."

"That must be a great feeling; to know that somewhere in the world someone cares that much about your welfare."

"It is."

"I know the perfect place for dinner; someplace I believe you'll like. There's a place called Providence on the West Side. It's sort of like a piano bar. There isn't a performer there every night, but maybe, just maybe if we're lucky, there will be one there tonight."

"I'm feeling pretty lucky; how about you?" she asked.

"Luckier than I've felt in a very long time."

In fact, there was a performer, an R&B singer whose voice was not only beautiful but hypnotic. He sang a song she had always loved called "Always and Forever" and as she sat basking in the ambiance of the candlelit paradise she found herself in, enjoying good food, great wine and even better conversation, she hoped the night would never end.

"Would you like to see the dessert menu?"

Belinda always hated this moment, even when she was spending time with her girlfriends. It always seemed to her as though everything in life had this haunting expiry date. Something as simple as an enjoyable dinner would remind her that even that would eventually come to an end; especially when it was time for dessert.

"Don't you hate this part? That's why every now and then I eat my dessert first, to remind me that not everything has to come to an end. I know it's silly, but if it fools my thinking if only for a moment, then I have won."

Belinda was awestruck. It was as though he had reached inside of her head and responded to her thoughts. Dante himself wasn't even sure if he was using his special gifts or if there was a true connection to her. Either way, he too did not want the evening to end.

"You know the downside to not wanting an evening of dining to come to an end?" Belinda asked.

"What's that?"

"Having dessert when you're way too full. You may have to roll me out of here."

"I would carry you all the way home and back again, if that is what you needed."

Something in the way that he said those words told Belinda that it was important that she turn and face him directly, so that he could not only hear it, but also see the sentiment in her eyes when she spoke.

"And that you did, and for that I will be eternally grateful."

When they kissed, neither of them thought of time.

Their lips fit together like two pieces of an intricate puzzle. There were no awkward fumbles of their tongues, searching for that electrical charge that would set each one's passion ablaze. They simply fit. His tongue danced inside of her mouth, tasting hers. She gently flicked the tip of his tongue with her own and pulled away. Eager to make it last, while building the excitement, she held back, but just a bit; enough to leave him wanting more.

"Would you have a drink with me, at my place?" she asked.

"Are you sure?"

"I can't remember the last time I was surer of anything. I want you, Dante. I want you so much," she whispered in his ear.

"And I need you."

His manhood throbbed like a heartbeat against her thigh, coaching her wetness and making her legs weak. But this time it was different. He wasn't some sort of parasite feeding on the existence of another. She was simply a woman, and he was a man. The sensation was a distant memory, but one that was vaguely familiar.

"Should we get a cab?" he asked.

"I think so."

Once inside Belinda's apartment, her fear was gone. This place that had become foreign to her was suddenly home again.

She wasn't sure why, but she was suddenly nervous; not a nervousness borne of fear, but one of excited anticipation.

"What would you like to drink? I have vodka, gin, scotch, tequila, orange juice, green tea; or I could make some coffee," she prattled on.

His eyes followed every move she made and the nearness of his body, mimicking every step, thrilled her. It was as though an electric current ran between the two of them, even from a few feet away. He walked toward her, drawing closer, and with the gentlest touch, placed his index finger on her lips.

"Relax, Belinda. There is no need to feel nervous, no need to entertain me. My greatest desire right here and now is to bring you pleasure. I want nothing for myself."

He unbuttoned her dress, peeling the cloth away from her body and dropped it to the floor. Standing before him donned in the most beautiful white lace thong and lace-covered bra, she was perfection. And with that he lifted her, cradling her in his arms, and carried her to her bedroom to lay her gently upon her bed. He knelt down at the foot of her bed and removed her shoes, massaging the balls of her feet and eventually engulfing her tiny toes with his mouth, licking and sucking at each toe slowly and methodically, while his hands molded the shape of her calves. His touch was magical, and she couldn't imagine what it would feel like once he traveled further up her body, since, to her surprise, she was already building to a quiet moan. She couldn't remember when she had felt so desired and more than anything, she wanted to make him feel the same.

Her attempts to raise herself from the bed were met with tender resistance from Dante.

"I lied when I said I wanted nothing for myself," he whispered. "I do; I want to memorize every line, every slope, every part of your body, from head to toe. Surely, you wouldn't deny me that? I want to memorize every part of you; with my eyes, with my lips, with my mouth, with my tongue…and with my heart. Will you allow me to do that, Belinda?"

"Oh God yes, Dante. Yes."

He needed her to give herself over to him, willingly and wholeheartedly. With her consent, he could lavish her with the worship she so duly deserved.

The wetness of his tongue drawing invisible lines along the length of her lower leg elicited a spine-tingling shiver. She didn't think she could wait any longer. The anticipation was deliciously maddening.

"Dante, please… Now."

"Not yet, my sweet. There is so much more of you uncommitted to my mind's eye."

As Dante nibbled at Belinda's silky thighs, he was amazed and further excited by the obvious heat that traveled from beneath her panties. His hands were drawn to it like a magnet and he pushed her saturated lace thong to the side, his mouth starving for a taste. Her moans were his aphrodisiac.

"Hmmm...hmmm...hmmm."

The animalistic growl that emitted from his lips, combined with the paradise his tongue had taken her clit to, shielded her from even noticing his minimal transformation. In that split second, all caution thrown to the wind and her nectar on his tongue, the truth of what he was was forgotten by Dante, his eyes once again burned fire red, only to return to their greenish-blue hue just in time to meet Belinda face to face.

Careful to bring her only pleasure and suddenly mindful of his true nature, Dante proceeded cautiously, resting only the head of his manhood at the entrance to nirvana.

"Now! I've waited long enough. I want you inside of me now!"

Her hot, panting breath, her forceful words, spurred him on to action and he entered her slowly, taking up a rhythm that Belinda encouraged with the slow movement of her hips as they slowly built to a crescendo.

"It is a joy to be inside of you like this," he whispered in her ear.

And with his words, her grip on his member tightened and once again, Dante was close to surrendering control. He expanded and lengthened, due largely to his unspoken secret.

"Dante. Dante. Dante. Oh. Oh. You're, you're, you're so big inside of me."

Dante was terrified he might harm her. He was unsure if he was capable of controlling the effects of unleashed passion and an emotion he had little experience with—fear.

"I must stop. The last thing I want to do is hurt you."

"You're...you're...not hurting me. It's so, so very good. I want this. I want you."

Belinda was no longer capable of contributing even the slightest motion. He took over how deep he ventured inside of her and the pace of his rhythmic strokes. For a split second it occurred to Belinda that this was what white-water rafting must feel like—exciting as hell, with a hint of danger as you plummeted to the far reaches of the unknown. Suddenly, consumed by uncontrollable passion, Dante's eyes gazed into Belinda's as he released centuries-worth of unrequited lust, now returned by his beloved Belinda.

"Cum with me!" he bellowed. "Cum with me!"

With all control lost, Dante's eyes burned brightly. They were a deep, dark red.

SIXTEEN

Belinda was happy to learn that Diana would be going to Summer's family barbecue, since Belinda assumed that to mean that her two friends had arrived at a truce; even if it was temporary. She called Diana so that they could go to the festivities together.

Although she had finally completed the story she had promised *Newsweek*, she hadn't gotten any new assignments lately, so she was pacing herself with spending money. She silently hoped that Diana would do her usual and hire a car. Normally Belinda would've been fine with taking the subway, but she had been wrecked with such fatigue over the last week or two. She wasn't sure if it was the result of her marathon sessions with Dante or the mental energy expended to write the story she had agonized over for so long, but she was more exhausted than she had ever been. Not only that, she was sure that she was engaging in mild hallucinations; on more than one occasion she had imagined Dante's eye color changing into a vast assortment of colors, including red.

"Truth be told, I'm actually looking forward to this barbecue. I need a little normalcy in my life. Things have been so crazy lately, I'm starting to feel as though I'm losing grip. Not only that, I seem to be sick all the time; fatigue, headaches, nausea, diarrhea. I've been a hot mess. Yet, according to my doctor, there is absolutely nothing wrong with me. So I guess that means it's all in my mind."

"Belinda, you need to get some sleep, plain and simple. If you don't want to take something I prescribe, why don't you go see a specialist? I can refer you to someone who specializes in sleep disorders, if you'd like."

"I don't know, Diana. I'm starting to think I need a lot more than a sleep specialist. I'm seeing things that aren't there, feeling things that couldn't possibly be real. I'm starting to feel like I'm losing my mind."

"Exactly my point. That's lack of sleep. Most of us don't place near enough value on the importance of sleep. We've become a sleep-deprived society. Sleep, or the lack thereof, has been linked to everything from acute illnesses to depression, suicide, even murder."

"You're probably right. I must admit, as much as we poke fun at Summer, I'm hoping that her matriarch of 'believers' is at this barbecue to shed some light on what ails me."

"Belinda, no. You're not starting to believe all that hocus pocus crap that Summer talks about all the time?"

"No information is a waste of time. Starting today, that's my motto."

"Make sure you keep it all in perspective. Okay?"

"Okay, I will."

"So do you want to meet up? I can call a car and be at your place in fifteen. Her mom lives on the Grand Concourse, right?"

"No way, Diana! You mean you're really gonna go?"

"Yep. She invited me and I'm going. It'll be nice to show Summer that I've got a little chutzpah for a change."

"Well, good for you. But, if I were you, I wouldn't use that word *chutzpah* for the rest of the day."

Both girls laughed and, for the moment, Belinda's mind was on something other than her state of mind.

By the time they arrived, everything was in full swing. The barbecue was in the backyard and there were people playing cards and eating the vast assortment of foods that were laid out.

"I gained ten pounds just looking at this stuff," Diana whispered.

Summer's mom greeted them. "Hey, girllll! You mean you finally made it up to my neck of the woods."

"Hi, Mrs. Johnson," Belinda said.

"And, what the hell is with that Mrs. Johnson stuff? You know everybody calls me Tilly. You makin' me feel older than I am. And, you know damn well I ain't old!"

"You know it!"

Summer's mother grabbed Belinda and hugged her. Belinda was suddenly so happy she had come. It had been a while since she had seen any of the folks from the old neighborhood.

"Where's Mr. Johnson? I mean, Bruce?

"You know where he is. Over by the grill, trying to burn down the whole damn neighborhood."

Her laugh was suddenly cut short when Belinda introduced Diana.

"Oh, I'm so rude. Tilly, this is our friend, Diana. I'm sure Summer has mentioned Diana to you."

Tilly Johnson's dislike of Diana was readily apparent. Although, Belinda couldn't fathom how anyone could dislike someone so much they had just met.

"Summer never mentioned to me how beautiful you were."

It may have sounded like a compliment, but Tilly's words and her expression were completely deadpan.

"You must attract men like lambs to the slaughter."

"That's an odd expression," Diana responded.

"But one I'm sure you've heard before."

"Yes, I have, but not in quite some time."

"I bet."

In an attempt to alleviate some of the discomfort Belinda thought Diana might be feeling, she called out to Summer. "Girl, look who's up in the *Boogie Down!*"

Summer was shocked. "Oh hell no. You mean you both actually came?" Summer ran over to both girls, just in time to see the expression on her mother's face. "Mama, don't worry about showing Diana and Belinda inside the house to hang up their jackets; I'll take them."

"No problem. I'll let you entertain your guests."

"We usually don't have barbecues this time of year, but it's been so doggone warm and we didn't do a lot this summer so we figured what the hell; a last hurrah before the hawk starts biting. But, if it's too cool we can hang out inside the house."

"It's pretty nice today," Diana remarked.

As they all walked to the house, Summer couldn't resist making a face at Belinda; a questioning gaze, communicating that she caught the strange moment between her mom and Diana; especially since Summer knew it couldn't have anything to do with Belinda. Her mother always treated Belinda like she was her own child.

"I don't know," Belinda mouthed silently.

Belinda, Diana, and Summer sat outside for a while, until it got too chilly. Just about everyone from the neighborhood was there, including one of Kaleel's old running buddies, Red. He couldn't keep his eyes off of Diana.

"I think you've got an admirer," Belinda mentioned.

"Oh really. And, who might that be?" Diana asked.

"Who are ya'll talking about; Red?" Summer inquired. "He was asking me all about you, Ms. Diana."

"Yeah, and what did you tell him?"

"Nothing. Just the obvious. You know, single, doctor, blah, blah, blah. So what do you think?"

Diana frowned slightly. "What's his name; Red? Somehow, he doesn't sound like my type."

Summer said, "But you don't know a thing about him."

"His name is Red and he's an old friend of Kaleel's," Diana said. "I'm sorry if you're offended."

"Naw, I'm not offended. I realize that my ex is a piece of shit. No big deal. I was passin' on the info. You do you. If Red ain't your cup of tea, that's your call."

"Okay."

"Can we go inside?" Diana asked.

"Tryin' to escape, huh?" Summer asked.

"No, I'm just getting a little cold. That's all."

"What about you, Belinda? You ready to go inside?"

Belinda replied, "Yeah, I wanted to say hello to your grandmother anyway."

Summer's grandmother was sitting in the living room and drinking a cup of tea when they came back into the house.

Summer said, "Hey, Nanny, did you meet my friends? This is Diana and you know Belinda."

"Hello, child, come on over here and give Nanny a kiss."

Diana approached and Summer's grandmother visibly recoiled. There was fear in her eyes and she began fingering the gold crucifix that hung from her neck, mumbling words that none of them could quite make out.

"There is evil afoot, children. Don't give in to the demons. Do you hear me, child?" she said, speaking directly to Belinda.

Belinda wasn't sure what to say. Summer's grandmother had to be at least eighty-five years old, but somehow she thought it was more than that. Belinda wondered if this old woman, half-blind from diabetes, might actually be able to see more than any of them were capable of seeing.

"I said, do you hear me, child?" Nanny said again.

"Yes," all three girls answered in unison.

"Demon, be gone," she said to Diana. "I'm an old woman, but not so easily fooled. You may have these young ones bamboozled, but you ain't tricked me."

"Now be nice, Nanny. Diana is our guest."

"She ain't no guest o' mine. I don't break bread with evil. And if you knew what I knew, you wouldn't either."

Mere seconds passed between the time the old woman spoke and Diana's eyes went from her usual amber brown to a razor-sharp, piercing, emerald green and eventually blood red, before they converted to her customary shade. Somehow, though, no one noticed. No one, that is, except Summer's grandmother.

Summer suggested, "I can get our jackets and we can go back outside if you want."

"Yeah, that sounds good. We can watch the sunset," Belinda said.

"Yeah, I'd like that," Diana agreed.

In a show of respect to her grandmother, Summer said nothing until they left the living room and went back outside.

"I'm sorry, Diana. I don't know what got into my grandmother. She's usually such a sweet old woman, but she is getting up there in years. I apologize."

"No apology necessary. I understand," Diana said.

Belinda had known Nanny Douglas ever since she was a little girl and she had never seen her behave in such a way. That was twice tonight that someone had reacted oddly to Diana's presence. The night was winding down and, given the events of the day, she was sure Diana would soon be announcing her departure. She would expect them both to leave together, since they had come together. Belinda wanted a chance to speak to Nanny Douglas again...alone.

With Summer busy helping her mom clean up and Belinda heading back into the house, Diana crossed the backyard and walked over to where Red was sitting.

Before going back into the house, Belinda stopped in the doorway long enough to see Diana coyly whispering something in Red's ear.

"Hey, baby. I was waitin' for you to come on back," Summer's grandmother said.

"How did you know I was comin' back in here to talk to you?" Belinda asked.

"I'm old and I'm wise. Once you get to be my age, that's the greatest asset you can depend upon...being wise. It's almost a guarantee; a reward for living this long."

"Okay, so you're wise, but are you clairvoyant, too?" Belinda joked.

"Oh, so I see you tryin' to test me. I know what you wanna know. You wanna ask me about that heffa you runnin' around wit. All I can say, baby, is watch your back. 'Cause that one is no damn good. Ooh, and now she done got me to swearin'."

"Nanny Douglas!"

"In my day, we used to call 'em harlots and vixens or even seductresses. Now I see them for what they are. Women like her are demons; plain and simple."

"You can't be talking about Diana. Summer and I are bigger seductresses than she could ever be," Belinda joked.

"That's what she wants the world to think. Don't fall for it. If you do, it will be too late for you to save yourself. I realize that this sounds like the ravings of a senile old woman, but these ole eyes have seen things I hope you girls will never see. Have a seat, girl. I've got a story to tell you."

Belinda pulled up a chair and sat directly in front of Nanny Douglas.

"Do you know where our family is from?"

"Summer told me her momma grew up in Louisiana."

"Yes, child; the bayou. Did she tell you why we left Louisiana?"

"No, I don't think she ever mentioned it."

"It was 1944. Girls got married young in those days. We didn't have as many choices as you girls today. I was twenty years old when I married Chester Douglas. He was a good man. Not much to look at and I didn't fall head of over heels like you see in a lot of these movies these days. But, he was a good provider and he was a decent man. Treated me good. Treated our kids good.

Then, after about two years of marriage, Chester started to change. At first I thought he was ill. He slept all the time. Didn't want to go to work. I thought maybe he was on opium or something. But, then one night, I was lying right next to him in the bed and this...this thing appeared; out of nowhere. She was beautiful; beautiful and lying on top of my husband in our bed, with me lying right next to him. At first, I thought I had to be dreaming. Then suddenly I realized this wasn't no dream. She was there. I leapt out that bed lickity split and started beating the shit out of her. That's when she changed. That beautiful, shapely woman, having her liberties with my husband, suddenly changed into the most grotesque thing I had ever seen.

"I grabbed Betsey and fired at her and she just disappeared, like she had never even been there. I tried to tell people what happened and nobody believed me; not even Chester. He swore on a stack o' bibles he didn't remember a thing. Everything was quiet for a while and then about a month or so later, she showed up again. I took my two kids, got in our car, and drove to my sister's place a few miles away. Chester tried to convince me to come back, but it was obvious he was too far gone to be anything more than that thing's slave. He kept tryin' to get me to move back, so about a month later I moved here, to New York, where one of my cousins lived. I figured the farther away we were, the easier it would be. We've been here ever since. Tilly and her brother, Bruce, were too young to know what was going on, but I know. I'll always know. I think certain people attract certain forces. I think my family may fit into that category of people who attract. You see, I've seen others like her since. Maybe not every day, not even every year, but I've seen others; and believe you me, child, that one you brought up in here today, she is just as much a demon as that one that visited me and Chester all those years ago.

"I've known Diana for a few years now. I've never seen anything about her that would indicate she's bad."

"Yeah, and I bet she makes sure of that; wears sack clothes, like she's wearing today; acts like butter wouldn't melt in her mouth; no cursing, no swearing. She plays the role well. But I can see past her façade."

"But how...how can you see past it? How do you know evil when you see it?"

"You know it, child. When it's staring you in your face, you know it."

"If that's the case, why don't I see it in Diana? You think she's evil. You're sure of it. But all I see is a friend."

"It's not that you don't see it; it's that you don't see it yet."

"I've met someone, Nanny Douglas; someone I really like...a lot. And, it's been so long since I've felt this way about anyone. But, I feel like there's so much more to him than meets the eye. I'm afraid I might not like the things I don't know."

"Trust your instincts. That's all I can tell you, is to trust your instincts. Something tells me your instincts are pretty doggone good. Because, you know what, you say you trust your friend, Diana, but if you truly do, why are you sitting here with me? You realize when something doesn't fit. In your heart, you know."

SEVENTEEN

"I just love this body!"

While she typically took the form of Diana, she enjoyed the opportunity to transform. Through time she had been several different women, and men; even certain animals. It was one of the advantages to being what she was. The power to hide in plain sight.

"If I were you, I would lay low for a while; stay in that body. What is she called again; Felice? That's one of the reasons I limit my contact with mortals. When you get too close, there are too many questions to answer. Distance allows certain freedoms."

"Yes, but the isolation can be daunting."

"Now you're starting to sound like Dante."

"Don't compare me to that pussy."

"How is he any different than you? You both seem disenchanted with this existence. And as I see it, you're even worse than Dante."

"What the fuck does that mean?"

"Think about it. It's a matter of time. I could better understand Dante's desire to be done with it. He's been at it for centuries. What's your excuse?"

"I don't know, René; maybe I'll wait until Dante gets here and we can commiserate."

Brilliant senses announced Dante's arrival before he even made it to René's door.

"Why don't you make yourself scarce?"

"Why should I?"

"Because I have no interest in refereeing the two of you while you rip one another apart and you have work to do."

"Did you secure a residence for them?"

"Yes. It's large enough to hold them all for now. But, if things progress as we have planned, we will have to expand. We can cross that bridge when we come to it. Speaking of which, when will we be done with this most recent one? We've spent much more time with her than any of the others."

"This is no longer just about survival. There's now much more at stake. As we increase in numbers, our strength also increases. There will come a time when our power will be immeasurable."

"I understand that, but why is it so important that it be her? There have been others before her and still others will follow. She's not worth the time."

"I'll decide who is and isn't worth the time."

He didn't like her tone and for a moment considered the ramifications of challenging her imagined authority... or was it imagined?

"I just don't get what the big secret is. There's obviously something you know about her that we don't. Why does it have to be such a mystery?"

"There is no secret, no mystery. She's the one I've chosen and it *has* to be her."

"Just because that's what you want doesn't necessarily make it so."

"That's the difference between you and me. I will not concede. She will be the one, one way or another."

"Let's not forget she is nothing more than a mere mortal; a mortal that is getting dangerously close to figuring this whole thing out."

"I've forgotten *nothing*."

"Oh, so what you're saying is it's okay for you to fuck with Dante, to question things, but it's not okay for me?"

"You always take it too far. You forget his place and ours. You may not like it, but Dante has ushered more souls into the abyss than any other. That guarantees him reverence. Now go. He's here."

"Where is she?" Dante asked as soon as he entered.

"Come on! She had things to do."

"I sincerely hope none of those 'things' had anything to do with Belinda."

"What concerns me most, Dante, is why you care."

"Haven't you ever wanted more than this?"

"More than what?" René asked. "We are omnipotent. Who, other than you, could want more than that what we are right here and now?"

"Yes, we are powerful, but we are not omnipotent. No

being is; not even us. I realize that now. There was a time when I thought as you, but if I can suddenly regret and wish for something better, something else, if I can feel loneliness, how could I be all-powerful?"

"Maybe it is time for you to return home, brother?"

"This is my home. No other place has been more of a home to me than here."

"Surely you must realize that one day you will return to whence you came. The souls you have delivered have ensured your place."

"I have made my decision. My place is here. It is where I have lived. And, eventually, it is where I will die, if I am lucky."

"You're speaking nonsense."

"Maybe I am but, brother, I have a request I must make of you. I have never asked anything of you, but, I need you to do this for me."

René already knew what he was going to ask.

"You asked me if I loved the mortal, Belinda. If I am even capable of love, then I believe that I do. I never knew that our kind was capable of anything akin to love. But, if we are, this is surely what I am feeling. I don't know what any of this means. I don't even know if I will even have an opportunity to share this love with her, but I don't want her harmed; not anymore and not like this."

"What are you asking me?"

"René, don't play this game. You know exactly what I am asking. There are many others to choose from. All I am asking you is to leave this one alone. Leave her to me."

"And what am I to expect in return for this 'favor' you expect me to grant you?"

"What do you want?"

"I'm not sure yet. But surely you knew that any sacrifice on my part would have to come with a price. Or have you truly forgotten what we are? The essence of our survival is contingent upon trading our existence for mortal souls. You may not have allowed yourself to see beyond this temporary conversion to your original being, but eventually you will also have to trade one desire for another. These mortals are so protective of their beliefs, so obsessed with their faith, and so arrogant in their efforts to maintain the status quo, that they can't see what's staring them right in their faces. Good and evil must always coexist. Otherwise, how would you explain us? We are descendants of Lilith and her legacy is boundless. Through centuries, the story of Lilith being created by God as Adam's first wife have been reduced to nothing more than folklore. But she was so much more than mere folklore. Her existence is infinite and so is ours. We are all nothing more than a consequence of our duality. You were once able to survive without drawing life from mortals, but now you cannot. Yet, you want to believe that you can have that existence once again. I think you are kidding yourself, but who knows, maybe I am the one that is wrong. But, don't fool yourself, brother, your existence as a demon came with a price and so, too, does existence as a mortal—or even anything close to it.

"If it means I will enjoy even a moment at Belinda's side, I will pay that price."

"We'll see, brother. We'll see."

While Dante agonized over what price he would have to pay for Belinda's freedom, René prepared to take what was his.

What plagued Dante most was the realization that René, who he once mentored, had now become so much stronger and more calculating than he had ever been.

As quickly as Dante left René, Diana emerged from a corner of the room; this time the body that housed her was a far cry from Felice or even Diana. Her body was awkward and unshapely, her face was littered with acne and her teeth noticeably crooked. René chuckled.

"That's different."

"I..."

"No, please." he laughed. "No explanation necessary. Please."

"Whatever. We have bigger fish to fry anyway. I don't care what you say; something has to be done about him. He's going to ruin everything."

"Slow and steady wins the race, my dear. All things will happen in their own time. You're just as tense as Dante. You both have forgotten the immeasurable joy of being what we are. It's not supposed to be work. It's supposed to be fun."

"Fun, fun!" she yelled. "It's getting more and more difficult to lure these mortals. When I settled here in New York City, I thought for sure there would be more than enough tainted souls to allow me a steady flow of sustenance to survive. That assumption has proven false, so many times since I've been here. Do you know how many times I've been close to the end?"

"That's because you have done exactly what Dante has done."

"Don't you dare compare me to that weakling!"

"I didn't say you were weak. But, you are much too connected to these mortals. That's what makes me different than you and Dante. I think of them as little more than food; or at the very best, pets. They are not my equal, will never be."

"But think of how many times you have almost been destroyed."

"Yes, but I am still here. They can get close, but they will never touch me, not truly."

"Don't underestimate them, René. I've seen that done before and the end-result has been catastrophic."

"That's why we're here. It is of utmost importance that our kind evolve into something greater than themselves. Until now, the older ones like Dante have been mainly concerned with preserving their energy, and preserving their place. We need to focus on more than that. We need to think about tomorrow."

"Dante may very well prove to be a hindrance to that tomorrow."

Diana rolled her eyes and left.

After leaving René's place, Diana's principal goal was to silence another hindrance.

She stood in front of an awning that read Golden Arms Assisted Living Facility. Before going inside, she smoothed the sides of her hair, adjusted her clothing, and walked up the ramp and straight to the front desk.

"I'm here to see Mabel Douglas."

"Your name is?"

"I'm Tamara Moore. I'm from Bethel Baptist Church."

The woman at the desk buzzed Ms. Douglas and let her know she had a visitor. Thinking it was a representative from her church, she said it would be okay to send her up.

"Ms. Douglas is on the third floor, room 302."

"Thank you."

The hairs rose up on the back of Mabel Douglas' neck as soon as she heard the knock on the door. For a moment she considered refusing entry, then thought better of it.

"Who are you?" she asked when she opened the door.

"Didn't the person at the desk downstairs tell you? I'm Tamara Moore. I'm from your church," she said, a villainous smile etched upon her face.

"You can take whatever form you like, demon! I know you! I'll always know you!" Mabel screamed.

"Not for long, old woman. Not for long."

The rancid odor of rotting flesh that accompanied her transformation would usually cause her victims to wretch uncontrollably. That was the thing about reaching a certain age; Mabel knew all too well, not only the look of death, but the smell. She was prepared. And, at that moment, Diana felt some small level of respect for this feeble being's apparent courage. Instead of screaming and begging for mercy, like most would have done, Mabel Douglas was smiling; a most peculiar smile, given the predicament she found herself in. And as Diana's bloody talons extended from her grotesquely malformed hands, Mabel's parting words were fearless.

"Is that all you got?"

EIGHTEEN

"I can hook you up with another gig, if you like."

"No, I want the job at Potion."

Summer's promoter friend, Que, often contacted her when he had a bartending job. Summer even helped him with some of the promotions for his events. But, this time it was Summer who had contacted him.

"You ever been to that place?" he asked.

"Yeah, I've been there. I'm trying to figure something out. It's personal. I need a day or two; maybe a week tops. You think you could arrange that for me?"

"Please, girl! Anything for you! You've helped me out so many times. That's the least I can do. I just wish you needed my help getting into a more upscale establishment."

"Hey, Que, I didn't take you for a prude."

"I'm not a prude. It's not the sex I have a problem with. It's the establishment itself…the sticky floors, the nasty-ass bathrooms. I don't roll like that. I try not to even schedule any of my events there, but I try to appeal to all of my clientele and the place gets a lot of play."

"Yeah, I know. I was there a few nights ago."

"And what were you doing there?"

"I was trying to find a friend. I found her, but now I'm checking some stuff out. I think somebody's been doing some foul shit, and I want to catch them in the act."

"Well, if they're hangin' at Potion on a regular, they are definitely into some 'foul shit.' Just be careful. Even though management swears by the safety of their establishment, there have been a lot of disappearances connected to that club and more than a handful of people who frequent that place have popped up dead."

"Speaking of which; I went there with Pookie. You know Pookie, right?"

"Yeah, of course I do. We were boys back in the day. But, we've all kinda gone our separate ways through the years."

"I talked him into going to Potion so I could check something out. He didn't even really want to go. But, when it was time to go, he was nowhere to be found. He told me to make sure I stayed close to him because the place was crazy. When it was time to leave, I had to go home by myself because I couldn't find him anywhere. I've been calling him on his cell ever since and nothing."

"Like I told you, there've been quite a few disappearances connected with that place. Which, I guess, makes sense. Some people probably go there out of boredom with their sex lives or whatever. You can bet there are probably some sickos up in there. It's the perfect place to go if you want to do some wild shit. I could see it attracting some crazies."

"You wouldn't happen to know another way I could get in touch with Pookie, would you?"

"His moms still lives in Jefferson Projects over on 115th and First. She's still in the same apartment. You could probably find him over there. His moms is getting up in years and I know they were always close."

"Thanks, Que."

"No prob. I hope you find whatever it is you're looking for."

"I hope I don't."

The next morning Summer couldn't shake the feeling that something bad was going to happen. She considered calling Que and cancelling her plan to work at Potion, but changed her mind. Instead, she called around and tried to find someone who could give her Pookie's mother's phone number, to no avail. She remembered Pookie's mother from when they were kids in the neighborhood and she had even come to her and Kaleel's wedding. She figured it wasn't too far a stretch to just show up and knock on the door. By the time she got to the building, she realized she wouldn't have to knock on his mother's door. She saw the flyer as soon as she walked in the building. The words MISSING PERSON were emblazoned on the front of a bright yellow sheet of paper. He had been missing since…the night the two of them went to Potion. There was other pertinent information such as his height, weight, age and hair color, etc. and in the middle was a picture of Pookie along with his name: James Percival Anderson. Summer couldn't help but smile…Percival. If his boys had known that was his name back in the day, they would've fucked with him about that to no end. Summer was sure something had happened at Potion the night they were there and she suddenly felt guilty for dragging him into her drama. She was so deep in thought, she didn't even hear her cell phone ring. It was her mother calling to tell her that her grandmother had passed away.

Summer was sitting in Belinda's place, on the brink of tears.

"I can't deal with Diana right now. She probably hasn't even considered going to the funeral, but just in case she has, I want to make sure she doesn't. My mother is convinced she had something to do with it."

"Something to do with what?" Belinda asked, on the edge of her seat.

"With GG's death."

Belinda shook her head in dismay. "I know your family didn't take to Diana, but, Summer, murder? Does your mother really believe that, or is she that grief-stricken? She doesn't even know Diana."

"You came with her to the barbecue. You saw the way

that my mother reacted to Diana. She didn't like her from the very beginning. What did my grandmother say to you at the barbecue anyway? Did she say anything about Diana? My mom said that, after you guys left, Nanny couldn't stop talking about Diana and that she was a bit shook up. You were the last person to talk to her. Did she say anything at all to you?"

"Pretty much the same stuff she said when you were there. She told me a story about a demon she thought she encountered when she was young. I googled it when I got home that night and there was actually a name for what she was talking about. It's called a succubus. I got a little shook up myself after reading it. According to old folklore the succubus would tempt men by appearing as a beautiful woman and then literally suck the life out of them and the male version of the demon was called an incubus and he was even worse. Succubi were artful at seducing their victims, while the incubi weren't near as subtle. They were downright violent; intruding upon their victims' homes, lying on top of them and basically raping them. And, not only that, they were oppressively heavy and, if you can believe this, their dicks were ice cold. Try reading something like that before going to bed at night; especially when you've been having dreams exactly like that for months. Not exactly a bedtime story."

"Belinda, are you telling me you've been having dreams like this?"

"Yes."

"Well, maybe it has something to do with the conversation you had with my grandmother. They say dreams are just manifestations of what you saw or read during the time when you're awake."

"I thought of that, too. But my dreams started long before the talk I had with Nanny Douglas."

"Diana and I are friends and I know that I should be saying your grandmother was an 85-year-old woman, but I can't shake the feeling that something is going on here. Something that she is smack dab in the middle of. I don't know who to trust."

"Finally, she sees the light!" Summer yelled. "Maybe I shouldn't tell you what I'm about to tell you, but I'm going to anyway."

"Whatever it is, Summer; I need to know."

"Remember that guy, Red, that was checking Diana out at the barbecue? He's dead."

"What?"

"Yeah. They found him out on Montauk a week or so after the barbecue. He was a mess, after the water and all. His family could barely recognize him."

"Do they know when he disappeared?" Belinda asked.

Summer replied, "I think the last time anyone saw him was at our barbecue."

"Summer, I saw Diana talking to him at the barbecue. She walked right over to him and whispered something in his ear. It sort of surprised me; when we were all sitting together, she seemed to have absolutely no interest in him at all."

"No interest? That's an understatement. Her exact words were, he wasn't her type."

"Yeah, I remember that."

"Not only that, it seems to me that there have been far too many disappearances surrounding Diana. There comes a time when shit doesn't look like a coincidence anymore."

"Summer, tell me the truth," Belinda said. "Am I completely insane for even thinking what I'm thinking?"

"I'm the wrong person to ask that question. I'm a believer. Don't get me wrong. It's not that I believe in everything. We live in a world of possibilities, and maybe, just maybe, we can't see or know everything. I mean, who's to say that we as humans know it all?"

"I know one thing; I'm starting to realize that Diana is not all she appears to be."

"You just figured that out. I've been trying to tell you that for years. But noooooo, you wouldn't listen to me."

"Don't you need to get ready?"

"Yeah, I definitely don't want to be late. My mother is getting on my last nerve. I feel for her, losing her mother, and you know we all loved GG, but she is starting to drive me up a fucking wall."

"Be nice, Summer. At least you have a mom. I wish I had a mother to 'get on my nerves.'"

Dante approached Summer after the service. "I'm sorry for your loss."

"Did you know my grandmother?" Summer asked.

"I'm sorry, Summer; this is Dante Rivers," Belinda offered. "He's a friend. Dante has been very supportive. I've been telling him about how good your family has always been to me and he wanted to show his respect."

"Really? I appreciate it," Summer said. "My family appreciates it. Thank you."

"No thank-yous necessary," Dante responded. "I was looking forward to meeting you. Belinda has nothing but good things to say about you."

"Funny. She hasn't mentioned you to me at all."

"Summer, yes, I did. You must've forgotten. Dante's the one who rescued me when I took that spill in my apartment."

"Oh. So, you're the knight-in-shining-armor. Have we met before? You look awfully familiar."

"No, I don't believe we've met."

"Hmmm."

"So, did you hear from Diana at all?" Belinda asked.

"No surprisingly, I haven't. She did send some flowers to the funeral home, though. My mom threw them out; said they were probably laced with poison or something. Did she call you at all?"

"No, she didn't. I'm kind of glad she didn't. I was gonna try to make things easier for you and your family and try to diplomatically get her not to come to the service, but she didn't contact me, so I didn't have to. It made my life easier."

"Belinda?"

Belinda turned around to find Aidan standing directly behind her. Simultaneously with Aidan's arrival, Dante's hand protectively embraced her back.

"Aidan, hi," Belinda said.

"Hello, stranger. I thought you were going to call?"

"It's just, um...I've been so busy and there's been so much going on lately. I'm sorry I didn't get back to you."

"It's okay. I was worried; that's all."

"Well, you could've called me."

"True, true, very true. I didn't want to officially become a stalker."

"So, Aidan, how's the family?" Summer interjected.

"Good, everybody's fine. I was sorry to hear about your grandmother. She was our neighborhood matriarch. Every one of us spent some time in Momma Douglas' kitchen at some time or another."

"Ain't that the truth?" Belinda chimed in.

Dante's grip on Belinda was so firm, she was flattered. It was a possessive stance; and she had to admit she liked it. She wasn't sure it was an aspect of her personality she enjoyed, but Belinda, like so many other women had spent most of her life looking for someone to watch over her. There was a subtle strength about Dante that was unmistakable.

"Oh, I'm sorry. Dante, this is Aidan; Aidan, this is Dante."

The two men shook hands.

"What's up, man?"

Dante was unresponsive, nothing more than a tilt of his head.

"Well, we're all going back to the house. Did you drive, Aidan?" Summer asked.

"Yes."

"Would it be okay if Belinda and Dante rode along with you? That is, if you've got room. Your wife...your family isn't with you? Are they?"

"No, they're not. I've got plenty of room."

Belinda glanced at Aidan and he seemed somehow different; not at all like himself.

"Is everything okay, Belinda?" he asked.

"Yeah. Everything is fine."

"So you're ready to go?"

"Yeah. I want to say something to Summer real quick. I'll be right back."

As Belinda walked away to talk to Summer, Dante turned to Diana, who had taken up the form of Aidan and attended the funeral.

"What are you doing here?" Dante asked.

"I wouldn't be welcome in my usual form, so I traded bodies with someone more appealing to the masses. I really think we're going to have to do something about her."

"Who? What the fuck are you talking about?"

"Your little girlfriend's tacky best friend. She's going to ruin everything if her and her family keep sticking their noses where they don't belong. That's why we're all gathered here today. I had to get rid of the old woman; she was becoming a nuisance."

"And you couldn't think of anything other than killing her?"

"I could have, but she pissed me off. Getting rid of her was an added bonus."

"I'll tell you the same thing I tell René; mind your arrogance. It may very well be your downfall."

"Mind your compassion; it may be yours. Although I can understand your attraction to this one; she's absolutely delicious."

"Aidan, or Diana, or whoever you are, don't push me."

"Or else?"

"Or else, you might find yourself in worse shape than that old woman you killed. As I told René, stay away from Belinda Wilson."

"I don't think I can do that. You see, I'm one of her best friends and when Summer's gone, she'll need me. And, Dante, if I were you, I wouldn't test me. Summer's family tried that and look what happened. Summer won't be shadowing me at Potion now, will she? She's a bit preoccupied."

NINETEEN

"So, what do you think?" Belinda asked Summer. "Is he gorgeous or what?"

"Yeah. He is definitely fine. Now that I've actually seen him, I really think I've seen him somewhere before."

"How could you see someone like that and not remember where?"

"I know, isn't it weird; especially me. I never forget a good-looking man. I must be more preoccupied than I thought."

"Yeah. That's probably it."

"I can't wait until this day is over."

"I can imagine. That's the only reason I didn't kick your ass."

"What. What did I do?"

"Aidan, Dante, and me in the same car. What were you thinking?"

"You and Aidan always kept everything so much on the down-low, I almost forgot about the two of you."

"Really? I thought you were just fuckin' with me."

"No, I wouldn't do that. I was trying to coordinate everybody with their rides to my parents' place."

"Well, everyone's leaving and see Dante standing over there, looking awkward. I hope Aidan isn't saying something he shouldn't be saying."

"Why would he? He'd have to be a fool. He's the one that's married."

"I still can't believe I did that. Never again. I don't care how lonely I get or how well I know someone, I will never fool around with another married man again. It's counter-productive. I'll see you at the house, okay? You holding up okay?"

"Yeah, Bee, you go on. Your friend looks like he's in pain over there."

"Belinda, why don't you sit up here with me? You don't mind, do you, Dante?"

"No, not at all."

"So, Belinda, what have you been up to? You've been a little scarce lately."

"You know, the usual; working hard. What about you?"

"Pretty much the same. Any new articles I should be looking for?"

When he was alone with Belinda, Dante felt like they just fit. Sitting there now in this car with her and Diana masquerading as Aidan, he realized time had marched on without him. All those centuries, he had done his best to keep up with all the changes, but listening to Aidan and Belinda's banter, he realized that he hadn't. This time he was living in was no longer his.

"You okay back there?" Belinda asked.

"Yes, I'm fine."

Once they arrived at Summer's parents' home, Dante felt even more out of place than he felt during the car ride on the way over.

"Are you okay?" Belinda asked.

"Yes, I'm fine.

"Hello, Mrs. Johnson, I'm so sorry to hear about your mother."

"Thank you...Aidan? Thank you for coming."

Mrs. Johnson stared at Aidan so intently.

"Honey, everything okay?" Mr. Johnson asked.

"Yeah, I guess so. You know Aidan pretty well, don't you?"

"Yeah, I've known him since he was a kid, like most of the kids here. They all grew up with Summer."

"He seems different, for some reason."

"It's been a rough couple of days. You're probably just tired; that's all."

Tilly Johnson's instincts told her it was more than that. She had known Aidan since he was seven or eight years old and standing in front of her, everything about him seemed different than the man she had last seen only a few weeks earlier.

"Summer, come here for a second. I've gotta ask you a question."

"Yeah, Mom?"

"You know Aidan pretty well, don't you?"

"Of course I do."

"Do me a favor. Look at his eyes for me. Don't make it obvious or anything, but tell me if you see anything different. I could swear the color of his eyes are different."

"They're probably contacts."

"They don't really look like contacts. They look pretty real to me. They look blue."

"I would've remembered that. Aidan's eyes are definitely not blue. They're contacts."

Summer found Belinda standing near the food table. "My mother just asked me the strangest question about Aidan."

"What?"

"She wanted to know what his eye color is. She swears that Aidan's eyes are suddenly blue."

Belinda laughed. "Those are contacts. Trust me; they freaked me out the first time I saw them."

"Maybe he's going through some changes at home."

"Maybe."

"I'm probably going to leave soon. Do you need anything before I go?"

"No, I'm good. And, I'm even better because she didn't show up."

"Did you really think she was going to show after the way things were the last time she was here? That would have been a bold move on her part."

"Nothing about Diana would ever truly surprise me."

Belinda hugged Summer and kissed her on the cheek.

"You hang in there. Okay? Call me. Where are your mom and dad? I wanted to say goodbye."

"They're probably in the kitchen puttering around. The two of them can't seem to keep still, now that they're retired anyway. Since my grandmother passed away, they've been ten times worse. It's like they're looking for something to do."

"I'll find them."

They were exactly where Summer said they would be.

"Mr. and Mrs. Johnson, I'm so sorry for your loss. If there is anything you need, please don't hesitate to call me."

"Thanks, Belinda. We appreciate it," Mr. Johnson said.

"Yes, Belinda. Thank you so much. My mother always liked you so much. She would have felt like she missed a hell of a party with all of her favorite people here."

Belinda and The Johnsons managed slight chuckles.

"Yeah, I think she would have enjoyed this," Belinda agreed. "My friend is looking like a deer in the headlights over there. I think I'll go rescue him."

Belinda walked over to Dante. "I only wanted to show my respects. So, we can leave whenever you're ready."

"No, don't worry about me. I'll be fine."

Belinda sat down with Dante for a moment. "Are you hungry? I can get you a plate of food."

"Thanks, Belinda. I think I will have something to eat."

While Belinda and Dante sat eating their meal amidst the somber setting, Aidan and Summer were in the the Johnsons' bedroom with the door locked.

"So, you're telling me you never thought of us in any way other than friends?"

"No, not really," Summer lied.

"Besides, I tend to steer clear of my best friends' men. Not to mention the fact that you are married."

"Best friends?"

"Yeah, best friends. Or, are you going to tell me you've never slept with Belinda…on more than one occasion?"

"That was a long time ago and my marriage is one of convenience."

"Hmmm."

Summer stood there, considering the possibilities, yet bound by the friendship code. She had done a lot of things, but she had never slept with a friend's man; past, present or future.

"As tempting an offer as it is, I'm going to have to pass. I make it a point never to break the code."

"The code?"

"Yeah. Thou shall not sleep with thy girlfriends' men."

"Wow! If men had such a code, they'd probably never get laid."

Done playing with Summer, Diana decided she would take her leave and go have a little fun elsewhere.

"Aidan, were you going to leave without saying good-bye?" Belinda asked when she saw him heading for the door.

"Of course not. I was just going outside to get some fresh air."

Belinda made it a point to look directly into his eyes when she spoke to him. They were clearly blue and for the first time, she realized they were really *not* contacts. That didn't make sense.

Right before she left, Belinda found Summer again.

"I am ninety-nine percent sure that Aidan's eyes were brown when we were growing up together. Now they're blue. For the longest time I thought they were contacts, but they're not. His eyes are absolutely blue. Your mother was right."

Once in Potion, Diana surveyed the club, searching for what she needed. She found it in one of the lounge areas. There was a tangle of bodies emitting such a strong level of energy, she needed to be a part of it. From the moment she got even close to the group, their awareness of her was obvious; moans intensified, hands beckoned to her.

She knelt down before the group, wrapped her hot mouth around an unoccupied cock and licked and sucked relentlessly until he begged for mercy. Each time she engulfed his mouth, her inner temperature intensified. As someone entered her from behind, she knew this restoration would be plentiful. There was so much to choose from. His hands were more powerful than she was accustomed to from most mortals. He gripped her ass and drove himself into her, over and over again, pulling all the way out and then plunging deep. She willed herself to keep her natural instincts at bay. The last thing she wanted at this moment was to transform. But, she wasn't sure she could resist. Just when she thought she might reveal herself, the skilled cock fucking her doggy style exploded inside of her, slapping her on the ass as he went in search of other ways to entertain himself. As he did, Diana removed her mouth from the dick she was sucking off, just in time to climb on top of him and ride him, feeling the rhythm of the others. Before she left Potion she was afforded the opportunity to sample each and every man in the group.

Satisfied with what she had accomplished and feeling invincible, Diana could leave Potion, but not without taking someone with her.

She found the jackhammer that was fucking her from behind.

"How would you like to come with me back to my place? I have a car waiting outside. The car can take you wherever you need to go when you're ready to leave my place."

"Lead the way," he said.

He also made his living satisfying rich lonely women and he thought he had hit the jackpot with Diana when she mentioned her Christopher Street address.

"Is there anything in particular you would like when we get to your place? I do anything. There are no limits."

"I hope that's true. If so, I may not let you go."

If he had known Diana wasn't joking, he probably would have never left Potion. But, he was already calculating in his head how much cash he might be able to get and what he would do with it.

"Shall we go?" she asked.

"I'm ready when you are."

While he calculated the amount of cash he could get, Diana was doing her own calculations. She wondered how long this one would be able to sustain her before he perished; one day, two, a week, a month?

While in the car, Diana leaned over and whispered in his ear. "Do you want to be my love slave?"

He chuckled.

Diana chuckled, not because of what she had said, but because he didn't realize she meant every word she said. Yet another John Doe had joined her in her lair. She hoped that this one would keep for longer than the others. They all started out the same; monster fucking machines that lost all vigor much quicker than she expected. Just once she would have liked to find one that could keep for a month, maybe even two.

Then she could vest her interest in more important things.

TWENTY

"Hello, may I speak to Belinda?"

Belinda already knew the answer to the question before she asked it. She had known her for years. They had grown up in the same neighborhood, but the last thing she wanted to hear was her voice at the other end of the line.

"Hello, this is Belinda. Who's calling?"

"I don't know if you remember me, but my name is Nicole. I'm Aidan's wife."

"Oh, yeah. Of course I remember you. You went to Our Lady of Faith, right?

"Yes, I did."

"How are you?"

The abruptness of Nicole's words was more than enough to let Belinda know that this was not a friendly call.

"Actually, I'm not so good. I haven't seen Aidan for three days now. The kids are worried. I'm even a little worried. And, I guess I was calling you to see if he's at your house."

"Oh. No. Uhm. I haven't seen Aidan since..."

"Wait a minute, before you say anything. I didn't call to give you a hard time. Even though he doesn't flaunt it in my face, I know Aidan has affairs. I'm ashamed to admit it now, to you a practical stranger, but I have them, too. We don't have the best marriage and truth be told we probably should have gone our separate ways a long time ago. I'm sure we're not the only couple that lives like this and I'm sure we won't be the last. Anyway…I've known for some time that you and Aidan were seeing each other. I even knew when you stopped seeing each other. I could tell. His personality kind of changed a bit. It was you that broke it off, wasn't it?"

Belinda suddenly felt like a complete and total bitch. What the fuck was she having an affair with a married man for anyway? Was she crazy? Even though she had already stopped seeing him, the remnants of her actions still followed her.

"Nicole, I'm so sorry. I'm really not this kind of a woman. It was the first and only time I ever had an affair with a married man," she lied.

In fact, she had had an affair with one other married man a few years before Aidan. But, she didn't want to admit that to Nicole.

"You don't have to explain it to me. Really. I'm just trying to find Aidan. No one's seen him for a couple of days now and at first I thought maybe he was weighing his options or something and would eventually come home and tell me he was leaving. But now three days have passed and nothing. Even though he cheats, he loves his kids. He would never drop out of sight and not let them know what was going on. So you really don't know where he is?"

"No, I haven't seen Aidan since Summer Johnson's grandmother's funeral. As a matter of fact, he drove a friend and me, a male friend of mine...to The Johnsons' house after the funeral.

"Everyone there did say he seemed a little different though. A couple of people even said they thought he looked different."

"I noticed that, too," Nicole mentioned. "The last time I saw him, I asked him what he was doing with colored contacts. It was so unlike him. He told me that he didn't know what I was talking about and that he wasn't wearing any contacts. I've known Aidan since I was twelve and his eyes have always been dark brown. Not blue, not green, not light brown...dark brown, almost black. But, the last time I saw him, it was like he had a few pairs of contacts that he was interchanging. One minute they were blue, the next minute they were green and then they were light brown. It was weird."

"That's what someone mentioned at The Johnsons. I think it was Mrs. Johnson that said that."

"I'm sorry to have bothered you; and again, I didn't call to give you a hard time or anything. Don't be too hard on yourself about the whole married man thing. I sound like a nut, since that was my husband you were with, but if there's one thing I've learned over the past few years, it's that relationships can be hard and things don't always work out as you planned. Not only that, it can get damned lonely out there, even when you are married. So, every now and then, people find one another under less than ideal circumstances. I've done it, and suffered from the same guilt. But what I realize now is in life we're going to make mistakes. The truly admirable quality is how we come back from those mistakes and what we learn from them. Please let me know if you see or hear anything from Aidan. The kids and I are starting to get worried."

"I will and again, I'm so sorry."

Once off the phone, Belinda wondered why Aidan was cheating on his wife. She seemed like such a nice woman. She was attractive and she seemed to be a good mother. There was no accounting for the reasons why married people had affairs; or why single people had them either.

The first thing Belinda did was call Summer.

"You're not going to believe who just called me."

"Nicole."

"And how do you know that?"

"Because she called me and asked for your number," Summer whispered quietly. "She seemed really worried and she didn't seem mad at you at all, so I thought I should give her the number. I thought about calling you first. But, when she explained what was going on, I decided to give the number to her. You're not mad at me, are you?"

"No, not this time. But in the future, could you call me first before you just give out my number?"

"What did she say?"

"She was actually pretty cool. She acknowledged the fact that Aidan and I were having an affair and that we had cut it off, but she didn't do it in an accusatory way or anything. I think she really was worried about where he is. She said he's been missing for three days.

"Summer, I felt so guilty when I was talking to her. I am never going to have an affair with a married man again in life."

Summer didn't want to tell Belinda about what had taken place between Aidan and her. Right now, she was feeling her own guilt.

"Don't feel guilty. I heard that she's had affairs, too. So, that's probably why she was able to be so understanding."

"But still, it really sucked to have to talk to Aidan's wife on the phone about the fact that I had been screwing him. I felt like trash; plain and simple."

"I wonder where he is?" Summer said.

"You aren't the only person wondering that," Belinda responded.

TWENTY-ONE

"Don't you even bother to conceal your true form any longer?"

"I have no need to. There are no mortals here."

As much as Diana enjoyed the numerous bodies she had to choose from, she enjoyed her natural form so much more. The frightened shudder from a mortal as he watched her transform was enough to make her want to maintain that appearance all the time. The fear it inspired in them was her aphrodisiac. Often, she had plans of preserving a life in order for her to have a steady flow of restoration available. But, she would become so carried away once she transformed, before she knew it, they were depleted of all remaining life.

"There are mortals everywhere. This is their plane; not ours. Why is it so easy for you to forget that? We are merely visitors. We take these souls not only to restore, but also to secure a place in our true home."

"I haven't forgotten anything. It's impossible to forget something that isn't indeed true. Humans don't own this 'plane,' as you call it. We decide who lives and who dies, we decide who will sacrifice themselves to us next. If we hold all the cards, how then can they control *anything?* Your inability to see just that is what keeps you not many rungs up on the ladder from where they are."

"I have no desire to compete with mortals. All I want to do is survive."

"You want to survive, yet you'd rather commit yourself to one weak, paltry mortal, probably incapable of maintaining her own life force, let alone yours. You have resigned yourself to perish; and why?"

"Because I want more."

"Do you read their papers, their magazines? They're no different than we are. None of them truly maintain lasting relationships; divorce, separation, patricide, matricide, mothers killing their own children. The only difference between them and us is they make a show of love. We're demons; we don't need to perform an act for anyone. We are what we are."

"Well, if that's how you see it, then I guess I'm ready to trade in my reality for an act. It's got to be more interesting than what I've been doing for the past several centuries."

"I can't believe, I used to respect you. I always thought that in order for you to have survived this long, you must be all-powerful. You are nothing at all like what I expected."

"Nothing ever is; not even these mortals you claim to know so well. If you don't listen to anything else that I say, I'm going to give you this one. Don't assume you know all there is to know about mortals. They might just shock you."

"Can't wait," she said sarcastically. "You know what I've learned about mortal women, and you listen, because this is *extremely* important. It's something you would do well to remember. I saw it on a bumper sticker or something and it stayed in my head, it's actually pretty profound, in a mortal kind of way: 'Dick is fleeting, but friendship is forever.' Isn't it amazing how priorities change when it isn't a question of survival? It doesn't mean the same thing to them that it does to us. How can you expect to forge a relationship with a mortal? It's impossible. The differences that divide us from them are too numerous. Yet, you have decided that you are going to laugh in the face of all reason and go against the grain. Poor disillusioned Dante. Always wanting more than he has.

"I heard you had another mortal woman once, a long time ago, and you killed her. Didn't that teach you anything? It can't be done!"

"I would be careful if I were you, Diana, or whatever it is you're calling yourself these days?"

"Another thing I enjoy about being a demon, I can be anyone I like. So, yes, I am Diana, among other things, people, animals, whatever. My power is endless. Although Diana is definitely the one I kind of like more than the others. What do you think? Do you like Diana best of all?"

"I think that you are a loathsome bitch, in whatever form; and that you can set up your little medical practice and play nicey-nicey with Belinda, but you will never, ever touch her. Because if you do, I will kill you. That's an absolute promise."

"Such anger and, I might add, totally unwarranted. How can you condemn me for doing what I have always done; for doing what *we all* have always done? Or, have you forgotten that you are no mortal and your survival is arrived at the same way mine is?"

"I wish I could forget. Just because I must do something doesn't mean I have to like it. And, over time, I have come to abhor this way. If I could wave a magic wand and suddenly change things, I would."

"But you can't!"

Diana knew she would have to draw whatever energy she required early this particular night. She had a busy day ahead of her tomorrow at her practice. So, she dressed and headed to Redemption for the evening. It had been a while since she had gone there. She was looking forward to finding a lawyer to extract from. The only emotion more stimulating for her than fear was arrogance.

"Eenie, meenie, minee, mo..."

He was perfect; like a peacock spreading his feathers. He would most definitely be her choice for tonight. The Dolce & Gabbana suit, the Berluti shoes, the Armani tie. He was begging to be noticed and, tonight, he would get his wish. Unfortunately, some long-legged bimbo with fake boobs obscured her view and captured his attention. She wasn't worried, though. She had something the long-legged blonde didn't.

"Can I buy you a drink?" Diana asked.

"Hell no! Can't you see that he's already having a drink with me?" the blonde said.

Oh, Summer thought. *She's a lively one, but not for long.*

"I'll be happy to buy both of you a drink," Diana offered.

She seldom sought to control others' minds. She enjoyed the hunt so much more when they were completely aware. But in the interest of time and a desire not to draw too much attention, she made an exception. Her plan was different for each.

For him, a glance at her ever-changing kaleidoscope of colors in her eyes. The vivid burst of blues, greens, reds and browns and the assortment of shades for each were like fireworks.

Diana was fascinated with his childlike state. She thought she actually saw him stretch out a single finger to touch, like a baby mesmerized by a mobile. All that was left for him to do to make the image complete was to utter the words: 'Ooh shiny.'

He was sure it was the alcohol or maybe someone had slipped him a surprise in his drink. He couldn't remember feeling so high in his entire life. It was impossible for him to look away; in her eyes he saw more beauty than he had ever seen. Just when he thought it couldn't get more spectacular, there was a moving picture of him fucking both her and the other girl doggy-style, as they each bent over a stool. He was sticking his dick in one, then the other; short quick jabs, then long, tight strokes.

"You're something else," he said.

He realized she was something different, but he was too drunk to recognize how different. If so, he probably would have ended the little cat and mouse game they were playing with one another right then and there.

"So, what brings you both to Redemption on a Tuesday night?"

"Massive quantities of alcohol," he said.

"Oh no, we can't have that. If you drink too much, you won't be able to fuck me and that's why I'm here. I'm Diana, by the way."

"I'm Bobby; and this is Candace."

"What do you do, Bobby?"

"I'm a lawyer and Candace here is a secretary. I was thinking about inviting her back to my office for some *dick*tation! Ha, ha, ha, ha. Get it? *Dick*tation!"

"You're a riot, Bobby. You must keep them rolling in the courtroom, huh?"

"Not a laugh to be heard, baby; I'm the best. That's why they pay me the big bucks."

Diana suddenly hoped he didn't have a small dick. Often when men found it necessary to brag about their prowess in the workplace, it was because they had tiny dicks. She could still create something, if need be, but she preferred something larger to serve her purposes.

She then turned her attention to Candace, the secretary.

"Candace, huh? I bet a lot of people call you Candy."

"Yeah. That's because I'm so sweet," she said, directing her comment at Bobby.

She mistakenly thought she was in a competition. Candace had probably come to Redemption hoping to snag herself the chance at a prospective rich husband, somewhere down the line. She would gain more than that tonight. She would gain a bit of perspective.

While Bobby's head was turned, Diana flashed Candace a glimpse into her eyes that she wouldn't soon forget. She played out Candace's death in intricate detail in her eyes, as if she were watching a movie on a screen. Diana was expecting a scream. Instead, Candace slowly backed away from both Bobby and Diana and ran from the club like a banshee.

"What got into her?" he asked. "Did you do something mean, Diana?"

"Me? No, not at all. Scouts honor," she said, holding up a sign meant to indicate she was a girl scout.

"I bet you were never a girl scout in your life."

"Why don't you come with me outside and I'll show you my scout uniform."

"Absoposifuckinglutely," he uttered, through his alcohol haze.

He didn't see it coming. She whipped his pants down to the ground and began pawing at him with her hands. The alcohol he had consumed was delaying his hard-on, which only served to infuriate Diana. She stripped down completely naked, hoping the excitement of her red bare nipples and her pubic bush out in the open air might inspire him. She was accustomed to her satisfaction being immediate and his semi-hard dick contributed to her inclination to transform. She tried to control it and fortunately for him especially, she did. Finally, after stimulating him extensively with her mouth and hands, he was hard. She slammed him hard against the brick wall. Climbing his body like she had webbed fingers, she grabbed at his dick with her pussy lips, tighter and tighter, encouraging him to stay hard inside of her. Each time it got softer, she squeezed tighter and stroked harder. Eventually he could feel something prickly scraping against his cock, not hard enough to cause pain, but enough to boost his hard-on. She laughed outwardly.

"What's so funny?" he asked.

He assumed she was making fun of his difficulty with staying hard. She wasn't. Her chuckle was about how close he had come to losing his pitiful appendage. In the end, she decided the renewal she received from him wasn't worth the time and sauntered off, down the back alley, completely naked, but not before she converted to her demon form.

She could hear him pissing himself out of fear as she left. He had no idea. He had been far luckier than most.

TWENTY-TWO

Dante walked into his apartment only to find René steadily pumping away at two women on *his* bed. Dante seldom brought mortals back to his apartment. He always considered the ramifications of being discovered and was careful not to leave too many trails. His apartment was his sanctuary. It was where he escaped for another kind of restoration. And, it was rare that he shared his domicile with any mortal. He chose to allow his restorations to take place in clubs, in dark alleys, even in restaurants, if need be, but hardly ever in his home. Now, René had breached that refuge.

"René, what the fuck are you doing in my apartment?"

"I brought you something," he said, pointing to the redhead reclining beneath the blonde on his bed.

"I can find my own women."

The redhead turned her head and surveyed him up and down before she commented, "I bet you can."

"These two are for hire. There are so many options to choose from, aren't there, brother?"

"Yet, I am perplexed. With all these options you could think of no other place to bring them but here."

"I told you it was a surprise, for you. I didn't think you were going to be a party-pooper and refuse me. Besides which, there are things I believe we need to discuss."

"As far as I'm concerned, everything has been said."

"Believe me, Dante. You'll want to hear what we have to say. You want something from us and now we want something from you."

"Who is we?"

Diana suddenly appeared from nowhere.

"I thought I told you to stay away from me," Dante said.

"Well, technically, you told Aidan to stay away from you," she replied.

"What made you think you could fool me anyway? Just because I've been spending time with mortals, doesn't make me one. Did you think I wouldn't figure out that was you at the funeral?"

The two girls on the bed were sure they were playing some sort of a game when they heard the words mortals. The redhead wondered if they were fans of Dungeons and Dragons. She always thought that was a game played by college kids.

"I wasn't trying to deceive anyone. Not really. I didn't think I would be welcome as Diana, so I made some temporary alterations. You got a problem with that?"

"Yes. As a matter of fact I do. I want the two of you to leave Belinda the fuck alone, whether you're Aidan or Diana or anyone else you decide to be."

"Unfortunately, at this point, we can't do that," Diana said.

"I must admit, Dante, she's right," René said. "Until now, I was just having a bit of fun with both you and Belinda, but now she's got something we want."

"What could Belinda possibly have that the two of you could want?" Dante asked.

Diana grinned as René answered. "The Cambion she's carrying belongs to us."

Now, both girls were sure this was a game of some sort. Either that or they were all crazy. In which case, it occurred to the blonde that they should probably leave.

She was just about to tell René that they were leaving when she found she couldn't speak. Within minutes, the redhead discovered the same. They were convinced he had slipped them some sort of a drug that had seized up their throats and decided to remain calm until their voices returned. After all, this wasn't the worst they had been through while on the streets.

"What did you say?" Dante said.

"She's carrying Cambion; and we want it."

"And, what makes you think it's yours? It could be mine."

"Possible, my friend, but highly unlikely," René said. "You see, I've been visiting her just about every night for months; long before you even laid your eyes on her; and long before you started bedding her."

"That proves nothing."

"You're right, it doesn't. It doesn't matter whose seed impregnated her; the Cambion is part of our clan and we want it, no matter what."

"You can't have it! I'll never allow it!"

"You'll never allow it?" René chuckled. "It's not up to you. Look at it this way. At least now I will no longer be visiting her bed."

Within seconds, Dante had transformed. He leapt at René, catching him off guard, and ripped open his face with his jagged talons. René simply stood there, eerily calm. Diana wondered why he hadn't struck back. He wiped the blood from his face and by the time he pulled his hand away, the gaping hole in his face was gone.

"Once again, Dante, you have made my point for me. Every moment you spend with these mortals weakens you. There was a time when you would never have wasted vital energy, simply to satisfy some sense of anger...a purely emotional response; a weak response. And, for what? It is you who are more severely weakened for it. You haven't restored, have you? The sex you are having with Belinda, it's not restoring you, is it? Did you even bother to question why, or are you too caught up in trying to live a lie? The more powerful the Cambion inside of her becomes, the less energy she will be able to supply for you. Quite frankly, Dante, you're damned if you do and you're damned if you don't."

The energy it had taken for Dante to convert to his natural form now left him feeling physically spent.

"Ironic, isn't it? If you continue along this path much longer, you'll cease to exist and you won't be with her anyway. If you give in to your natural urges, she'll most likely abandon you. Or, she could end up like Brenda.

What a dilemma." René paused and looked at Diana. "Diana, dear, can you hear the clock ticking? I can."

Diana moved closer to Dante. "I tell you what, Dante, what do you say we all make a trip to Potion tonight? That place has got the cure for what ails us all."

Dante stood there, staring at them both, before storming out.

Dante left his place angry but fully aware that everything René was saying was absolutely true. He was right. He didn't have long. And, with Belinda pregnant, her energy would not be near enough to sustain him. The pangs of guilt he was feeling now, once foreign to him, were now becoming a part of him. He had to admit to himself that he would have to ignore those feelings and do what he had to do. He hoped that René and Diana would not be at Potion, because that's where he would be going. At least there his guilt would be minimal.

He realized he would need all the energy he could get in coming months, so he returned to his apartment and spoke up.

"Leave the two of them here."

While Diana and René were discussing their next move, Dante was doing what came naturally to him. The effects of René's silencing were still in effect and Dante preferred it that way. With both girls lying face down on the bed, he pulled them both down to the very edge, positioned their bodies so that their upper bodies were on the bed and their lower bodies were draped to the floor below. He spread them both as wide open as they would go and proceeded to slide his cock into each of them, one by one, taking turns; first one, then the other, until each of them and he had cum. His goal accomplished, he instructed them to dress, led them to the door, and returned their voices to them just in time for the door to close behind them. He wondered if they would be trouble, since they had been to his home, but that was probably why René had chosen them. Prostitutes were just as careful and cautious about their safety as he was. They wanted to fall below the radar and so did he.

TWENTY-THREE

Diana mistakenly assumed that once Summer's grandmother was gone, Summer would forget about her plans to spend some time at Potion. Diana was wrong. If anything, she was more committed than ever to following her hunch to completion.

Summer looked around the club, wondering who on earth had designed the place. There wasn't a corner of the club that wasn't sexually-themed. Even the bar stools were equipped with vibrating dildos. She watched as a woman, who clearly spent a great deal of time there, positioned herself in the middle of a bar stool, pushed a button and undoubtedly was filled up with an impressive mock dick. It was only a matter of minutes before she was gripping the side of the bar, while she rode the wave of an earth-shattering orgasm. There were dick-shaped glasses, stirrers, even ice. And, in every available space there were all manners of sexual acts taking place. Just walking into the bar, Summer had one tall dark brotha slap his uncovered cock against her ass. And the women were no different. While Summer tried to lift the open-

ing to the bar area, a woman whispered in her ear and
told her how much she'd like to cum on her big titties.

While she surveyed the club looking for any signs of
Diana, Belinda's new friend, Dante, walked in. Summer
had to admit to herself, she wasn't surprised. A lot of her
memory of the night they had spent at Redemption was
fuzzy, but every now and then she would see glimpses of
Dante, even before she met him. At first she thought
they were dreams, but she now realized they were probably memories. She followed him with her eyes, hoping
he didn't recognize her. Within minutes, she saw her.
It was Diana in all her glory…wearing a vinyl skirt and
matching vinyl bra top. She noticed Summer immediately and made a beeline for the bar.

"Hello, Summer!"

"Hey, Diana! Thanks for the flowers."

"Oh that…it was the least I could do."

It was all Summer could take to keep from jumping
over the bar and whipping Diana's ass. It was as if she
were admitting what she had done. If ever there was a
doubt in Summer's mind as to Diana's involvement with
all of the recent events taking place around them, Diana
confirmed for Summer that she wasn't crazy. Diana was
indeed evil and Dante had something to do with it.

"Dante's here," Summer said as a test.

"Oh really. Then, I'll have to say hello."

Summer realized she hadn't slipped Diana up. She
was toying with her. In essence, she was communicating

to her that she wasn't afraid of her and she was laying all her cards on the table.

"So, you admit you know him?"

"Why, of course I do. But, you already knew that, didn't you, Summer? You're so much smarter than I ever gave you credit for. I always thought you were just some under-educated piece of ass, but you're so much more than that."

Summer knew she probably should have been afraid. But, she didn't care. Just as she was about to swing at Diana, Dante intervened.

"Summer, don't!"

It was more for Summer's protection than anything. Dante knew better than anyone how powerful Diana was and what she was capable of and the last thing he wanted was for Belinda's friend to be harmed.

"Mind your fucking business!" Summer screamed.

"Yeah, Dante. We're both big girls," Diana said lazily.

"Summer, I think you've seen what you came here to see. It's time for you to go."

He grabbed Summer's arm and she read the meaning in his eyes and completely understood. It was time for her to cut her losses and listen for a change.

As she exited Potion, a painfully pale man, who seemed vaguely familiar, passed her and looked directly at her, smiling before joining both Diana and Dante. And, suddenly, as if a light switch had suddenly been turned on, Summer's memories of that evening at Redemption all came flooding back. The memories were like shooting pictures in her brain; flashes of pictures and events that she had somehow forgotten. These pictures reminded her that they had all been at Redemption the night all this craziness started. And the younger one was the same man she saw following Diana downstairs that night. She wished Belinda were there to see this. She decided a picture with her cell phone would have to suffice, and she snapped a picture quickly and discreetly before leaving.

"Your little girlfriend is gonna be none too pleased with you," René said.

"I can handle that. Let's get to the point of why you're here. You are here to see me, aren't you?" Dante asked.

"I've had a lot of time to think about what we discussed. What if Belinda and I were to give the Cambion to you? What then?"

"What do you mean, what then? Then we all move on with our lives."

"And what about Belinda?"

"What about her?"

"You know as much about Cambions as we do. Don't be naïve. You know the fate of mortal women who give birth to Cambions."

"Don't tell me you actually thought she'd be able to survive the birth?" Diana laughed.

Dante said, "I will be here to see her through it. Yes, she will survive it. I will make sure of it."

"There are some things even you can't control, Dante," René offered.

Dante was anxious to return to Belinda, but he would have to do something about his greatly diminishing strength. Standing in a corner was a woman who seemed to beckon to him. She was alone, but it appeared that she was unsure of what she should do next. Without even the preliminary of conversation, Dante approached her, pressed her body against the corner of the wall that she almost seemed to be supporting, then slid his stiff, frigidly cold dick inside of her. She shivered once he was inside of her. She was fixed to the spot, only moving when the pressure of his dick raised her body a few inches off of the floor. The angle from which he was entering her and his height allowed her to feel every inch of him, from her standing position. Her nipples hardened even more each time his jacket rubbed against them.

"Oh yes," she moaned.

Gravity influenced the flow of her cum and Dante's cock was drenched with her torrential downpour. Her lubrication only served to preserve his release. He continued, taking up such an easy tempo, it was reminiscent of a dance.

"Don't...don't...don't stop...keep going...keep going... Oh...Oh. You are so, so good. So good!"

Dante continued to dance inside of her, his hands braced against the wall, his jacket brushing against her hard, full nipples. That was the only contact he had with her, besides his dick inside of her pussy.

They continued like that for at least an hour, both in

the standing position. Her legs were beginning to turn to jelly and her pussy had cum more than she thought possible. She was drained beyond understanding. However, Dante was still actively engaged in vigorously fucking her. He was unaware of how long it had been since he had been in his true element, where he could unleash his hunger freely without fear of judgment.

He bared his teeth as he approached satisfaction. She watched as the veins in his neck protruded and bulged. What she didn't know was that if he didn't finish soon, she would be staring at bloody horns sprouting from that neck. She bit him in the exact spot where his veins seemed about to explode and he released a deep, guttural moan. His eruption was enough to raise her six inches from the floor. As soon as he removed his dick, their mingled juices cascaded down her thigh. She was eager to taste him, so she ran a delicate finger inside her thigh and slowly brought her fingers to her mouth.

"Uhm. I didn't think it was possible. You taste just as good as you feel inside."

Dante walked away and headed straight for the door to leave Potion. His dick no longer inside of his restorer, he was plagued with guilt, yet pleased to find that his energy had multiplied in the short period of time that he was there. There had been several women watching him, as if he were a performer on a stage, while he fucked his shy participant against the wall. He wasn't sure when he would be able to return to Potion again, so he took another. This one he bent over one of the barstools and fucked her from behind; long deliberate strokes designed to maintain the act. When he was sure his efforts would afford him a longer period of time to restore, he gave one final punctuating and propulsive force, which drew an agonizing, yet satisfied cry from her lips. He had done what he came there to do and so he immediately left.

As soon as Summer was far enough away from the club, she dialed Belinda on her cell. "What are you doing, B? We need to talk."

"Nothing. I was just taking a nap."

"Is it okay if I come over? There's something we need to discuss."

"Okay."

"And Belinda, don't mention to Diana or Dante that I'm coming over. Okay?"

"Okay. But, why?"

"I just saw them together…at Potion."

"Summer, make sure you come straight here. Dante was supposed to be here hours ago and I'd rather you didn't run into one another. Okay?"

"No problem. I don't want to run into him either. I should be able to get there in a half-hour."

"See you then."

As soon as Summer was inside Belinda's apartment, she pulled out her phone to show her the picture. What she had seen in the viewer while taking the picture was dramatically altered. It was as though she had photographed characters in a horror movie or maybe guests at a masquerade party; except they were too monstrous to be anything but real. As much as Belinda believed from the very start that something sinister was taking place, even she was shocked by what she saw in the picture she had taken.

"I swear to you, Belinda, when I took this picture it was of Diana, Dante and another man; a young pale man."

Surprised at how calm Belinda seemed to be, Summer's agitation persisted as she tried in earnest to get Belinda to believe her.

"Summer, it's okay. I believe you."

Belinda's placid state was more unnerving to Summer than the photograph. Her first thought was that Belinda must be in shock.

"Who is the third one?" Belinda asked calmly.

"I don't know if you remember or not, but they were all at Redemption the night all of this started."

"Dante, too?"

"Yes, Dante was there. But, what's even stranger is you were supposed to be the one with amnesia, but even I didn't remember any of this until today." She paused to gauge Belinda's reaction. "Belinda, I don't like this. These three are up to something. You want to trust both Dante and Diana, but I'm worried that they're dangerous. What on earth would they be doing together?"

"I agree with you, Summer, but what should I do about it?"

TWENTY-FOUR

After Summer left Belinda's apartment, she forwarded the picture to Belinda as a reminder. She didn't want her to lose her resolve in confronting Dante.

Dante and Belinda ate in silence. Each of them was so steeped in their own thoughts, trying in earnest to think of a way to say what needed to be said.

After his confrontation with René and Diana, Dante knew that he would have to tell Belinda everything... and soon. He had been embroiled in such a web of lies involving Belinda, he was sure she would despise him with every fiber of his being. However, he had to risk her turning her back on him if it meant her safety and the safety of her unborn child. He and Belinda had achieved such a symbiotic state with one another, Dante was often hard-pressed to differentiate between who was the mortal and who was the demon.

While Dante pondered how he would tell her, Belinda made it easy for him.

"Dante, what are you?"

"For you to ask that question, I think maybe you already know."

"Yes, I believe I do, but I want to hear it from your own lips. I want to know that I'm not crazy. I've always known there was something too good to be true about all of this, but I didn't want to know. Are you human? Were you ever human?"

"No, Belinda, I'm not."

She hadn't expected him to be quite so direct in his reply. It was one thing to believe something to be true. To hear it out in the open with your own ears and straight from the horse's mouth was another thing altogether.

Belinda had no plan for what she would do when he answered; especially if the answer was yes. Now, all she wanted to do was run. Yet, she was rooted to the spot where she sat.

"I read somewhere that your kind can hypnotize people, make them do things. Is that why I'm still sitting here? Is that why I haven't run?"

"No, I wouldn't do that to you."

"Have you ever?"

"No, I've never controlled you. I've always enjoyed your free will. I've welcomed it. You are the closest thing to good that remains of me."

"So say it, Dante. Tell me what you are?"

"I have had many names through time. But I'm best known to mortals as an incubus. I draw my continued existence from the sexuality of others."

"In other words, you're a rapist?"

"Well…. No…. I mean, sometimes. I don't know what to call what I do. I require it to survive. For the most part, the women I am with go with me willingly, but I must admit, there have been times that, through necessity, I have had to take what I needed."

"What would happen if you didn't? If you never had sex with another woman ever again, including me?"

"Then I would most probably cease to exist."

"It always seems as though you're talking in riddles, even now. What does that mean? When you say cease to exist? Do you mean die? Would your body just disappear in a puff of smoke? What would happen?"

"I'm not sure I know myself. I survive by feeding off of the souls of others. Many believe that the souls that we bed were already tainted by evil of some sort. The souls we gather are a return for our existence on this plane…in the mortal world. Therefore, chances are if I were not here, sustaining myself with the souls of mortals, I would still exist but in the demon world."

"You mean hell, don't you?"

"That's the easiest way to explain it, although it is not as simple as what you've seen in movies."

"Nothing ever is."

"There's so much more you need to know. But, I need you to listen to everything…everything I have to say, before you react. Then, you're free to respond to the information I give you however you see fit."

"How free am I to respond when I'm dealing with a demon? I mean, couldn't you control me any way you want to? How would I even know if I were doing what I wanted to do or what you were influencing me to do?"

"After all this time, I would like to think that you have enough trust in me to know that I would not do that."

"Dante, you have to admit that we're way beyond mere trust here. You just revealed to me that not only are you not human, but that you exist by raping innocent women. We're way beyond a question of simple trust here."

"Unfortunately, Belinda, there is so much more that you need to know."

"Let me have it."

"Do you remember the very first time we met?"

"Yes, it was when I woke up in your apartment. Wasn't it?"

"No."

"Another lie? You told me you never used your powers to influence me in any way."

"And that was not a lie. I didn't, but someone else did. I am not the only…incubus here. In fact, there are many. Our numbers are growing with each passing day. The night I first saw you there was another of us, whom I spent a great deal of time with. His name is René. At first, because he was younger, I felt an obligation to be sort of a…mentor to him. I tried to encourage some level of humanity and survival by encouraging him to not take more than he needed, but René has always been a hothead from Day One. Eventually, he was venturing out on his own. He was careless about his actions and arrogant about the threat to himself and others. Mortal women began to die and disappear in alarming numbers before he realized that what I tried to explain to him made sense. The night I first saw you, I knew you would change me forever. I tried to fight it. At first, I even considered walking away and avoiding ever seeing you again. It was the night you were at Redemption."

"The night all of this started," she interrupted.

"Yes. Well, as I was saying, I saw you and everything stopped. I waged an inner battle and compassion somehow won out. I was prepared to leave Redemption when I saw René. I knew he would recognize all of the same qualities in you that I saw. And, while I wanted to preserve what you had, I realized that René would want to deface you in all ways imaginable. That night I thought it was the first time he encountered you, but I now realize he had been visiting you over a much longer period of time."

"Dante, what are you saying! No! You're not saying what I think you are!"

"Yes, Belinda, I am. I didn't know what this would do to you if you knew. But under the circumstances, you have to know."

Although Dante heard no sounds, her tears fell in abundance. She sat with her shoulders hunched, her head lowered. She was utterly dejected. The realization of what had been happening to her hit her like a ton of bricks.

Still crying, she raised her head after mentally going over everything he had just told her. As if she had hit the rewind button on all she heard in the last few minutes, she questioned Dante about one of his statements. "What 'circumstances' were you talking about?"

"Huh?"

"You said that under the circumstances you thought I had to know. What circumstances?"

"Belinda, know that I had nothing to do with this and until René…and Diana told me, I didn't have a clue."

"What? What does Diana have to do with this?"

"I went to René and I told him how I feel about you and I asked him, brother to brother, to leave you alone. He assured me that if you gave him and Diana what they wanted, they would never bother us ever again."

"What could I possibly give either of them that I haven't given already?"

"Your baby."

"What are you… What? What are they talking about?"

"Belinda, you're pregnant."

"You're all stark raving mad. I'm not pregnant. Thanks to the two of you and your nightly depletions, I've been plagued with fatigue and nausea and all manner of illnesses. I went to the doctor and he found nothing. If I was pregnant, the doctor would've told me!"

"Belinda, I know how much you'd like for this to not be true, but there are several explanations for why your doctor might not have known you were pregnant, including the fact that the life created by a mortal and an incubus is very different than a mortal life. They are called Cambions and they are born with strengths that surpass even us. That's why Diana and René want your baby. They are hell-bent on ultimate power. They believe that a race of Cambions will help them to achieve that goal."

"I'm not sure whether there is or isn't something growing inside of me. If there is, be it Cambion, mortal or incubus, it's mine and they will never have it!"

"Belinda, you've got to think about what you're saying. On your own, this could kill you. Most mortal women never survive the birth of a Cambion."

"Most mortal women probably don't have their very own incubus demon to see them through it. Will you help me?"

"Belinda, do you really need to ask me that?"

"Dante, I want this. I believe in the power of fate. And I believe this child is my fate. It's part of me and I cannot simply turn it over to René or Diana. I have my child's best interests at heart, not Diana's or René's. I could use your help, but I can assure you that I'll fight them, with or without your help."

Dante was impressed with her courage, but he didn't think she had a clue about what she was letting herself in for.

"I'm here for you, however you need me."

Belinda felt violated by both René and Dante, but it would be best if Dante stood with her, not against her.

"Dante, I need you to tell me everything about your kind. I know nothing and that could be my downfall."

"What do you need to know?"

"Can your kind die?"

"Not in the traditional sense. Some have been disposed of temporarily with fire, but they have always returned eventually. We can be exorcised. In the exorcism, the demon leaves the body, leaving the person free of the evil that has plagued them. That would be problematic for demons such as me."

"Why?"

"I've been here for centuries. Without the demon that inhabits this body, I am nothing more than an ancient, dilapidated host."

"What about Diana and René?"

"They are young enough that if their demons were exorcised, the bodies they possess might still survive."

"Then that's what we have to do."

"Belinda, exorcism is no guarantee."

"What are my alternatives? I will not allow those two to have this baby. Not only that, I feel like the world needs to know about this. I'm not a demon; I'm a mortal and I'm not prepared to see my kind become the minority. Can you understand that?"

"Absolutely."

"What will all of this mean to you?"

"I'm not really sure. I do know that before you and I even met, I was already growing tired of this existence. So, my survival is the least important thing here. I'm more concerned about your safety and the safety of your child."

"Dante, I've noticed something."

"What?"

"Every time you mention me and the baby, you say 'my baby.' Isn't there even a small possibility that this is 'our' baby."

"A small possibility, but it's much more likely that it's René's."

"I need to know who the father is. How will I find that out? What will a doctor say if he examines the baby? Will he be able to tell it's...different?"

"Usually after seven years, Cambions appear no different than mortals. So, you would probably have to wait until then to allow the child to go to a traditional doctor."

"Do Cambions ever kill their mothers?"

Dante's silence spoke volumes.

TWENTY-FIVE

Chained to this stranger's bed, all he could think of was his wife's azu. Such a simple dish that his wife made from lamb. How many times had he complained about having azu for dinner yet again? At this very moment, he would have given anything just to be able to sit down at his modest dining room table and see the faces of his wife and kids enjoying some of that azu along with him.

At first, he was annoyed more than anything; sure that he had been the butt of some harmless prank or female hazing. That is until he watched her transform. The beautiful woman he had followed home became a ghastly, vile creature when her orgasm was at its strongest. Her stench was like nothing he had ever smelled before; a mixture of death and bodily waste. Even when he tried not to look at her, or held his breath, there was nothing he could do about her bodily secretions. Through the horns that sprouted from her neck and head, gobs of blood dripped and coagulated upon him. Her skin was what death must look like after a body was buried and before it became dust. But, of all these things, her eyes were the most frightening of all. They were like blood boiling in a pot on the stove. Red and bubbling, a cross between blood and pus running from the corners. Whenever possible, he tried not to look at them. It was like a horrible accident in which the victims are mangled and dead; you didn't want to look at it, but you couldn't help it. It was so unreal, you couldn't force yourself to look away, even if you wanted to. What worried him most of all was the remnants of her cum left lingering on his shaft, nauseating him. He was sure if by some miracle he survived this nightmare and was returned home, he would probably walk away from this with some horrible disease. He wondered what kind of STD you could contract from a monstrous creature such as this.

His days were filled with fitful sleep and his racing thoughts…always trying to come up with a way to free himself. He had a cell phone when he arrived at her home and he wondered if it was still somewhere in the apartment or if she had destroyed it. But none of that mattered; the chains he was bound by were impenetrable.

When he thought of freedom, he wondered what he would tell his wife. Would he tell her the truth or some carefully crafted modification of such? Whenever he went over the truth in his mind, he abandoned it. He could just imagine the conversation: 'Honey, I was lured to this beautiful woman's house, one of my passengers, in order to have sex with her, but then she changed into this hideous monster and kept me captive… That's where I've been for the past several weeks.'" Yeah, that would be sure to guarantee him a divorce.

She provided him little food and he wasn't even allowed to go to the bathroom. He was sure that the only reason she fed him was so that she could continue to defile him whenever she liked, which was constantly.

Never could he have imagined that one single indiscretion could have such a devastating outcome. If only he could go back to that night. There was a moment, the night that he first arrived at his prison, that he sat there on the comfortable couch, sipping the finest scotch he had ever tasted, and he considered leaving, while she was in the shower. There would have been no uncomfortable explanations; no temptation, he could have simply walked out the door. And, maybe, if he was lucky, she wouldn't have cared and he would never have seen her again.

He heard the key turn in the lock and knew she had returned; his hell was not over.

"I see you've been pulling at the chains again. You're doing nothing more than causing undue pain for yourself. Look at your wrists; your ankles. They are bloodied and soon infection will set in. Is that what you want?"

Her question was clearly rhetorical since she had yet to remove the heavy tape adhered to his lips. Even when the tape was removed, he was only capable of speaking when she allowed him to. He had tried several times to yell, to scream, even to beg her for mercy and if she decided she didn't want to hear him, the only words spoken were in his head. So, he had taken to body language, as he was doing now. Shaking his head by way of communicating, "Please, have mercy." All his actions produced were mere smiles from her lips. She must have felt some iota of benevolence, if even for a moment, because she allowed him to speak.

"I can't. I have nothing left."

"The only reason you're still alive is because you have plenty left. As long as you're alive, you have something left to nourish me. You do, indeed, have something left; and I will have it. You just need a bit of encouragement; that's all."

Diana had converted her one-bedroom apartment into a two-bedroom. The second bedroom was cleverly concealed in order to allow her privacy for visitors such as Vlad.

She kept him chained to the four-poster bed, with his mouth taped shut, while she was out for the day. When she returned, she removed the tape, since all she needed to do was control him to keep him from screaming.

She joined him on the bed, her hair fanning about his naked and bound limbs. She took his dick into her mouth and sucked him until he sprang to life. Vlad would have liked nothing more than to remain limp and unresponsive. However, with each lick of her tongue, with each deep suctioning suck from her mouth, he became stiffer. It was sick; and he was repulsed by his own involuntary moans, which escaped as his body writhed beneath the chains that kept him prone.

"Let me know when you're ready. Don't you dare waste a bit of your nectar in my mouth; it will do me no good there. Don't test me, or your penalty will be quite severe."

He listened to her words and wondered how much more severe it could possibly be and assumed she must be talking about death, since that was the only way this could get any worse.

"Oh. Oh. Okay."

Up and down she stroked him, holding him firmly with her mouth; opening up, the tingle of the slight air which got in exciting him, keeping him from cumming. Her tongue traced the head of his dick, flicking the hole at the tip, sucking on his balls, before he was ready.

"Now, now, I'm ready now. Just do it. Just fucking do it!"

She mounted his dick and the grip her pussy held on him was at first excruciating. He had never felt anything so tightly wrapped around him. Not even with the control of his own hands had he felt such a vise grip on his member.

"You beg me to let you go, but your dick is so hard. You don't really want to go, do you? I can feel that you don't want to leave me. So, just give it to me. Give me what I need. I want your seed for more than just my pleasure, Vlad. I need it to survive. Would you deny me my own survival? Give it to me. I need it."

She rode him relentlessly; her body maintaining a speed and rhythm impossible for mere mortals.

"You like that, don't you, Vlad? Don't you? I can feel how much you like it. Don't hold back. You were meant for this. You were chosen to preserve me. It is a great honor."

"GRrrrrrr!" Vlad couldn't resist. He knew he should have had more self-control. But he couldn't. His response was purely a byproduct of nature. There was nothing that could have kept him from giving her exactly what she wanted. His hot cum blasted deep inside of her and Diana knew it. His purpose had been served, at least for tonight.

Dante had begun to make things very difficult for them all and if it were up to Diana, she would have destroyed him a long time ago. For all his condemnation of mortals and their *feelings*, René had grown just as soft as Dante. There was a time when no demon would think twice to preserve its own existence, no matter what the price to another's. Although he never spoke the words, she knew René had a certain respect for Dante that prevented him from carrying out the actions of a true demon.

For so long, Cambions were ostracized by mortals and demons alike. Diana and René decided a long time ago that the stronger, more powerful Cambions would ensure every incubus and succubus on earth invincibility. Instead of hiding in plain sight, afraid of being recognized by mortals, it would be the mortals that would be forced to hide. They would become little more than animals on a farm; their only purpose being to maintain the demon life force. Cambions were cunning creatures; and they were now angry creatures. They were sick and tired of being abandoned by their mortal and demon parents and René was working toward harnessing that anger and strength and garnering trust from the Cambions so that their only alliance would be with the demons that bore them.

Other demons agreed with their plan of action. But there were some of them, like Dante, who were resistant to change and preferred things remain as they had been. An existence which René believed left them; the stronger beings, subservient to mortals, while they stole what they needed in order to survive. René no longer wanted to exist like some sort of thief in the night. He demanded that the mortals recognize his power and bow to it, as it should be.

From the very first moment Diana began to consider the possibility, she thought of nothing else. Her every action was set into motion to achieve that very purpose.

And, whether René wanted it or not, Dante had to either submit or be destroyed. She would discuss with René one more time, the ramifications of Dante's constant opposition to their purpose.

If René chose to disagree, she would have to take matters into her own hands.

Before leaving for the night, Diana proceeded with

her ritual with Vlad. She proceeded to tape his mouth.

"Please don't. When you're not here, I can barely breathe. I promise, I won't scream. Please don't put the tape back on."

Diana considered his request and decided he had submitted enough to allow him this small freedom.

Vlad heard the door shut and uttered a sigh of relief. One more night, and he was still alive. But that wouldn't last for long. For the umpteenth time, he looked around the sparsely furnished room, searching for anything he could use as a weapon. He had been doing the same thing since the very first day he arrived. Yet, now, he noticed something he hadn't before. There were curtains. And where there were curtains, there had to be a curtain rod. He had no idea how much time he would have. But it was now or never, he would have to find a way to pull that curtain down along with the rod, tuck it away somewhere out of sight, and use it against her when she returned.

TWENTY-SIX

"Just how much do you want this?" Diana asked him.

"Need you ask me that? I want it just as much as you do. But, why are you asking me that question now?"

"Because before we go any further, I need to know just how important this is to you. And, if it is as important as you say it is, there is only one solution to this. Dante's got to go. He's become far more trouble than he's worth."

"Diana, we've got to think about this."

"Oh no, don't tell me. Now you've got cotton balls like your friend, Dante."

"My balls are just fine. Thank you very much. I'm not as quick as you to forget about the possible outcomes of our actions. And, may I say, you, my friend, need to slow your roll before you get somewhere you can't get out of."

"Don't worry about me. My balls are just fine. And, my fear is in perspective. But, I'm sick of playing this game with Dante. He changed the rules and now he expects the rest of us to play along. Well, I'm not playing. I liked the game just the way it was. And, I intend it to stay that way."

"What are you talking about?"

"You know exactly what I'm talking about. We hand-picked the incubus that would sire the Cambions. They had to be the brightest, the strongest and the most powerful; just as we handpicked the human female that would give birth. Not just any mortal/demon combination will do. We are working toward the best of the best here. However, none of this means anything if we allow a mortal to raise these Cambion offsprings."

"That is, of course, not going to happen. And, I'm not sure why you're spending time worrying about this. I believe there is more going on here than meets the eye. You have always been envious of Dante's power. Are you sure that's not why you're trying to create dissension among us?"

From the moment the words escaped his lips, Diana knew any action she took against Dante would be on her own. The line in the sand had been drawn.

"It is most important that we stand together, Diana. Each day Dante is becoming more diminished. Eventually survival will allow him to see what is truly important. But your pushing him will only encourage an even greater divide. You must, for once, sit back and allow the inevitable to unfold."

Diana couldn't stand to listen to him yammer on any longer. She left René's luxury high-rise and, mostly out of anger, she lured his doorman into a laundry room and drained him until he was just barely skin and bones.

If she had known what was going on back at her apartment, she would have spent less time exacting petty revenge and more time ensuring that her secret was not found out.

"Shit!"

Vlad had worked tirelessly to pull the curtain from the window; swinging his feet to pull at the end of the curtain with the heel of his shoe. He would have liked to be able to plant his entire foot on the curtain and slowly tug at it until it fell. But his foot just barely reached and his heel was all he could muster within the short distance. He became frightened at every noise, since he didn't know when she would be returning. He had listened as his wife shouted at the kids in their native tongue enough times because they had knocked the curtain down. He could almost hear her voice: 'Прекратите тянуть занавески от окон.' Why then was it taking him so long to do the exact same thing now?

Finally, it fell and with it came the intended object. It didn't appear very menacing, but most anything could be fashioned into a weapon with a bit of effort; especially something made of metal.

He was sure that she would be returning soon. But, it would take very little time to prepare the rod to act as a weapon. Then he would be free. At first he considered attempting to use the pointed end of the curtain rod as a key to free himself from the chains, but that would take far too long and by that time, she would have returned. Instead, he continued with his original intention. He first flattened the rod so that it was no longer rounded in the middle but completely flat. He then extended the ends, flattening the areas closest to the end, so that the points were much more pronounced. Just minutes before, he heard the key turn in the lock, he folded it in half and secured it in a corner of the mattress, preparing to strike at the most optimum time.

Along with draining his manhood, apparently his time spent here had also drained him of logical thought. It never occurred to him that she would most probably walk in, and immediately notice the missing curtain. He hoped she would be so preoccupied with the nasty things she was going to do to him, that she would pay no attention to the window; especially since the shades still blocked out any light.

He was relieved when she removed all of her clothing and set about her usual routine. He would have to wait until he was inside of her, but before she transformed. He believed that was the only way his plan would work. Once inside of her, her body rising and falling on top of his, Vlad slowly slid the rod from beneath the mattress.

"Oh, Vlad, you weren't going to use that on me, were you?" she whispered in his ear, before transforming and biting into that very same ear, removing it from his head.

Vlad's gurgled screams became trapped in his throat along with the blood that eventually choked him to death, but not before Diana secured one more ounce of liquid energy for herself.

René watched the news as remnants of Diana's actions unfolded on the screen:

"Forty-seven-year-old Vladimir Shoelenko, a driver with Delta Car Service who was missing for several weeks, was found dead this morning, an apparent victim of a homicide. His car was found abandoned and stripped in an alleyway in Harlem three weeks ago. Shoelenko's dispatcher at Delta became concerned when radio calls made to Shoelenko went unanswered and Mr. Shoelenko failed to return home to his family. Mr. Shoelenko leaves behind a wife and five children. His murder is still under investigation and The New York City Police Department is asking anyone who may know anything about Shoelenko's murder to contact NYPD's CRIME-STOPPERS Tips Line at 800-577-TIPS.

"And in other news, a doorman, Frank Micesso, at a luxury high-rise located at 112 East 84th Street, was found dead in a laundry room on the premises. Apparently, a resident contacted police when she arrived home to find no doorman on duty. An autopsy is pending and police have not out-ruled foul play as a cause of death."

His apartment building was teeming with police officers, news reporters and countless others. René resolved to keep a low profile all day, never leaving his apartment. He knew exactly who had wrought this havoc so near to where he lived. It was clearly Diana and she had probably killed the driver as well. With all her talk of

Dante ruining things, she was creating far more problems for them than Dante ever could. Instead of concerning himself with Dante, he wondered if he should be focusing his attention on Diana instead.

While he had begun to learn from his mistakes and had grown more and more careful about maintaining a low profile, Diana had not.

He called Diana as soon as the news broadcast went off.

"So I see you've been a busy little beaver."

"What are you talking about?"

"Don't play dumb with me, Diana. I know your trademark well."

"So, what if it was me?"

"You know what I never do, Diana: 'Shit where I live.' And, quite frankly, I don't appreciate *you* shitting where I live either. You will control yourself and you will do it now. Do you understand me?"

"What are you, my keeper? When did it become your responsibility to guide me? That's you and Dante, not me. I am in control of my own guidance."

"I don't give a shit what you do, but when it starts to affect me, that's another story entirely. You will keep your drama from my door, or suffer the consequences!"

"So, now you're threatening me? You're becoming more and more like Dante every day."

"Right now, looking from my window at the police cars and news reporters and countless others gawking at the scene you played out here last night, I consider that a compliment. I now understand Dante cautioning us all to remain below the radar. Your actions may indeed draw attention to us all and undo all that we have worked toward."

"Dante is a frightened mortal wannabe. I don't walk in fear. I embrace my freedom and my power over these mortals. Dante will never be capable of knowing such dominion."

"Yes, Diana, but how long will you last? Surely, not as long as he has."

"I'd rather not walk the earth as long as he has, if it means me doing it with shackles upon my feet."

The knock on René's door ended the conversation.

"I'm sure that's probably the police now, going door to door. Thanks a whole fucking lot, Diana," he whispered.

René hung up the phone, so he could open the door. The last thing he wanted to do was to create suspicion.

"Is your name René Vitale?"

"Yes, officers, it is."

"We're investigating the death of your night doorman. He appears to have been killed late last night."

"Oh, it was murder? I've been watching the news and they hadn't mentioned that he was murdered."

"That's why we're investigating."

"I guess that makes sense. He was a young guy. What was he? Thirty-seven? Thirty-eight years old?"

"Yeah, about that… So, Mr. Vitale, were you home last night?"

"Yes, I was."

"Did anyone visit you?"

"Yeah... A friend of mine, Dr. Crandall, stopped by, but just for a few minutes."

"How long is a few minutes?"

"I'm not really sure, maybe fifteen minutes; a half-hour? I wasn't really paying that much attention to the time."

"Do you have Dr. Crandall's phone number?"

"Yes, I believe it's in my cell phone." René crossed the room to get his phone. "It's 212-555-3814."

"Thank you, Mr. Vitale. Are you a doctor as well?"

"No, I'm not."

"What do you do?"

"I've made some very savvy investments over time that afforded me the opportunity to retire young."

"And what did you do before you retired?"

"Pretty much nothing." He chuckled. "I'm what would be called *old money*. My parents were kind enough to leave me well-fixed when they passed away."

"Must be nice."

"Yeah, I guess it is."

"Well, if you think of anything that you may have noticed last night, don't hesitate to give me a call. You can ask for Detective Simon."

The detective handed René his card.

"I'll make sure I do that."

René closed the door and sighed. Diana's actions were now ushering New York City police detectives to his door. This was no longer just annoying. It was starting to affect his very way of life.

TWENTY-SEVEN

Summer wouldn't have even considered asking Kaleel for help if she were not completely desperate. She considered bringing Keyanna along to soften the encounter and also to allow her daughter to see her father, if even for a moment; and from within the walls of a prison. Instead, she maintained her resolve, and decided that wasn't what was best for her daughter.

The bus ride alone was enough to make her appreciate her decision. Standing on line, waiting to board the bus, looking around at the people that were boarding the bus with her, she was happy she had taken steps to ensure that this did not become her life. After all, she had a strong foundation, good parents, and a good education. There was no reason at all she had to fall prey to the stereotype and she wasn't going to allow her daughter to do so either. She had to work on herself a bit more; become more motivated about her future. But, at least, she wasn't married to a jail bird and she wasn't in prison herself, while a family member raised her child—like so many other women she knew.

That's one of the reasons she wasn't sure it was a good

idea to reach out to Kaleel. With her divorce from their marriage, she had also divorced herself from so many other things. When she remembered the days when she stood by and watched as Kaleel sold drugs out of their home, she couldn't believe she had been that stupid. She often thanked her lucky stars that she hadn't ended up in prison right along with Kaleel and if he had been a different man, she probably would have. Kaleel may have been a criminal, but he was also a good man. Some people didn't believe that the two could walk hand in hand. But, she had seen it up close and personal and she knew it was possible.

The bus ride was long and the bus itself was smelly and the conversations that went on were not to be believed. There were crying children and pregnant women, some of which looked ready to pop at any moment.

Once she arrived at the prison she felt as much like a criminal as the person she was visiting. She brought a few things for Kaleel that were on the list of acceptable items; like soap and toothpaste. The one thing she was sure *not* to bring, however, was cologne. It pissed her off to no end, when he asked her to bring him some cologne. What the hell a man in prison needed with cologne she didn't know, but she had no intention of bringing him any. She almost felt offended by him asking. Here he was in prison while his daughter constantly asked her where her daddy was, and he had the fucking nerve to fix his lips and ask her to bring him some damn cologne. Not a chance in hell!

"Singer, you have a visitor."

Kaleel was more than a little surprised when he first learned that Summer would be visiting. He never got visitors anymore. His own mother had stopped coming years ago. Although he would have liked to see his daughter, deep down inside he knew it was best that her memories of him not be that of prison bars. Still, he would have liked to at least see her every now and then.

Kaleel and Summer had been together since they were kids in school, so Kaleel was shocked when Summer divorced him. He always thought there would be an unbreakable bond, no matter what came between them; especially after they had a child together. What Kaleel couldn't realize was it was *because* they had a child together that Summer had to let him go.

"Hey, Summer. I was hoping you surprised me and brought baby girl. But, I understand why you didn't."

"She's with my parents. I considered bringing her, but I still don't think it's a very good idea to bring her here. This is really not the place for a small child. I would much rather you see one another under different circumstances."

"I guess by then, she'll be old enough to come and visit me herself. Or, have you forgotten how long I'm in here for?"

This was a never-ending. It was difficult for Kaleel to understand why Summer couldn't bring his daughter to see him every once in a while.

Before Summer could quote her commonly used mantra, Kaleel stopped her.

"I know, we're going to have to agree to disagree on this one. The problem with that is, you pretty much hold all the cards, since I'm a captive prisoner here and all."

"Kaleel, can we talk about something else? It's actually something pretty important. And, it affects both me and Keyanna. I need your help."

"What do you need…money?"

"No. We're okay in that area. Thanks for that, by the way."

"It's the least I could do, right?"

"Yeah, but not every man would have."

"I keep trying to tell you, baby, I ain't your ordinary man."

"That's damn sure the truth. So will you help me or not?"

"I have to hear what you need first. As you can see, I'm not exactly at maximum potential here."

"Yeah, but you still got more connections than most men on the outside."

"Okay, that's enough. You can stop stroking my ego. What do you need?"

"I knew you would help me."

"You know it, girl. I've always got your back, no matter what.

"You remember my friend, Belinda, right?"

"Of course I do; a little bourgeois, mocha-brown, nice legs, cute face. Yeah, I remember her vaguely."

"My friend's not bourgeois."

"I'm just messin' wit ya."

"Anyway, she met this guy and I think he might be bad news."

"You want me to get somebody to fuck him up?"

"No, no! It's nothing like that; at least not yet. I just want to know who he is…all of who he is. Do you know someone that can check him out…really check him out? Not just the surface shit, but a complete run-down."

"Yeah, I think that can be arranged."

"What do you need from me?"

"Well, first, I'm gonna need a name. An address, if you got it; any family members? Anything you got, no matter how unimportant it sounds. If this guy is obsessed with tangelos, give me that too…everything."

"Oh, and Kaleel could you also have Diana checked out?"

"Not your friend, the doctor?"

"Yeah, one and the same."

"Okay, Summer, so what's goin' on? You sound like you're into some deep shit here."

"It could be; I just want to see how deep."

"Don't forget you've got our baby to take care of."

"How could I ever forget that?"

Summer knew there were more important things to think about, but right then and there she felt like reminding him who was sitting in a jail cell while *she* had all the responsibility of caring for *their* child. She still needed his help, so she held her tongue.

"Thanks, baby," was all she said.

Summer knew they would most likely find nothing, but since Diana and Dante knew all there was to know about them, she felt it was time she stepped up her game and did some of her own investigating.

Even after all these years, Kaleel never ceased to amaze her. Three days after she had gone to see him in prison and given him all the information he needed, her doorbell rang and when she looked out the window, there was a FedEx truck parked out front. For a split second, she was afraid to open the door. She was always on edge lately and not keen on surprises of any kind.

"I have a FedEx delivery for Summer Johnson," the deliveryman announced through the intercom. She buzzed him in.

"I need your signature."

She signed the envelope and took it inside her apartment and sat down at the couch.

It was an honest to goodness report, from a detective agency. She couldn't believe it. It was definitely not what she expected from Kaleel, but better than what she anticipated.

The report outlined everything; social security numbers, former addresses, former employers. There were even pictures included. The interesting thing was, according to Dante Rivers' report, he was 115 years old. And, Diana Crandall's report listed her medical license as suspended.

The report had not revealed much more than she already knew, but there was definitely something not right. If nothing else, it had given her an ace in the hole, if things got out of control.

Kaleel called Summer collect the next day.

"You know I had to read that report before you got it, right?"

"Yeah, I knew you'd be all up in my business."

"So what's up with that? Diana's license is suspended. And who the hell is Dante Rivers? His info can't possibly be legit. Anybody could look at that shit and see dates don't match up. How the hell has he gotten away with that? If that was my peeps, he wouldn't be out there like that. According to that shit, he's 115 years old. What kinda shit is that and how is he even able to use those papers in any kinda way?"

Summer had no intention of telling him the real deal; that both Diana and Dante were some sort of creatures and his ass probably really was 115 years old; maybe even older. At least she knew that Diana was indeed from this century, although she was a damn sight older than she was pretending to be.

"So what do you plan on doing with this information?"

"I'm just gonna use it as a sort of…insurance policy. And, that probably won't even work. But, if nothing else, it might buy me some time. I do appreciate it though. Thanks a lot, Kaleel."

"You know I love you, girl!"

"Kaleel, you are as crazy as a damn loon!" She laughed. "So, when do you want me to bring your daughter to see you?"

"You for real?"

"Yeah. I guess so. We all make mistakes. And, it's not like we didn't all enjoy the fruits of your labor. Far be it for me to be a hypocrite. So, what about next week?"

"Yeah, that's good!"

Thinking of Kaleel grinning from ear to ear, she had to admit that there were some fathers that could not care less whether or not they *ever* saw their children again. She wasn't thrilled about riding that bus and she was even less thrilled about the prospect of bringing Keyanna into a prison, but like she said, she too could have been sitting exactly where Kaleel was sitting.

"We'll see how it goes when Keyanna visits and maybe we can have her visit on a regular basis. But, we'll have to see. Also, I've been considering sending my parents and Keyanna on a little mini-vacation, but I'm not sure yet, so if I do, the other visits would have to happen after she gets back."

"What's the occasion?"

"No occasion, just a little vacation. They've been retired forever and still haven't gone someplace really fun."

"You gonna take Keyanna out of school just so she can go on vacation with your folks? Summer, what the fuck is going on! You know damn well, I know what that means. You don't just pick up and decide to send your folks and Keyanna out of town on a dime. So what kind of shit you got yourself mixed up in and how can I help?"

"I'm okay, Kaleel, really. None of this is anything serious. It's nothing I can't handle."

"You sure about that?"

"Yeah, I'm sure."

Kaleel let it drop, even though he didn't believe her.

TWENTY-EIGHT

"There's one thing I neglected to mention to you, when we had our talk."

"You mean there's something else. I don't think I can take one more surprise."

"Belinda, my life-force is leaving me with each passing day. I haven't restored in weeks; and with you pregnant I'm afraid to count on you for my restoration."

"But, Dante, I'm fine. I actually feel healthier and stronger than I've felt in a long time."

"Yeah, probably because René has stopped visiting you and I haven't touched you in a few days."

"No, I don't think it's that at all. I think it's the baby. He's very strong. I can feel him, growing inside of me, bringing me strength. It's incredible."

The last thing Belinda wanted was to consent to Dante returning to his old ways. But, he would eventually be gone if he didn't.

"If I can't help you, then I think you should go back to Redemption or some other club and get what you need."

"I can't. Now that I've found you, I am different. I don't think I could just continue where I left off."

"But you have to. You can't leave me here alone, with a baby. But, for now, let me give you what you need."

TWENTY-NINE

S tanding in the middle of his cell, poised and ready to mount the raging hard-on he had gotten started with his hand, was a beautiful naked woman...a woman that bore a striking resemblance to Summer's doctor friend. He was sure he had to be dreaming and that it was probably brought on by the investigation and his talks with Summer. For the moment, all Kaleel could think of was Lady Godiva and how much he was going to enjoy this wet dream.

Her hair reached past her impressively round ass and tickled her hard, red nipples. He should have been banging the bars for the guards to come, but his cock was doing the thinking.

"Oh, baby, you're big. I've been lookin' for a man like you my whole life."

"I should be asking you what the fuck you're doin here in the middle of the night, but sweetheart, all I'm thinkin' about right now is those lips of yours slobbin' my knob."

"Uhm, I love a man who knows exactly what he wants."

Diana had a gift for knowing what most men needed to get off. She had to know. If they didn't get off, she didn't replenish her energy supply.

She bent down and quickly spit on Kaleel's cock. As her spittle slid down the length of his steed and landed on the floor, Kaleel began stroking his own cock with his right hand.

"Come here, baby. Let me feed you some of this dick."

And that he did. He was surprised to find that no matter how much of his long, thick cock he shoved into his mysterious visitor's mouth, she met his thrusts with an equal level of hunger, spitting and sucking, until his member was fully bathed. He was so engaged, he almost forgot about his cell mate, until he saw him standing there, cock in hand, spewing wildly onto Diana's back.

"Uhm," she moaned, with her mouth still firmly planted on his cock. "I do believe I'm being double-teamed," she uttered between licks and sucks.

For a moment the presence of his cellmate brought Kaleel back to the reality of the situation he found himself in. He was in a prison cell in the middle of the night and being visited by a beautiful naked woman. He wasn't that far gone that he couldn't recognize this was no dream. And he knew damn well he wasn't insane. So, the only choice left was that he was being set up.

"Yo, yo, yo, hold up, Shorty. How the fuck did you get in here? Brick, you know this?"

"Naw, man. I thought this was you. You the big man. I thought you had the hook up."

"See, now I know your ass is as crazy as they say. How the fuck you think I got some pussy delivered to my cell like a damn pizza and shit?"

"How the fuck am I supposed to know? Didn't you just ask me the same damn question?"

Diana's complete and total lack of concern allowed her to continue her efforts on Kaleel's cock, but sadly, he had begun to lose momentum. She definitely couldn't have that. Since 'Brick' was clearly the dumber of the two, Diana decided the only way to get what she needed would be to get a little rivalry going. Hell, she would be ahead of the game, since it never occurred to her that she would be able to get two for the effort of one.

"Brick? Is that what your name is? Are you ready to put it to work? I think maybe I'm not Kaleel's cup of tea. But you know what to do with a steaming hot pussy, don't you?"

It took no more effort than that. Any questions about how a woman had made her way to their locked prison cell long forgotten, Brick lifted his cum-coated dick to Diana's mouth and fed her. She could tell from his movements that he had little to no control and sucking him off did nothing for her. She needed him inside of her in order to reap the benefits. She removed her mouth from his tool and bent over spread eagle, while gripping the bars of the cell. Brick's eyes were saucers, while Kaleel also abandoned any thoughts of the absurdity of Diana's presence. While Diana waited impatiently for Brick's cock to enter her, she could hear both men begin to fight over who would be first. Diana turned, and with more strength than the clueless men even considered, she pushed the near 300-pound Brick to the floor with ease, mounting him just as swiftly as he landed.

"You like that?" she said.

"Hell yeah. This pussy is tight, baby. Real tight."

"You want some more?"

"Shit yeah. Damn, baby, are you a virgin. I...I...never felt any...any...anythinnnggggg...

His breathing soon became extremely labored and he was incapable of speaking. While Kaleel stroked his own cock, waiting his turn, he watched as the life physically drained from his cellmate. At first, he thought it was just tricks the lack of light was playing on his eyes; until he saw the 300-pound Brick appear to decrease in size. Yet, he was still alive. What she was doing to his cock far outweighed any other sensations he might have felt.

"Brick, man! Yo, Brick! Something's wrong with that bitch! Oh shit!"

Diana finally dismounted Brick's cock, just in time for Kaleel to see the jagged teeth that had undoubtedly severed his cock at the root.

"Now it's your turn."

Diana saw to it that Kaleel's screams were never heard by the rest of the prison. And, despite his anguish, there was still enough of an erection present to allow her to leave with what she came for. Summer would no longer be able to call on him and his associates to interfere with her intentions. She had not only seen to that, but she had also secured two more souls to sustain her.

Before she left, she stopped and spoke to Kaleel's life-less figure.

"Maybe now your ex-wife will keep her nose out of my affairs," she said.

"Hi, Gramma! You sound funny."

"Mommy! Gramma's on the phone!"

Summer was running the dishwasher and hadn't even heard the phone ring.

"Keyanna, what did I tell you about answering that phone before asking me?"

All she heard was sobbing.

"Mom, you've gotta calm down. I can't understand you."

"Summer. It's...it's Kaleel. He's dead!"

Suddenly it dawned on her. This wasn't her mom; it was Mrs. Singer, Kaleel's mom.

"He can't be. I just saw him. I went to the prison and spoke to him face to face."

"It happened last night."

"He can't be!"

"I'm sorry, baby, but he is."

"I went to see him and I didn't even bring Keyanna. All this time I didn't want her to see her father behind bars. Now, she'll never see him again."

"Don't do that to yourself, Summer. Only a good

mother would even consider that. At least you got a chance to see him. I stopped visiting. I couldn't stand to see my son behind bars any longer."

"Momma S, Kaleel loved you very much. He knew how you felt about him."

"Really? I did love him. I wanted so much more for him than he chose. Now look, he's gone."

"Do you need anything?" Summer asked.

"No, everything should be fine. I'll make all the arrangements. I will probably need a suit, though. You know how Kaleel liked to look clean. That boy could dress. And, he didn't like that cheap stuff either. Boy, he could dress."

Her voice trailed off into a fresh set of tears as she reminisced about her only son.

"A mother ain't supposed to bury her child. It ain't supposed to happen."

"You want me to come over; keep you company?"

"No. I'll be alright; Kaleel's sister is here."

"I still have a few of Kaleel's clothes here. I'm pretty sure there's at least one suit in there, maybe more than one."

"Thanks, Summer. I'll talk to you later, okay?"

"I'll give you a call later, check on you."

"That would be nice. Maybe I'll be calmer by then and I can talk to my granddaughter."

"Yeah. She would like that."

"What are you going to tell her?"

"I don't know. Momma S, you didn't say how it happened."

"One of those jail birds must have done it or one of the guards. His brother told me one of his boys inside said Kaleel was torn apart...and in the middle of the night. How could something like that happen without anyone knowing?"

Summer agonized all day over the news. Although she had divorced Kaleel, she still cared about him as Keyanna's father and as a friend she had shared so much with him for so many years. Now he was gone. His mother had no son, his daughter no father, and she had lost her protector.

She considered calling Belinda, but realized she was dealing with enough and didn't need to hear any more bad news. When the first tear fell, she realized how much Kaleel's death had affected her. That's when her mind grasped the truth; she would never see him again, nor would their daughter. Keyanna had not only lost her great-grandmother, but now she had no father. Summer had always been such a strong woman, never leaning on anyone. She had always been the person that everyone else leaned on. Now, she felt so alone. Even though she initially talked herself out of reaching out to Belinda, she quickly changed her mind because no matter what Belinda was going through, she would still have her back.

"Belinda," she spoke through her tears.

"Summer? Is that you?"

"Yes."

"What's wrong?"

As soon as she asked her what was wrong, Summer fell apart. "He's dead, Bee! Kaleel is dead!"

"Oh no, Summer! What happened?"

"According to his mother, the official report from the prison is that he and his cellmate killed one another, but I don't believe it. Kaleel had that same cellmate for at least three years. It doesn't make sense. There was never any conflict between them. If anything, Kaleel always told me how much respect his cellmate had for him. Do you think they could have gotten to him somehow?"

"Summer, there was a time when I wouldn't have believed any of what has happened, but now, I just don't know. None of this makes any sense in the real world. But, the world we thought we were living in was just a façade. Never in my life has that old cliché made more sense: 'Ignorance is Bliss.' I wish I could go back to the way things were, when I had no awareness of what was taking place around me. Have you told Keyanna yet?"

"No. I'm such a coward. I'm afraid. I don't know what to tell her. She's only five. She's lost her great-grand-mother and now her father. How is a five-year-old supposed to understand that?"

"First of all, Summer, the last thing you are is a coward. You're the strongest person I know. I know it's probably not fair, but every time I think about the situation I find myself in, I know I'm going to be okay, because I've got you."

"All I've been doing is crying. I'm a fucking mess."

"You're entitled. How is Kaleel's mom doing?"

"Even though Kaleel was a career criminal and she had probably already resigned herself to Kaleel's fate, she's a mother. No mother wants to bury their child."

"I'm starting to understand that more and more."

Summer was so focused on Kaleel and Keyanna, she completely missed the meaning in what Belinda had said. Belinda decided now would probably not be the best time to talk to her about it anyway. She had enough on her plate.

Summer wasn't sure what to tell Keyanna or how. She hadn't seen very much of her father in her five years, but she still knew she had a father. Summer decided honesty would be best.

"Keyanna, come here. I have something very grown-up that I need to speak with you about."

"Okay, Mommy, I'll be there in a minute. Okay?"

Normally Summer would have insisted that Keyanna drop whatever she was doing when she called her and come right away. Under the circumstances, she thought it best to wait patiently. Hearing that her father was dead was more than enough to swallow in a day, without adding to it.

Keyanna came tearing out of her bedroom like someone was chasing her.

"Yeah, Mommy?"

"Keyanna, I explained to you what death means, right?"

"You mean like when GG died?"

"Yes, like when your great-grandma died."

"Yeah, I know. GG went to heaven and if you're bad, you go to hell. When you go to heaven there's your favorite foods and there's a ginormous toy store and everybody you ever loved that died is there…including your pets. But when someone goes to hell, there's a devil dressed in red with horns and a lot of fire and you have to burn in the fire without dying because you're already dead."

Summer made a mental note to more closely monitor what her daughter was watching on TV.

"Well, everybody sees heaven and hell differently. But, yeah, GG went to heaven. Someone else died and I wanted to tell you about it. You'll probably be sad, like you were when GG died, and it's okay. If you feel really sad, you can come and talk to me or if you want to cry, you can cry. It's okay."

"Who died?"

"Your dad, honey."

Summer picked Keyanna up and put her on her lap. She could see that Keyanna's young mind wasn't quite sure how to process the information she had just received; whether she should be sad or confused or curious.

"Will Daddy go to heaven?"

"Of course he will."

"But I thought bad guys went to hell. Daddy was a bad guy."

"Your dad made mistakes. But, Keyanna, your father wasn't a bad man. He just made bad decisions."

"So when I go to heaven, I can see Daddy again."

"Yes, honey, you will. But that probably won't be for a very, very long time. Okay?"

"Okay, Mommy. Can I go play now?"

Summer had never been a strong believer in therapists, but at this very moment, she silently wished there was one she could call upon to ask for advice about her daughter. She wasn't sure if she should be concerned about her daughter's apparent nonchalance. After all, what was the normal reaction of a five-year-old to the death of a parent you only remembered seeing a handful of times from the confines of prison?

Both Belinda and Summer were becoming concerned about the mounting death toll and disappearances that seemed to be suddenly surrounding them.

THIRTY

"Why did you give those detectives my name and number?"

"Survival of the fittest, my dear. Besides, aren't you the one so proud of being able to walk around shackle-free? Deal with it! I wasn't about to sacrifice myself for the sake of you. You walk into my home, kill my door-man, and expect not to leave some sort of a trail. Yes, I understand they are stupid mortals. But, they are not completely brain dead. That detective was very inter-ested in both of us. You wanna know why? I'm sure it's either because you signed in downstairs when you came up to see me or, if you disposed of your signature, then it's because they've got you on camera."

"Do I look like a fucking amateur to you? Of course, there is no signature and no camera."

"Um, I am gaining a newfound respect for you. So, they will find nothing?"

"Nothing."

"Excellent. Then I guess you have nothing to worry about."

"No."

Dante would usually show up at René's place unannounced. As he watched the drama unfold on his television screen, he knew the best place for him was far away from René and Diana. He knew it was her as surely as he knew his own name. Only Diana would be brazen. He understood her psyche well. Without even knowing the specific circumstances of the previous night, she and René had most probably had a disagreement of some sort and in her rage she had done something that was sure to anger René. She was out of control. Her latest demonstration made him fear for Belinda all the more. He realized he had to put some thought into moving Belinda someplace safe. And, maybe even Summer along with her. Belinda didn't have much family, but Diana would know who to get at to hurt Belinda the most. That would be Summer and her family.

Dante began to wonder if their disagreement might have involved him and/or Belinda. If it had maybe he had some leverage to work on René. He knew it was all a game for René and maybe if he grew tired of playing, for whatever the reason, both he and Belinda could slip away, undetected.

He tried to slip into René's apartment undetected, so that he wouldn't be noticed by all the curious onlookers. He was in René's apartment within minutes, anxious to appeal to him for what was left of Belinda's soul.

"René, I've never asked anything of you, but if I have

to I will beg you now. Please leave her alone. She's an innocent. You don't need her."

"You want to liken her to an innocent, but she isn't. I would never have been able to enter her world if her thoughts were not deeply entrenched in exactly what I offered to her. I opened up her world to something she already wanted. If anything, I freed her. She was drowning in her ordinary life. Most of these mortals are."

"There was a time when I told myself that same lie. That is, until I realized that what a mortal thinks and what he does can often be greatly contradicting."

"Yeah. Whatever you say. All I know is I've seen more women than I'm capable of counting that would rather die than close the door on the opportunity to fuck me one more time."

"Especially when you're controlling their minds."

"You believe what you will, Dante. But, your Belinda, she wanted it just as much as every other mortal woman that came before her."

THIRTY-ONE

Summer ran the conversation in her mind over and over again; sure she had misinterpreted something or misunderstood something. But, she hadn't. The truth had been staring them in their faces for weeks now. The plain and simple truth was, neither of them wanted to admit it. There was evil among them. And, now, Belinda had been touched by it more directly than any person ever should be.

"Summer, I don't know any other way to say this but directly. I'm pregnant."

"See, I told you you were pregnant. Did you tell Aidan?"

"It's not Aidan's baby. It's Dante's; or at least I hope it's Dante's, since the alternative is far too horrifying."

"That freak. Why would you want it to be his?"

"Come on, Summer; let me explain before you condemn. Okay?"

"Okay, then explain."

"This is not an over the phone kind of conversation."

"Okay, then just give me the gist of it."

"Well, the gist of it is, it looks like your grandmother

was probably right. Dante is what you would call an incubus and I believe his friends are as well, including Diana."

"You're awfully calm about this."

"What else can I be? Ranting and raving isn't going to help me any. What's done has been done."

"Have you given thought to an abortion?"

"I tried. I made an appointment and everything, got to the place and it was like something prevented me from following through. I couldn't even set foot through the door."

"Belinda, you can't just let all of this unfold. You've got to come up with some sort of a plan. You know that, don't you?"

"Of course I do. It's just at this very moment, I'm all out of ideas."

"You know what they say, don't you: 'Two heads are better than one.'"

"Bee, I've got some things I need to take care of, but when I'm done, I'm gonna call you, so we can hook up. Okay?"

"Okay, Summer. I'll be here. I haven't got enough energy to be anywhere else. At least, until they kick me out of my apartment. I haven't worked for weeks. I've got a little saved, but that's gonna run out quick, fast and in a hurry."

"Don't worry about a thing. We'll talk. For every problem, there is a solution."

"You think so, huh?"

"I know so."

Summer had plenty of money. The illegal ventures Kaleel had been engaged in before he was arrested left both Summer and Keyanna well-fixed. In fact, for quite some time, the Feds were sure that Summer knew where all of Kaleel's money was. And, that she did. Fortunately, for her, she had hidden it someplace where no one could find it. It seemed now she would most definitely need it.

She called her father.

"Daddy, what are you doing now?"

"Nothing, baby girl. I was gonna go downstairs and hang out with some of the boys."

"The boys?" Summer laughed. "Some of those boys are seventy, eighty years old."

"You mean like your daddy?"

"You'll never be old to me. You're too cool to be old. Instead of hangin' out with the boys, you think you could come by my place? I need to discuss something with you. It's kind of important."

"I'll be there in a half-hour."

By the time Mr. Johnson got there, Summer had extracted some of her cash reserve and it was sitting on her kitchen table; $25,000 to be exact. Even though she knew her father wouldn't want to take it, she was going to make him.

"Baby girl, where did you get all of this money from?"

"I've always had it. It was money I saved when I was with Kaleel. I know you think I'm not very responsible, Daddy, but I was able to put a bit of money away; you know, for a rainy day."

"And, is it raining now?"

"Yeah, it is, Daddy. I can't go into details right now. And, quite frankly, you probably wouldn't even believe me if I did, but your life is in danger and I've got to get you and Mom out of town, far away from here. Can you just believe me? Trust me."

Summer's father looked at his daughter. A change had come over her over recent months. He had noticed it even before today. He hated to admit it, but he always wished his daughter was more responsible. It seemed like she was taking some steps in that direction.

"And, Daddy, I need you to take Keyanna with you."

"Whatever you say. Hell, your momma and I haven't had a vacation in I don't know how long."

"Yeah. That's it, think of it as a vacation. A few weeks in Jamaica, visiting old friends. I called Momma's old friend, Sandy, and told her you guys would be coming to visit. I got you a room for two weeks at the Jamaica Grande, but I wanted to make sure you had someplace to stay, in case it took longer than that to take care of things here."

"You still haven't told me what things you're talking about. You're not in any trouble, are you?"

"Not the kind of trouble you may think. I haven't done anything wrong, nor has anyone close to me, but Belinda needs my help and I think maybe everyone around us will be in danger if they stay here, you and Momma included."

"Okay, I can tell you're not gonna tell me anything, so I'll wait until you can."

"Thanks, Daddy. I promise I'll fill you in when I can. I just can't now."

"And what should I tell your mother? You know how stubborn she is. And she doesn't do anything people tell her to do."

"I'll tell her Keyanna's in danger. I'll have to lie and tell her it's related to Kaleel. If I tell her that, she'll do whatever we ask. I'll tell her she needs to take Keyanna somewhere safe. She'll do it."

"Yeah. You know your mother well. I think that probably will work."

"I got you guys on a six a.m. flight tomorrow morning. You think you can be ready by then?"

"Yeah. That's doable. But, baby girl, should I be worried here?"

"No. You guys should be fine in Jamaica."

"I'm not talking about us. I'm talking about you and Belinda. How serious is this?"

"It's pretty serious, Daddy, but nothing I can't handle."

"I know how hard it is for you to ask for help. And, I know you don't want to tell me what's going on. But,

I'm gonna say this one last thing... Don't be afraid to ask for help; if not from me or your mother, then from someone else."

"I'll keep that in mind. Thanks, Daddy."

"For what? You won't let me do anything."

"Just trusting me. That's all I need right now. Thanks for that."

"No problem. Well, do you have 'Mini You' packed up and ready to go?"

"Yeah, pretty much. But, I wanted to talk with her before she goes. Okay?"

"I understand. I'll be in the living room."

Summer went into her daughter's bedroom where she was playing with her dolls.

"Keyanna. honey, I need you to do something for me."

"What. Mommy?"

"Aunty Bee isn't feeling very well and I need to stay with her and take care of her. So, I'm gonna need you to take care of Nanna and Grand-Pop while I'm with Belinda. I need you to be a big girl. Can you do that for me?"

"Yeah! I'm a big girl!"

"Yes, you are. Nanna and Grand-Pop need a vacation, so you're going to go with them to Jamaica for a couple of weeks. You remember Jamaica, right? Remember we went there last year and we stayed at the nice hotel where the doors opened to the beach. Remember how much you liked the ocean?"

"Yeah! That was fun!"

"So, what I need you to do right now is to pack a bag with just your favorite toys and I'm gonna pack you a bag of clothes and a couple of your bathing suits."

Summer went into the hall closet and pulled out a couple of suitcases. One of the suitcases she took back to Keyanna so she could pack her toys.

"I bet I'm faster than you."

"At what?"

"I bet I can pack your clothes waaaayyyyyy faster than you can pack your toys. I'll bet you a big bag of candy from Dylan's Candy Bar that you can't pack your bag faster than I can."

Keyanna sprung into action, darting around the room like she'd already had that bag of candy from Dylan's. Within minutes, she was packed and ready to go.

"I beat you, Mommy! I win. Dylan's! Dylan's! Dylans!"

"Wow! You are fast!"

Summer's father appeared in the doorway to Keyanna's bedroom, smiling and shaking his head.

"You learned that trick from me." He laughed.

"What trick, Grand-Pop?"

"Nothing. Don't worry about it, Mini-Mouth."

Summer's father always called Keyanna Mini-Mouth because he said she was the only person he knew who talked more, and faster than Summer.

"Daddy, you drove here, right?"

"Yeah. I was lucky, too; I got a parking spot right in front of your place."

"Can you give me and Keyanna a lift downtown? I'm

gonna get her that candy from Dylan's that I promised. I'm not gonna give her any before you guys leave for Jamaica tomorrow morning, or else she'll be up all night. So, make sure you don't let her have the whole bag in one sitting. I know how you and Momma spoil her rotten."

"We raised you, didn't we? I think we can handle it, smarty-pants."

"Daddy, I'm gonna take Keyanna's bags, since she's already packed, and put them in your trunk. You might as well take Keyanna with you after we go to Dylan's. There's no point in me traveling all the way to the Bronx with her way over in the morning, unless you need me to drive you to the airport?"

"Naw. I'll just get a cab to the airport."

Summer picked up the cash from the kitchen table and put $15,000 in one envelope and $10,000 in another envelope. She scrawled *Daddy* on the front of the envelope with the $15,000 in it and *Belinda* on the other.

Keyanna always loved Dylan's. Summer was happy to be able to spend a little time with her there before she left. The place was magical; and magical was just what they both needed. By the time Keyanna exited Dylan's she had not one, but two bags of candy and she was wearing one of their signature T-shirts.

"Grand-Pop, look what Mommy got me!"

"Oh, but it's your Momma and I that spoil her," he joked. Summer just smiled.

"Well, I guess this is it, Daddy. Don't worry about me, okay? Everything is going to be fine. And when it's all done, Belinda and I are gonna join you guys in Jamaica. Something tells me by then we'll both be ready for a vacation."

Summer hugged her dad tightly and then Keyanna and handed him the printout of the e-tickets for their flight, along with Keyanna's passport and an envelope.

"Okay," her dad said. "I've got the tickets, Mini-Mouth's passport. What else do I need? What's in the envelope?"

He opened it to find a stack of cash.

"No, Summer. Your momma and I don't need this. We're doing okay on our retirement and this is the first vacation we've taken in God only knows how long. We don't need your money."

"It's not for you; it's for Keyanna. You know, for food and if she wants any souvenirs or anything."

"What is she, a linebacker for the 49ers? How much could she eat? And, we can buy her whatever souvenirs she wants. That's what grandparents are for."

"Please, Daddy, just take it. I'm gonna worry that you guys don't have what you need, if you don't."

"We won't need it."

"I tell you what. Why don't you take it and if you don't need it, you can give it back to me when I see you."

"And what are you gonna have, if I take all this money?"

"One of these days, we'll have to have a talk about what happened to most of that money the Feds were looking for when Kaleel got arrested."

"Summer! You told me you weren't—"

"Daddy, that's a conversation for another time. Okay?"

"Okay," he conceded.

"Let me get that red bag out of the trunk. That one's mine."

"Where are you going? I can drop you off."

"I'll be at Belinda's. She's only a few blocks from here. Daddy, use this when you call me," she said, handing her father a prepaid cell phone she had purchased earlier that day. "I've already programmed my new cell phone into your phone. Only use this phone to call me. Okay?"

Bruce Johnson was suddenly more worried about his daughter than he had ever been.

Summer watched her father and daughter drive away and planned her next step. Once her parents and daughter boarded that flight for Jamaica early the next morning, she could rest a bit easier. For now, her biggest concern was Belinda. She decided to walk the ten or so blocks to Belinda's apartment. She popped the luggage wheels into place and with her bag in tow, walked, rather than took a cab. She thought the brisk walk might help to clear her head.

She considered calling Belinda before she arrived, but remembered the prepaid phone in her bag that she had also bought for Belinda. She would explain to Belinda that no calls should be made on anything but the cell phones she purchased. She's wasn't sure if any of what she was doing would work, but all she could think of was that old saying: 'An ounce of prevention is worth a pound of cure.'

"Apartment 6F. Ms. Wilson is expecting you. You can go right up."

"Come on in. The door is open."

"Are you sure it's wise to leave the door open, under the circumstances?"

He was standing there as soon as she entered. It was Dante. Summer was suddenly very disgusted.

"Hello, Dante," she said coldly.

"Hey, sweetie."

Belinda walked over to Summer and they hugged one another.

"Are you okay?"

"Yeah, I'm good. I'm okay. Dante has been watching me night and day."

"Oh really?"

"Yeah. That's how he knew you were coming. He's been monitoring every movement near the apartment. I guess there are some advantages to having a demon as a boyfriend," she joked lamely.

"Yeah. I've gotta run right out and get one of those," Summer responded sarcastically.

"Well, I'll tell you why I'm here. I've been thinking and thinking about this situation night and day. And, I'll tell you what I think. We need to come up with a plan.

We can't just sit here and wait for all of this to unfold."

"Dante was just saying the same thing."

"Oh was he now?"

"Yeah.

"Does he know?"

"Yes, Summer. In fact, he was the one who told me."

Dante was careful not to interject. He felt that Summer and Belinda needed to talk.

"Belinda, are you hungry? Summer, how about you?" Dante asked.

"I'm fine," Summer answered abruptly.

"A sandwich would be nice," Belinda responded.

Dante excused himself to the kitchen, allowing Summer and Belinda to talk freely.

Summer filled Belinda in on everything that Dante had told her.

"Whoa! I knew I did the right thing."

"What did you do?"

"I sent my parents and Keyanna out of town. The death toll is mounting around us and I won't even get into the number of people who have disappeared since Dante and René arrived on the scene."

"Where are they? Where are your parents and Keyanna?"

"I think it's best that as few people as possible know where they are. It's not that I don't trust you, but under the circumstances," she said, pointing in the direction of the kitchen, "I think I should keep their whereabouts to myself; at least for now."

"That's cool."

"You up for a guest?" Summer asked. "I'm afraid to go back to my place alone," she lied.

Her real reason for staying was to keep an eye on Belinda and Dante. She still didn't trust him, even though Belinda obviously did.

Belinda glanced near the front door and spotted the suitcase.

"And, what were you going to do if I said no?"

"No, about what?"

"The bag. The really big bag, I might add." She laughed.

"You mind if I take a nap?" Summer asked.

"You know where your room is."

"I thought maybe Bèla Lugosi was using it."

"Summer."

"Okay, okay, I'll behave. In the meantime, you should go check on the man of the hour; make sure he's not adding a little extra garnish to your sandwich."

"Is that behaving? No! You're awful. Be nice."

"Well, that's a first."

"What?"

"This is the first time in my life anyone's ever told me to be nice to the devil."

"He's not a devil."

"Oh, I forgot. He's only a demon."

"Not just a demon; but a demon who has turned over a new leaf. I know you don't trust him. But something about this situation reminds me of you. Remember, how everyone kept saying you were bad news and I defended you. My instincts were good then and I think they're good now."

"Touche! I'm gonna take a nap, with one eye open, I might add. And, I suggest you do the same."

"Summer, you know I love him, right? And I can't do it."

"You can't do what?"

"I can't... Actually, I won't let him go."

Summer simply shook her head and left to take a nap. However, she wasn't sleep for very long.

"Aidan, what are you doing here?"

"Why, do you want me to leave?"

"I...I don't underst..."

"Shhh."

He was already lying on top of her. Aidan only appeared to weigh 185 pounds tops, yet his weight seemed triple that, crushing her. Slowly, his hips began to glide and swivel against hers. Something cold lay flatly between them, increasing in size. She should have been afraid but somehow, she wasn't. Hadn't she often fantasized about just this? She had silently envied the time Belinda spent with Aidan.

He entered her and the lifeless cold spread throughout her entire body. Yet, his appendage was only cold for a moment. It was as if they traded body temperatures. His icy manhood transferred to her entire body and her heat warmed him, just long enough for her to forget the cold.

She awakened to hands shaking her.

"Summer, Summer, wake up! Wake up now!"

It was Dante.

"What are you doing in my room!"

"You seemed as though you were in distress."

"I'm fine. Get out of here!"

"There's something I don't understand. Belinda told me you believed in the possibility of demons long before she did."

"So?"

"So, you're open to the possibility of the existence of demons, but you can't open your mind up enough to believe that not every demon is the devil himself."

"No, I can't. You may have Belinda fooled but, as far as I'm concerned, you're no different than the others. You're a demon; plain and simple. And, I don't know what it is you want from Belinda, but you've gotta know that I would do anything to protect her from the likes of you."

"I have no right to ask you to trust me, but I may not be around for long and you and I are all she has."

"I don't know about you, since you're the one who brought all this hell upon her. I, on the other hand, have always had her back and always will."

"I know that and that's why you and I have got to come to some sort of understanding."

"I'm listening."

"They will never stop, René and Diana and their kind."

"Don't you mean your kind?"

"Yeah, I guess I do. It's funny. I've gone through my entire existence without even a thought of love, but now that I've had a taste of it, it's far more enticing than the life I draw from my sexual encounters. I would surely trade each and every life sustaining act, for just a moment more with Belinda."

"Okay. So what has that got to do with me?"

"Nothing. I simply need you to believe everything I am about to tell you."

THIRTY-TWO

Dante wondered if there was any way to prepare for what lay before him. He actually began to consider the possibility of ending the existence he had endured for so long. He chuckled to himself. Even his thoughts betrayed him. What an odd word to choose: 'endured?' It didn't demonstrate enjoyment or a great lust for existence. Endurance was a word that spoke of resilience. Was that all his time on earth had been, a study in resilience?

He had to admit, that was all it had been; that is, until now. It was ironic that the very thing that had encouraged him to truly '*live*' would most likely be the exact same thing that ended his time here. But, before that happened, he would have to prepare. Either he would continue to draw life from those around him, or he would depend solely upon Belinda; a choice that could prove detrimental to both her health and life, whether she was pregnant or not. That is why he had remained alone for so long. Once, centuries before now, he had felt very similar for someone else. Unfortunately, his passion…and hers, had gotten the better of them, and she slowly slipped into an illness she could not recover from. He would not see the same thing happen to Belinda.

"There will come a time when I won't be here to protect her. My kind can only survive when we sustain ourselves through sex. No more sex and no more existence. With Belinda pregnant, she is no longer able to sustain me. I have sought female comfort, but it pains Belinda so, I can't bear to put her through it. So, all I'm saying is when the time comes when I no longer have the strength, I wanna know that there's someone here for her."

"I've always had Belinda's back and I always will. Your presence or lack thereof has nothing to do with that. We were good before you got here and we'll be good after. I don't know what else to tell you. I don't think I'll be able to change the way that I feel about you. I was raised in the church. I was raised to believe that the word demon was associated with evil. I never, in my wildest imagination, thought that demons might actually be real. So, how do you expect me to respond when my best friend in the whole world is now spending most of her time with none other than a demon? And, not only is she fucking a demon, but that same demon or maybe even one of his friends has knocked her up. Can you see this from my perspective? And, as far as your sustenance problem. If that's what is going to keep you strong, especially now, then maybe you just need to do what you have to do. Ordinary mortal men have skipped out on their women for far less. You just need to do what you have to do. You're telling me you're a demon; an incubus who survives by visiting nameless, faceless women in the night, but you can't do this without your woman finding out."

"Belinda might not know, but I'll know."

"Ain't that rich; a demon with a conscience. Where was that conscience when you were scaring the shit out of women in the middle of the night?"

"Why can't you see that Belinda has changed me? I'm not the same. I never will be."

"What I see is my best friend, completely and totally screwed; both literally and figuratively. I did a little research on all of this. Cambions; isn't that what she's carrying is called? Every site I found predicts that Belinda's chances of survival are minimal at best. Belinda has always been somewhat fragile. How do you think someone like her will fare in a situation such as this? It doesn't look good for her."

"You don't give Belinda near enough credit. She's stronger than you think. I have faith in her. She will be fine and Belinda has a rare advantage. She's got me. Seldom do demons and mortals forge an alliance. I don't intend to leave her side if and until I no longer exist."

"According to you, that could be very soon."

"I will do all I need to do to ensure that will not happen."

"Well, isn't she lucky?"

"I wish I could have kept her from this, but my existence here has nothing to do with that. René found her long before I did. So did Diana or Aidan, or whatever vessel your friend has been using."

"Diana was never really my friend. That was all Belinda. She met her, in of all places, yoga class. Could you see me in a fucking yoga class?"

"And Aidan, what about Aidan! What has he got to do with this?"

"He's one of the bodies Diana has been using."

"Oh my God! Diana, Aidan, the letters are exactly the same! How could I have never noticed that?"

Summer hadn't thought about Aidan for quite some time until he showed up at her grandmother's funeral. Typically she wasn't attracted to the same men Belinda was attracted to. Aidan was the exception to that rule. When Belinda first revealed to her that she was sleeping with Aidan, Summer had an uncustomary moment of envy. She eventually got over it, until she saw him at the funeral. Ever since that time, she had been having dreams about him, including just minutes earlier.

"Shit!"

"What?" Dante asked.

"It's nothing."

"You sure?"

"Yeah. I'm sure."

The prepaid phone Summer had purchased for herself rang. She glanced at the clock and it was 4:30 a.m. Her parents were always so early for everything, she figured they were probably calling her from the airport by now, since their flight was at 6:00 a.m.

"Hi, Daddy."

"Sorry, but this ain't Daddy. It ain't Mommy either. In fact, Summer, you're now a motherless and a fatherless child."

It was Diana.

"Bitch, you're dead."

"Now, now. I wouldn't make idle threats if I were you; especially while your daughter is still alive."

Summer's face was contorted with pain. She made every effort to keep her state of mind from being conveyed over the phone lines.

"So what the fuck do you want?"

"I think you know what I want. And, I'll trade you. Bring me Belinda and I'll give you your daughter. Even trade and I'm out of your life forever."

"Yeah, and I'm supposed to believe your evil, lying ass."

"Under the circumstances, I guess you're going to have to. Redemption…an hour."

Before Summer could say another word, Diana was gone.

"Summer, it has to be me."

Dante had heard everything.

Dante woke Belinda up.

"Baby, we haven't got much time. I've gotta get you and Summer somewhere safe. They've got her daughter and they want to trade you for her. It's not gonna happen."

"And what's gonna happen to Keyanna if I don't show? She can't die because of me."

"Belinda, trust me on this. Diana and René are gonna cut you open and take the baby and leave you dead, but not before they kill Keyanna. My way, maybe both of you will have a chance. In the meantime, I've got to get both you and Summer somewhere safe."

Dante considered transforming, but under the circumstances he thought it best to preserve any energy he might use until he absolutely needed it.

Once outside, the three hailed a cab.

"We're going to Hoboken."

Dante got a hotel room for Summer and Belinda in New Jersey.

"Don't open this door for anyone. I'll be back with your daughter before you know it."

As Dante headed for the door, Belinda stopped him and whispered to him quietly.

"Dante, you might have been able to do this a few months ago, but now? You're not strong enough."

"I'll be fine, Keyanna will be fine. Just have a little faith in me. Okay?"

"Okay," she said, with little confidence.

In the bathroom, Summer finally unleashed all the fear she was feeling. She sat on top of the toilet seat, sobbing uncontrollably. "I'm never going to see my daughter again."

"Yes you will! You've got to believe!"

"I've got to believe? In one demon saving my child from another? Even if I did trust him, I know what's been going on. He's diminished. He hasn't been doing what he needs to do to sustain himself. You better believe Diana and René have. What kind of fight is it going to be? He hasn't got enough strength to fight even one demon, let alone two."

"Dante, you're looking a little drained. You sure this is a good idea?"

"It's the only idea."

"So you're telling me you're willing to sacrifice all the souls you've gathered, the existence you've enjoyed for centuries, for a mere mortal?"

"That's exactly what I'm telling you."

"You know you can't win. They can't win."

"Give me the child."

"I will, as soon as you give me ours."

"That child is mine and Belinda's. You don't need that child. There are more than enough Cambions to serve your purpose. And, if there are not, you can produce others. Belinda, our baby and this child and her mother are going with me. We are going to leave New York, and you, alone. We will no longer interfere with what you're doing here. And, you will no longer interfere with us."

Diana laughed.

"You've got all of this tied up into a neat little bow, don't you, but you still don't get it, do you? We mean to get what we came for. It's the Cambion or nothing."

Diana tightened her grip around Keyanna's neck and lifted her entire body off the floor. Dante watched her carefully, but knew if he said anything, she would be more likely to hurt Keyanna even more. She squirmed in Diana's grasp and her whining seemed to infuriate Diana even more.

"Shut up!"

"I want my mommy."

"I'm gonna rip this bitch's head off in a minute. Stop making all that noise and keep the fuck still!"

"You're only frightening her more!"

"Oh, so suddenly you're an expert on the habits of mortal children."

"You might as well let her go, so I can take her back to her mother."

"You just don't get it. That's not going to happen."

"I have nothing more to say to you. René, is that where you stand as well?"

"Yes, Dante, it is. We both knew it would come to this eventually. I'm sure you had no illusions of any sort of alliances. You couldn't be that naive, could you?"

"As I'm sure you knew, I would do anything to protect Belinda and my baby."

"You really are disillusioned, aren't you? You're still calling it a baby, like it will be born some sort of mortal. Do you know anything at all about Cambions? The two of you want to live in the mortal world. What will you do when it is born? Cambions are not born like mortal babies. They're still born. They show no signs of life, yet they're alive; no pulse, no breath. And, it stays that way for years. You think we're devoid of a conscience? Cambions are devilishly cunning and their beauty is just as powerful. They can persuade even the strongest mortals to do what they want. Make no mistake about it, it will be born evil. And what will you both do then? It is best for all concerned if you let us have it. Belinda will thank us in the long run."

"I'm sure she won't and neither will I. I will leave here with that child Diana is holding and you will not have mine."

"Do your worst, brother."

"I intend to."

THIRTY-THREE

The facility that housed most of the Cambions that Diana and René had organized burned to the ground, with all of the children inside and René was convinced it had been Dante.

"Do you really think I could have done something like this?" Dante asked.

"Who else would have? Surely, no mortal would have cared, or been any the wiser. It would have had to be a demon. And you are the only demon that stood to gain anything."

Diana stood by elated to see that her plan had worked.

The facility was called CDA. Thanks to Diana they were able to maintain it with few questions from outsiders. It was where most of the Cambions were housed. They were brilliant children, with unheard of I.Q.s. If they were out amongst the rest of the world for too long a period of time and in too large numbers, questions would be asked that not dare be answered. In addition to their intelligence, they were capable of incredible feats of strength and power. They could make things happen once only imagined.

It was once Diana's hope that she continue to guide them and with her as their protector and benefactor, she would possess just as great as theirs. But, now, she would be on the run. Summer had informed the police that she was practicing medicine without a license and even though she was not fearful of the typical repercussions mortals were subject to, she would have to leave the city if she had any hopes of continuing with her mission. She could start over again, in another town, another city, but before she left, she would ensure that none of her work was discovered. She would also guaranty that Dante took the blame for what she had done, forever severing his ties with René. She knew, eventually, she would be reunited with René and she needed him. He was what Dante once was…the strongest of the demons and Diana would make sure that her union with René continued.

Throughout the years, the number of children at CDA had grown. When they first started there were only 20 children, now there were at least 300. She stood at the entrance watching them all, so proud of what they had accomplished with her help. Where Cambions were once disorganized and scattered separately and alone, they were now organized. She had proven it could happen. And, she would make it happen again. But for now, this had to be destroyed.

"And a child shall lead them," she whispered silently. "Only, sadly, it won't be any of you," she said before lighting the match.

Dante fought valiantly, but René was decidedly stronger and better equipped to win this fight.

"Just walk away," René begged of him.

He had no real desire to harm Dante.

"You know I can't do that."

"So you would rather I destroy you, for the sake of these mortals?"

With each strike of his talons at Dante's already exposed flesh, Dante weakened more and more. René took no joy in winning such an uneven fight. He lived for a challenge, and this was clearly no challenge.

For every one blow Dante served René, René pummeled Dante with a dozen more. They both wore a pained expression. Dante's was one of defeat, but Renée's was one of regret.

"We may not have been born of the same mother, but we are brothers in every sense of the word," René said. "Don't force me to do this!"

"You must!"

And, with that Dante released what little energy he still had left and flew at René, his wings, tattered and falling away. Just as Diana thought it would finally be over and she would have what she wanted, and once and for all be free of Dante, a shot rang out, hitting René dead center in the chest. The gun was then aimed again, fired and caught Diana right between the eyes.

Summer stood crying, holding the gun in her hand.

Summer still didn't trust Dante and feared that he

was just as much a threat to her and her daughter. He picked Keyanna up from a frightened heap on the floor and Summer raised the gun once again.

"I never wanted any part of this. You...you people, whatever you are...you came to us. He...he came to us. We just want to be left alone. That's all. We just want to be left alone. Just give me my child and leave us alone."

"Summer, please, put down the gun. All I want to do is give your daughter to you and go back to Belinda."

"Why don't you just leave her alone...now? Why don't you just fly out of here and pretend like you never met Belinda. You will ruin her life. Don't you know that? Her life is already ruined because of you."

He handed her daughter to her and she dropped the gun.

"Summer, don't you get it? Do you see any bodies?"

That's when she realized they were gone. Both of them were gone; even Diana, who she had shot right between the eyes.

"You still don't get it, do you? There is no end to this. They will continue to go after Belinda and her child wherever she goes. And, it is now my job to protect her. I couldn't leave her now if I wanted to."

Then it dawned on him. Where was Belinda?

"Summer, where is she?"

"She wasn't feeling very well. I believe she had an upset stomach and she was sleeping. I knew she would either try to keep me from coming or want to come with me if I told her I was coming to get my daughter, so I snuck out. I'm sure she's fine."

"We have to get back to the hotel…now!"

Dante knew better than anyone how quickly both Diana and René would be able to restore, especially from a gunshot wound. Bullets were nothing more than a temporary distraction, something to buy time, when dealing with demons.

"They're going to go someplace and lay low until they are able to restore. Possibly someplace where they can restore with a mortal's sexual energy."

"Is this really possible? They can actually survive those gunshots I pumped into them."

"Yes. They can and they will."

"How much time do we have? Is it enough time for us to leave town?"

"Probably not. It will probably only be a matter of a couple of hours, if we're lucky."

"This is unreal. So what you're telling me is they can't be killed."

"You can't really kill what's never been alive. These are not lives. They are souls; fallen angels, recruited by the devil. They capture souls to ensure their place of power. The need to replenish energy through these souls is merely an attempt to remind us that even we are not more powerful than our leader."

"Who is your leader?"

"He has many names. I think you would probably call him the devil."

"Why did he choose us? We're not perfect, but we're not the worst either. We're good people for the most part; especially Belinda. She's one of the best people I know."

"That makes perfect sense. That's probably why she was chosen. If her will and righteousness could be broken, then evil has won. It will always seek to challenge her; especially now that she is carrying a half-demon child."

"It's so sad. She will never know any real peace, will she?"

"I have lived among mortals for centuries, and I have seen enough to know that there is no such thing as *real peace*. Before this, did you know *real* peace? Did any of your friends? Did Belinda?"

"Maybe the most any of us can hope for is moments of peace. Right now, I would settle for that. What if we get back to the hotel and they're there? Then what? You didn't look like you were doing so well out there. And, now I'm sure they'll be pretty much pissed off as hell. We are going to be screwed big time!"

"I don't think they would have been able to restore that quickly."

"You don't think or you know? Because you don't think could mean we're walking into an ambush and that particularly concerns me, since I have my daughter with me."

"I know," he lied.

"You're full of shit!"

Summer was surprised that Keyanna had yet to awaken. She must have been in shock. She hoped that she would sleep through it all, whatever that meant. She went over places in her mind that she had always wanted to travel to, then she thought of her parents. They were dead because of her; so was Kaleel.

"You know, all I keep thinking is, I wish I had believed more. One thing I will say about us *mortals*, as you call us, we are so arrogant; always believing that we know everything. If we don't see it, taste it or smell it, we want to discount it. My grandmother told a story for years about an incubus that visited her and her husband and we listened to her story. Some of us, like me, even said we believed it. But even I didn't truly believe it. Because, if I had, it wouldn't have taken me so long to do something about everything that was unfolding around me. I just feel like so much of this could have been stopped if I had just opened my mind just a little bit more."

"That's not always so easy, not even for demons. We believe ourselves to be all-powerful, but the same way mortals don't typically believe in us, demons don't believe they are capable of human emotions. I now know I was living a lie for quite some time. I think I was even in love, once, before Belinda. And when she was gone, I told myself it was nothing more than a heightened reaction to her restoration of me. Now, if that isn't arrogance, I don't know what is. I do believe my arrogance is what led to her death. I often wonder, if I had not been so arrogant, maybe I would have been more careful with her and maybe, just maybe, she might have survived."

"What happened to her?"

"What happens to most mortals when exposed to an incubus over increased periods of time; she eventually was drained of all life. She gave her life so that I could continue to exist. And now, I ask myself what for, so that I can continue to drain others of their life force. Or, go on living a half life. None of it makes any sense for me. It used to make sense now it's nothing more than some ridiculous puzzle I'm unable to solve."

Dante paused and stared out into space.

"Promise me one thing, Summer? If I don't make it today, please, don't leave Belinda's side. She's going to need you. That is the only thing I can take comfort in, that hopefully you will at least have one another through this battle."

"Okay, you sound like you're giving up already. You can't give up now. You may not be the strongest demon, but you're the only demon we've got and you're still stronger than we are."

"I don't know about that; technically, you saved me. Speaking of which, where did you get that gun from?"

"You demons have got your firepower and we hood-rats, we've got ours." She laughed.

It was the first laugh she had in a long time, and with Dante no doubt.

THIRTY-FOUR

Dante and Summer arrived to find Belinda in labor.

"Oh my God, it hurts *so* bad, Summer. Is it supposed to hurt this bad? Something's wrong! It can't be the baby. It's too early. Look at me, I'm barely showing. I could only be five or six months pregnant!"

"Sweetie, you gotta calm down. We both know this is no ordinary pregnancy. We don't have all the answers, so we may need to make it up as we go along. Can you walk?"

"Yes. I think I can."

"Well, the first thing we need to do is get a cab. And Dante, you need to go someplace safe with my daughter."

"But I need to be with Belinda."

"We all need to be smart. And, right now I can't give Belinda what she needs if I'm worrying about Keyanna."

Belinda shook her head vigorously in agreement.

"Don't worry, Dante. I'll be okay."

One of Summer's customers at a hair salon she used to work at was a midwife and she had convinced her that Belinda had some legal problems that prevented her from going to a hospital; that story and the $2,000 Belinda paid her was enough to convince the midwife to be there to deliver her baby. Summer considered calling her now, but after all the research she had done on Cambions, she decided a hospital would be safer. They would have to answer any uncomfortable questions later.

Once in the cab, it hit Belinda. She would be giving birth to a demon child.

"Summer, I don't think I can do this. I'm scared. I don't wanna die. I'm…I'm just not ready."

"You're not gonna die, baby. You can't die. You know I'm too much of a mess to deal with all this on my own."

Belinda grabbed Summer's hand and squeezed.

"But you promised, Summer, right? You'll take care of Michael—that's the name I decided on—Michael; after the Archangel."

"Michael huh? How do you know it's a boy?"

"I just know; that's all."

"Don't even try it, Summer. After all these years, you think I don't know when you're trying to change the subject. You have to promise me."

"Of course, Belinda, you know I will. But, I won't have to, because you're not going anywhere."

"Summer, promise me. Say it!"

"I promise. Okay, I promise."

"I knew I could depend on you. I always have."

Suddenly, fond memories of their days as children in Our Lady Queen of Faith came flooding back to Belinda.

Along with those fond memories were thoughts of what Diana told her recently about what her child's life would be like. The last thing she wanted was for her baby to feel like he had no one. Belinda remembered what it felt like to feel all alone. When she was a little girl and her parents died she went to live with her aunt. Her Aunt Meg and her husband treated her like she was one of their own, but Belinda always felt like a square peg in a room full of circles. That is, until she met Summer. No matter what happened, Belinda knew Summer would always be there, just as she was now.

René and Diana were already waiting at New York Presbyterian when Summer and Belinda arrived.

"They wouldn't do anything here, in front of all these people, would they? Ah, shit!"

"What? What was that, another contraction?"

"Yes. I think it was. It hurts like hell!"

"I don't want you worrying about them right now. Let's get you and that baby taken care of, quickly!"

While Summer considered Belinda's question, it occurred to her that René and Diana hadn't exactly kept a low profile up 'til now. Belinda would be occupied. So, Summer knew she would have to be on point and ready for whatever happened.

"It's game time," René said, under his breath.

Once in the delivery room, things moved so quickly. Before Summer knew it, it was time for Belinda to deliver.

"Okay, Belinda. It's time. We're gonna need you to push. Now! Push! Push! Push!"

Belinda was panting and sweating, the pain so intense she thought for sure she would black out.

"And, again. Push! Push! Push!"

"I'm sorry sir, but we're in the middle of a delivery."

"She's my wife," he lied.

Summer looked up at Dante and Keyanna.

"I thought I told you to take her someplace safe. They're out there!"

"I couldn't abandon Belinda like that. Wait a minute; who's out there?"

"Diana and René. We're never going to get out of here; least of all with the baby."

"Yes, we will!"

"It's a boy!" the doctor stated.

Dante was just in time to see the delivery of Belinda's baby boy and to see her lose consciousness.

"Is she okay?" he asked.

"I need the paddles in here! Now!

"One...two...three... Clear!

"One...two...three... Clear!

"One...two...three... Clear!

"Belinda, don't you do this!" Summer yelled. "You wake up right now! Right now, wake up!"

"Belinda! Belinda!"

Dante began shaking her, hoping that his touch would awaken her.

The doctor's worked on her long and hard, but there was nothing they could do. Belinda was dead.

"The baby has no pulse, no heartbeat!"

"This is the damnedest thing I've ever seen. I thought he was dead. No heartbeat, no pulse. But he is damn sure alive. I can see him blinking and his arms and legs are moving. He needs to go to the neonatal unit."

With Belinda gone, Summer's only thought was to keep her promise. She would protect Michael at all costs. She turned to find Diana and René approaching. While Dante cradled Belinda in his arms, Summer grabbed Michael in one arm and Keyanna with her opposite hand, practically dragging her along the way and ran toward the hospital's emergency room exit. That's when she noticed the oxygen tank, less than three feet away. Trying hard not to drop Michael or lose sight of Keyanna, she searched for a book of matches in her pocketbook; she fished around in the bag's opening with one hand. There, tucked into the corner, was a book of matches, with only one match remaining. She lit it and tossed it directly at the tank, while she tried to wrap her brain around what she would do if the tank wasn't on. Or, even worse, what if the explosion was so intense it killed her and the children as well. She knew this could be her last and only chance. So, she took it.

CONCLUSION

"I should be grateful for just being alive, but every time I think about the people that never made it out of that hospital alive, because of us, I feel nothing but guilt. I keep thinking there could have been another way?"

"That is the mortal way, guilt and regret. But, survival is also the mortal way. All that's left for you to do is to reconcile your guilt with your survival instinct. Your friend, Summer, made a split-second decision. That decision saved your life and hers; and allowed Michael and I another day on earth. Maybe I will never feel things as you do, because I will always have one foot in the demon world, but I do understand. I also understand that, if you allow it, guilt can become crippling. And, neither of us can afford to waste that kind of time."

"But aren't we wasting time anyway? I feel like I am. I haven't seen my best friend in nearly seven months; with the exception of these visions I get through Michael. Hell, she doesn't even know I'm alive. And what about Michael? I haven't even held my own child. Hasn't enough time passed? Half of the year is gone; and nothing. No threats, no nightly visits. I feel like if I spend the rest of my life running and unable to be with my loved ones, then they've still won. Not only that, he's getting stronger. I can feel it. He calls out to me. Sometimes I can hear him as loudly and clearly as I hear you now. I won't let him feel as though I've abandoned him."

"If the bond is as strong as you say; and I have no doubt it is, he knows. He knows you're doing exactly what you have to do."

Indeed, her connection to Michael was very strong. Over time it had increased. Lately, she was even able to see things through his eyes. The first time she looked in the mirror and saw Summer looking back at her, she was terrified. She thought it was some sort of horrible omen. But, then the visions increased. They were un-remarkable events, played out behind her eyes. When she saw Keyanna one day, laughing and smiling, she knew. It was Michael. She was seeing everything he saw. And, it would be a way for her to never lose sight of her son, nor Summer and Keyanna.

"None of that surprises me," Dante said.

"You've got to know that if you can hear him, then so can they. And, they are very patient. They will hunt you both until they get what they want."

"Then I guess it's a good thing I have you to protect me."

"I will never be as strong as I once was. So far, you have been enough to sustain me, but there may come a time when you won't be. As it is, I have already lost the power to do some of the things I was once capable of."

"Do you miss it?"

"What?"

"Do you miss the power?"

"I have to admit, sometimes I do miss being able to do the things I used to do; being able to transform, that overwhelming sense of supremacy. But, when I consider what I've received in return; there's no comparison. If I regret anything, it's the part I played in condemning you to this life."

"You saved me. You saved our child."

If it were not for Dante, Belinda would have perished in the hospital explosion. Everyone, including Summer, assumed she was dead. After Summer threw the match that initiated the oxygen tank explosion, the hospital was chaos. Everyone was in a panic. As if someone had used a defibrillator to restart her heart, simultaneous with the explosion, Belinda's eyes suddenly opened. Although Dante's strength had already started to wane at that point, he still had enough power to transform to his natural state. He grabbed Belinda and took flight through a window that had been blown open during the explosion.

It took weeks for both of them to regain their strength and with Belinda ailing, Dante had no other choice but to return to his old ways; visiting women in the middle of the night, in an effort to restore himself to his former strength. When Belinda was well again, they agreed that if handled properly, they would both be able to endure and sustain Dante; maybe not at his former resilience, but enough for him to survive.

Belinda assumed Diana and René were both killed in the explosion. However, Dante assured Belinda that they were not. Nevertheless, Belinda had begun to relax just a bit, since she hadn't seen them for several months.

Thanks to Michael, they were always able to follow Summer well enough without being discovered. But lately, that wasn't enough for Belinda. She wanted to see him. Even a glimpse would be enough to satisfy her.

"Mommy, where did you say Aunty Bee was again?"

"Did you forget me telling you already, Keyanna? Remember, she went to heaven, baby."

"Is that why we get to keep baby Michael?"

"Yes, Keyanna, that's exactly why."

"What about Michael's daddy, did he go to heaven like my daddy?"

"I'm not sure where he went, Keyanna. I think maybe Michael's daddy was very, very sick and he went someplace to get better; and one day we'll all see Michael's daddy again."

"Is he nice, Mommy?"

"Who, honey?"

"Michael's daddy."

"I didn't know him very well, but I think maybe he is nice."

"That's good."

"Why?"

"You know why. Because Aunty Bee was nice, so if baby Michael's mommy was nice and his daddy is nice, then he'll be nice, too."

"Yeah, Aunty Bee was very nice."

Summer missed her best friend more than words could say; especially since this life was so isolating. She wasn't comfortable getting to know people, because in the back of her mind, she always questioned whether or not the person standing before her was some demon waiting to harm her or her children.

"Aunty Bee is an angel now. She watches over us all the time."

"Yes, I think maybe she does."

"Aw, Mommy. You don't really believe me. I can tell. You're just saying that because I'm a kid. But, Aunty Bee really is an angel. See, Mommy, she's right there."

"Keyanna, Mommy's trying to drive, so I've got to keep my eyes on the road, but if you say Aunty Bee is an angel, I believe you."

As much as Summer enjoyed her little talks with her daughter, she was happy she had finally quieted down. What Summer didn't notice, however, was Keyanna waving to the driver in the car behind them. She was much too deep in thought. Since Belinda's death, she, Keyanna and Michael had traveled from city to city; never settling in one place for long. Often, instinct would tell Summer it was time to leave; and when it wasn't instinct it was tangible threat. She knew they would never give up, so all that was left for her to do was stay one step ahead, at least until Michael was old enough and strong enough.

Belinda silently admonished herself for not being more careful. She usually made sure she drove at least two or three car lengths behind them. And, although she had promised Dante to stay away until Michael was older and stronger, she couldn't resist. No matter what he was, first and foremost, he was her child, her baby and she needed to be with him.

Belinda put a bit more distance between her car and Summer's. More than anything, she would have liked to have made her friend aware of her presence, to hold her baby in her arms. But, sometimes in life sacrifices had to be made. And, she knew, they were still looking for her. She had to put some distance between her, Michael and Summer. But one day she would let Summer know she was alive.

Summer knew that this momentary calm was just that...a moment. They would never stop trying to find Michael. Summer had sworn to Belinda on her death bed that she would keep him safe. Although, judging from what she had seen so far, that would probably be the other way around.

It didn't take a genius to figure out there was some-thing different about Michael. He wasn't quite a year old yet, but from the moment he was born, he demon-strated his propensity for great power. Summer was sure he somehow channeled his influence to her in order to keep them all safe. Whenever there was a threat, somehow, Summer was one step ahead of it. She was sure that was thanks to Michael.

"Do you need to go?" Summer asked.

"No, not yet, Mommy."

"Well, I do. So, come on let's go."

Summer pulled up in front of a rest stop.

"Can I wait in the car with Michael?"

"No, Summer, you have to come with me."

"Aw, Mommy, I'm a big girl. I can watch Michael."

"I know you're a big girl. But I'd rather you and Michael come with me. Besides, I might need your help."

Summer parked the car and maneuvered past the steering wheel and out of the driver's seat with great effort. She was getting bigger and bigger and she would have to make up her mind very soon who she could trust, since she clearly couldn't do this alone.

While Dante quickly ran into 7-Eleven to get provisions, Belinda watched Summer's car from a distance. She wondered why it was taking her so long to exit the driver's seat after parking and was concerned that something might be wrong.

Finally, she stood outside the car. For months, Belinda had watched her while she drove or through Michael's visions. She had never seen more than Summer's face and a few inches beneath her chin. But, she saw her now. She had to be fully seven months pregnant.

It was time. She could do what Dante had asked and

wait until Michael was a year old or more, but for what reason? What was going to change? Summer needed her now. She owed her that much and more. Belinda slowly exited the car, walking with purpose. She wanted to reach Summer before Dante came back and talked her out of it.

As Summer removed first Michael and then Keyanna, from their car seats, she was sure her ears were playing tricks on her. She knew that voice anywhere.

"Summer."

Her first thought was that it was a trap. She had pored through every website and bought every book regarding demons, incubus and succubus and she knew better than anyone that they could transfer into anyone they wanted. She didn't care. Belinda had arrived as if in answer to a prayer.

When she turned around, the tears that fell freely from Belinda's eyes told her all she needed to know. Belinda's tears matched her own.

"Where the fuck have you been?" Summer said. "I thought your ass was dead."

"Same old Summer, I see."

The girls embraced, afraid to let go of one another; afraid that if they did, none of this would be real.

"See, Mommy. I told you Aunty Bee was an angel that watched over us."

Belinda shot Summer a questioning gaze.

"I'll explain it to her later," Summer responded.

While the two of them stood there, elated and amazed at the other's presence, a loud noise practically deafened them.

Out of the gaping hole, that not two minutes earlier was a 7-Eleven, flames and billows of smoke emitted. And, out of the flames emerged René and Diana. They were even stronger than before.

"Are you alone?" Summer asked, hoping that Dante was somewhere close by.

Belinda looked at the entrance to the 7-Eleven with sadness.

"Yes. I guess I am."

"We gotta get outta here then…and fast!"

"What are we gonna do, Summer? Dante's gone. We're powerless."

"Don't you dare. Several months ago I made you a promise; a pretty big one—and I kept it. Now it's your turn. I'm gonna need you big-time, real soon and I can't have you falling apart on me. We're *all* gonna do exact what we've been doing. We're gonna survive. We have to survive. We've got babies to protect and at some point we're gonna have to make someone believe us. Otherwise, our world is doomed. Besides, little Michael here is definitely his father's son. He's got power you can't possibly imagine."

The pair was so caught up in their reunion, they almost forgot about Diana and René, but Michael hadn't. As the two closed the gap between themselves and Belinda and Summer, Michael saw to it that remnants of the explosion landed on Diana and René with enough force to allow them an opportunity to escape.

"Where to, Mama?" Belinda asked.

"I've always wanted to go to Detroit. How about you?"

"Detroit, it is."

"You think we'll ever be able to go back home."

"Anything's possible. These last few months have proven that. You want me to drive?"

"No," Summer responded. "I find that the driving calms me, keeps my mind off of all this."

"Okay. It'll give me a chance to write."

"You still writing? Isn't that what got you into all this mess?" Summer joked.

"Yes, you drive and I write. That's what calms me."

Summer maneuvered her belly behind the steering wheel and Belinda settled in the backseat with Keyanna and Michael. She couldn't stop staring at him. He was so beautiful. Yet, she was still a bit worried. Staring deeply into his eyes, she hoped to have the answer to her question. She saw no recognizable likeness to Dante. For so long she had allowed herself to believe that if he were Dante's child he would not be evil. But, what if he wasn't Dante's? She decided these were thoughts better left for another time. As if reading her thoughts, Michael reached out his tiny little hand and grabbed her finger, before drifting off to sleep.

"Summer?"

"Yeah?"

"Does he ever cry?" Belinda asked.

"That's a strange question. Why do you ask?"

"It's just, while Dante and I were on the run, keeping an eye on you guys, Michael found a way to connect with me. I could see things through his eyes. I never saw him cry. Don't you find that odd that a baby would never cry; even a demon baby?"

"I guess it's because he doesn't need to. He has other ways of communicating. He's only half-human, Belinda. You should *never* forget that."

Belinda was fully aware of that fact. She was also aware that Michael was half of her, too, and she was a normal, mortal being. Some part of her had to influence who he was.

While Summer drove and the children slept, Belinda retrieved her journal and began to write.

"Do any of us really even want to know the untold dangers that live amongst us?"

Belinda took comfort in the last remaining consistency from her former life. She could at least still write. Though it was doubtful the truth would ever be published, she knew the truth...Summer knew the truth. Her son Michael was a constant reminder of that truth. For now words hurriedly scribbled into a journal would have to suffice until she could make someone, anyone, simply believe. And, so, she wrote about it, hopeful that one day the world would be made aware of what awaited humankind. Though she tried to be hopeful, Belinda had begun to slowly embrace the reality that they might *never* be able to return to New York. This was their life now; a series of nameless, faceless people, city after city and so many hotels, she often awakened without even remembering where she was. She was stronger now than she ever believed herself capable of being. She had to be.

It was clear Summer was becoming very tired and Belinda suggested they stop at a hotel. As they did their best to leave the car quietly and check into the hotel just as quietly, Michael turned and looked behind them all, pointing down the road. He spoke not only his first but his only word until now.

"Father."

That single word brought Belinda hope. But, for Summer, it brought nothing but fear. Would they ever truly know who Michael's father indeed was? Yes, Belinda had convinced herself that it was indeed Dante. But, it could just as easily be Aidan or even René.

While Summer stood assessing the situation, she realized she could not allow foolish emotions to rule their existence. The demons that pursued them would not and to the best of their mortal capabilities, she and Belinda would have to do the same.

"Belinda, I know we're all tired. But I don't think it's a good idea to check into this hotel right now. I can't drive anymore. I'm too tired. You're going to have to drive. We'll make it to the next town and if it feels safe, we'll stop."

"But, Summer; did you hear Michael? It's Dante; Dante is coming. He said he would never leave me, that he would *always* look after me. I know it's him. I just know it is."

"You might be right, but it could just as easily be Aidan or René."

What Summer couldn't tell Belinda was that she didn't trust Dante much more than she did the others and the same went for Michael. As far as Summer was concerned the human side of Michael was little more than an accident. When it really got down to it, he was a demon; plain and simple. When this whole thing got started, she had looked up the word demon in the dictionary and was not surprised to find that there were several definitions of demon in the Wikipedia dictionary. One definition was: *a supernatural being described as something that is not human.* But, the meaning that rang most true for her was the Christian meaning: *a demon is considered an unclean spirit which may cause demonic possession.*

That was a fact that Summer assured herself she would never, ever allow herself to forget…even after her own child was born.

ABOUT THE AUTHOR

Urban Reviews says Michelle's first novel, *Color Me Grey*, is "full of non-stop drama and devastating secrets that will make you want to read future novels by Michelle Janine Robinson." Michelle has contributed several short stories to editor Zane's erotic anthologies, including *Purple Panties*, *Honey Flava* and *Caramel Flava*, and her short story contribution, "The Quiet Room," was the first featured story in the *New York Times* bestseller *Succulent: Chocolate Flava II*. Michelle is also a contributor to the oral sex-themed anthology, *Tasting Him*, with her story "A Tongue is Just a Tongue," edited by Rachel Kramer Bussel. Michelle recently put the finishing touches on her third novel, *Serial Typical*, published by Strebor Books/ Simon & Schuster in 2012. Michelle is a native New Yorker and the mother of identical twins. You can learn all about Michelle and what she is working on next on her website at www.michellejaninerobinson.com. You can also find Michelle at www.facebook.com/michelle. j.robinson, www.myspace.com/justef or follow Michelle at www.twitter.com/ MJanineRobinson.

CHAPTER ONE

"It's women like her...women like her that make the bad things happen. Yes, it is. Women like her have to go away or they make the world an ugly place. Yes, ugly women, ugly world. They wear disguises, really good disguises, these women, and masks, yes, masks and costumes to fool everyone. But, they don't fool me, for *I* am one of his disciples. No, I'm not fooled at all and I must save the world from the corruption of these demons. Yes, that's what they are, demons, and I can see beyond their disguises. So, I must save the world by destroying the monsters. They are everywhere, here, where I live, where I work, at the supermarket, movie theaters, restaurants, walking down the street as if they belong. They're even with the innocent children. They are everywhere. They pretend to be normal, just like *her*, but they're not. Oh no. Just like *her*, they have been sent here from hell, sent to alter the decency of our world, sent to alter this world to hell on earth. But, I *will* stop them! I will stop them *all!* And, I know just where to start."

Scattered throughout the tiny, damp, downtown apartment, were countless fashion magazines and newspapers, piled one on top of another, practically from floor to ceiling. Food was discarded throughout and flies, roaches and mice competed for residency. If anyone had ever gotten an opportunity to see inside, the place probably would have been declared an uninhabitable fire hazard. Along with the magazines, there were hundreds of cutouts of beautiful women, indiscriminately lining every available corner of wall space. Violent splotches of red clung to the walls. The pungent odor of cigarette smoke clung to the tattered black curtains, occupying the space like dense fog. Each and every window had been thickly coated with black paint, undoubtedly to completely block out any and all hope of sunshine entering, or anyone peeping inside. There was no furniture, not even a bed occupying the tiny studio. Instead, there was a dirty old mattress in one corner of the room, piled high with blankets, and at the center of the room, was a large metal container, filled with water.

"I exorcise thee in the name of God the Father almighty, and in the name of Jesus Christ His Son, our Lord, and in the power of the Holy Ghost, that you may be able to put to flight all the power of the enemy, and be able to root out and supplant that enemy and his apostate angels, through the power of our Lord Jesus Christ, who will come to judge the living and the dead and the world by fire.

"God, Who for the salvation of the human race, has built Your greatest mysteries upon this substance, in Your kindness hear our prayers and pour down the power of Your blessing into this element, prepared by many purifications. May this, Your creation, be a vessel of divine grace to dispel demons and sicknesses, so that everything that it is sprinkled on in the homes and buildings of the faithful will be rid of all unclean and harmful things. Let no pestilent spirit, no corrupting atmosphere, remain in those places. May all the schemes of the hidden enemy be dispelled. Let whatever might trouble the safety and peace of those who live here, be put to flight by this water, so that health, gotten by calling Your holy name, may be made secure against all attacks. Through the Lord, Amen.

"I am Your humble servant, Lord, one of Your angels, dispatched to earth to rid this world of the pestilent, festering boils of society. I will do Your work, Lord. I will destroy them, those that seek to corrupt and leave us all unclean.

"My work has only just begun. And it all will end as You intended, Lord. It all shall end with fire.

"I don't deny that this battle has become an exhausting one. Each day there are more. Who knew there were so many? As quickly as I destroy them, their numbers increase. Don't worry. I sit at the threshold of their arrival. The sooner I eradicate them, the better. It's only a matter of time before they will all be gone and my work here will be done. I *will* stay the course.

"I am so very tired. There is no rest for the chosen. Yet, it is my destiny to purify this earth, one way or another.

"More than anything, I long for the day when I no longer have to hide from those who simply don't understand. We have the same purpose. Yet, they continue to challenge me every step of the way. If only they were to join me in the fight, retribution would be even more swift and dealt with a far more crushing blow. I *will* make them see. I have faith. They will join me. My cause will become their own. Finally, the world will be pure."

Cloaked in layers of clothing and hunched over a vat of many months' worth of collected holy water, a nameless, faceless threat clipped even more pages from magazines. This time, instead of pictures of beautiful women, they were men—handsome, movie star-looking men. After a sufficient number of pictures were clipped, they were glued side by side with the pictures of women that lined every corner of the wall.

As much as the project appeared random, there was

nothing random about it. The trained eye could have detected how carefully the male and female pictures were matched to look alike. For every female photo, there was a matching male photo that could have easily been a sibling. The closer the photos matched, the more feverishly the work continued.

"No matter how much you look alike, you will never be one. It's not how it was meant to be. It was foretold long, long ago. This is my one true purpose, to maintain the balance of things. This unity was never meant to be. The others shall not divert me from my plan."

Searching for more pictures in the countless magazines that lined the floor, suddenly a clever advertising tool between the pages of a *Cosmopolitan* magazine revealed a mirror. It was likely nothing more than an attempt to grab its readers' attention, get them to stop and eventually buy the product being pitched. But, for the occupant crouched on the floor, crazily clipping pages, it was a trigger. In a fit of rage, a set of sharp scissors previously used only to clip pictures, was raised, impaling not only the magazine and its paper mirror, but the leg upon which the magazine rested.

As blood seeped slowly from the wound, the injured party appeared to feel nothing.

CHAPTER TWO

Candace listened to the sound of the buzzer, announcing her next client. She was tired. Recently, she had begun considering whether or not she needed to take a sabbatical. Between her practice, her support group, the work she did at the prison, and her own personal life, she was beyond overwhelmed. Helping others was what gave her life meaning, but she realized she was ignoring the same advice that she gave many of her clients. She wasn't taking care of herself. It was like the instructions given to passengers on a flight about securing your own oxygen before assisting others. She couldn't be there for everyone else, if she allowed herself to sink. She had three more clients to see today and she was free. Somehow it seemed as though her days were getting longer and longer. She had doubled her client load over the past year, in the hopes that the extra money would help her to have her long-awaited surgery much more quickly. Candace had chosen the field of psychiatry so that she could help others. She also had chosen psychiatry, and her unique specialty, to tackle her own demons.

Soon, she would be embarking on one of the greatest challenges in her life. She was sure she was ready, but hoped that it would still allow her to practice as a psychiatrist. She loved her career and found great fulfillment in helping others. She especially enjoyed the support group she had been conducting for the past several months. She often invited her patients to participate in the group, if she thought it might serve them well. In the beginning, she had been tight-lipped about her more personal reasons for feeling passionate about the work the group was doing. She felt it lacked professionalism to allow her patients a peek inside of her personal life.

Candace had spent so many years of her own life living in the shadows, she hadn't realized how damaging it had become, not only for herself, but for most of her patients, to spend most of their lives hiding from the world. One of her patients was so career-obsessed and adamant about Candace not documenting any sessions that Candace began to become concerned that her patient was slipping into a world where the lines of reality were becoming dangerously blurred and paranoia reigned supreme. Candace did understand better than anyone, since there was always that chance that her practice might suffer after her own transformation was complete. She had known since she was a child what had to be done. Yet, it was only now that her dreams were becoming real. As she encouraged her patients to discover, there were certain decisions in life that no one could or should make for you. All those many years ago, her parents had decided what they thought was best. They had been premature and had probably lacked a clear understanding of what they were dealing with. As far as Candace was concerned, it was high time she rectified their decision, and lived the life she was *truly* meant to live. If that meant abandoning her career, she was prepared to make that sacrifice.

Her next client concerned her a great deal. Candace had become expert at recognizing the subtle clues that indicated a patient was in real trouble. To start, she was sure that Shelly was not her real name. However, that was the least of it. With each visit, Candace became increasingly concerned about Shelly. Since her initial visit, she had presented signs of irritability, difficulty sleeping, and an obvious lack of emotion. Many of her thoughts and ideas were rambling, and often seemed to have no basis in reality. In addition, she demonstrated dangerous promiscuity on more than one occasion, while expressing a lack of desire to connect with anyone. She would pick up random partners frequently, and on many occasions, would become angered by their desire to see her again.

"Hi, Shelly. How are you today?"

"Everything is everything."

"I'm not sure what that means, Shelly."

"It means, nothing has changed. I still can't sleep. I'm

still pissed off, and don't know why. Everybody annoys me. I can't even walk down the street without thinking about how much I'd like to trip some random stranger up. I've stopped riding the subway to every place but here, because it's way too stimulating. Every time I get on the subway, I find myself thinking the most evil thoughts. Is that normal? Tell me. This is New York. Maybe my behavior is normal. What do you think, Doc?"

"That's what we're going to figure out, here, together."

"Yeah, I know that, but *when* am I gonna figure it out? I've been coming to you for months now and things are exactly the same. In fact, I think they may have actually gotten worse. Now, I'm starting to think I have a drinking problem. I woke up in a hotel last night alone and I couldn't even remember how I got there."

"Tell me the last thing you remember."

Shelly sat quietly for a moment, then she spoke.

"Okay. So, I remember leaving the hospital and walking to the bus stop. Then, it all gets fuzzy. I might have gone to a bar, but I'm not sure."

"We've established that things were a little fuzzy for you after you left work. What about before?"

"Nothing out of the ordinary...oh, except there's this one patient that I think the staff has been slacking on, since he's so incapacitated and incapable of voicing his concerns. I found these scars on his body. I'm not sure what to make of it, but something doesn't seem right. I only work part-time, but I make it a point to check in on him whenever I'm at the hospital. I believe he was the last person I saw before I left."

"Let's go back further than that?"

"All I remember is a smell. That morning when I woke up, there was this awful smell in my apartment. It smelled like someone had left some food out somewhere, but I couldn't find it or remember leaving any food laying around. It smelled like old bananas or corroded apples or something, but it was so strong, like an entire stock of fruit had spoiled over time in a supermarket and had never been thrown away. That's the only thing I remember."

"Could that have been the reason you were at the hotel?"

Shelly seemed miles away. Her eyes were suddenly vacant and empty. Candace thought she might be drifting off to sleep.

"Shelly? Shelly?"

Nothing seemed to be registering, then suddenly, like a light bulb had been turned on, her eyes blinked and she resumed where the conversation had left off.

"Yeah, Doc. You might be right. Maybe that's why I was at The Mercer."

"Shelly, you've never mentioned your parents. Are they still alive?"

"Uh...No. Actually, I'm not sure. I was adopted."

Candace sensed that she was lying, but resisted the urge to persist. She assumed that if Shelly was lying, she might retreat and maybe even leave. That's what she had done once, earlier in her treatment, when Candace had tried to persuade her to discuss her sexual trysts. She still would have liked to have known a bit about Shelly's parents.

"What do my parents have to do with anything?"

"Often, our childhood is the root of where many of our troubles begin. Even many sleep difficulties begin in childhood. They can manifest in different ways. For instance, as a child, one might sleepwalk, but when they grow up, the sleepwalking may be replaced with insomnia."

"Well, I don't remember anything about mine, so I guess we'll have to take another discovery route."

Shelly's show of agitation was nothing new, but what happened next most certainly was.

Candace watched as she shifted position. It was a small motion that, for most, would have been inconsequential, but for Shelly it was not. Her small adjustment brought about an obvious change. Her eyes appeared smaller and a bit squinted. Her posture was much more upright, so much so, she actually seemed taller, and her smile was broad and uncustomary.

"This is the first time I've ever noticed how beautiful your eyes are."

Shelly's tone was purposely seductive and meant to express her intent. The octave of her voice was of an obvious lower pitch.

She chuckled.

"Awww, you're so cute. Did my little compliment make you uncomfortable? I didn't mean it, really. I tried so hard to keep it tame. There are a lot better things we could be doing than sitting here and exploring the inner psyche."

"Like what?" Candace asked.

"Hmmm. Like fucking. I can smell your pussy over here and your nipples are so hard, pushing against that conservative silk top you're wearing. I can tell you feel it, too. We'd make incredible fuck buddies."

"We should explore why you imagine yourself suddenly attracted to me, sexually."

"I'm all for exploring. How about I start? I'd like to explore what your nipples taste like inside my mouth, or how much harder they'll get if I run my teeth against them."

Shelly stood up; her gait was seductive, yet lacked much of the sway her hips typically executed. There was a swagger to her step, similar to a man on the hunt. She crossed the room to where Candace was sitting.

"Shelly, I would like for you to go back and sit down where you were."

"Shelly? Shelly who? Shelly isn't here, Doc."

"You're not Shelly?"

"You can call me Kay."

She sat down next to Candace.

Shelly touched her own groin area, rubbing her hand back and forth.

"Oh, Dr. Phipps, you make me so fucking hot," she moaned.

Candace considered asking her to leave, but she would have to witness this transformation firsthand in order to make an informed assessment of what was happening with Shelly. She did, however, make a threat.

"If you don't move, I'm going to have to ask you to leave, *Kay*."

"Okay, don't get your panties in a bunch. I thought you needed tightening up."

"We're here to talk about you."

"You know this isn't going to work, don't you, Dr. Phipps?"

"What isn't going to work?"

"Trying to *fix* something that isn't broken."

"What is it you think I'm trying to fix?"

"Shelly."

It didn't go unnoticed by Candace that Shelly was speaking of herself in the third person.

"Aren't you Shelly?"

She laughed.

"Ever the shrink, huh?"

"What makes you say that?"

"Aren't you Shelly?" she said, mimicking Candace in a high-pitched, squeaky voice.

"I'm so much more than just *Shelly*. I thought you would have figured that out by now."

"Yes, I get it."

"Yeah, sure you do."

Just as easily as Shelly had slipped into her new persona, Kay, the *old* Shelly suddenly returned and the subject was immediately changed.

"Doc, I really wish your office was in another location. This is the only place that I now take the subway to; a bus to your office is a pain in the ass. I see by the clock on the wall our session is over."

"Don't worry about that. In fact, Shelly, I was thinking maybe you might want to add an additional day a week to your sessions."

"Wow! That's big. Am I really that fucked up?"

"No. You're not *fucked up*. I think it would be a lot easier to get to the root of things, if we had more time."

"I'll see you next week, Doc; *same bat time, same bat channel*. I'll think about that additional session."

As Shelly left Candace's office, Candace realized it was moments like these that made it more difficult to consider cutting back on her client load.